Other Books by Madeline Baker

Wolf Shadow
Hawk's Woman
Apache Flame
Lakota Love Song

UNDER
APACHE SKIES

❖❖❖❖❖

Madeline Baker

A SIGNET BOOK

SIGNET
Published by New American Library, a division of
Penguin Group (USA) Inc., 375 Hudson Street,
New York, New York 10014, U.S.A.
Penguin Books Ltd, 80 Strand,
London WC2R 0RL, England
Penguin Books Australia Ltd, 250 Camberwell Road,
Camberwell, Victoria 3124, Australia
Penguin Books Canada Ltd, 10 Alcorn Avenue,
Toronto, Ontario, Canada M4V 3B2
Penguin Books (NZ), cnr Airborne and Rosedale Roads,
Albany, Auckland 1310, New Zealand

Penguin Books Ltd, Registered Offices:
80 Strand, London WC2R 0RL, England

First published by Signet, an imprint of New American Library,
a division of Penguin Group (USA) Inc.

First Printing, September 2004
10 9 8 7 6 5 4 3 2 1

To my editor, Rose Hilliard,
for her encouragement,
support, and enthusiasm.

Chapter 1

The sound of gunfire rolled through the early-morning air like summer thunder. Muttering an oath, Ridge Longtree holstered his Colt. He hadn't wanted to kill the kid, but the young would-be gunman hadn't given him any other choice.

Swinging onto the back of his horse, Longtree urged the big black stud into a lope. The shocked faces of a young mother and her little girl flashed by in a blur as the black raced down the dusty main street, headed for the open prairie beyond.

So much for hanging up his gun and settling down. He had lost track of the men he had killed, the times he had tried to settle down, only to have some young gunsel discover who he was and push him into a showdown. The results were always the same . . . a blast of gunfire, the stink of death, a quick exodus from whatever town he was in at the moment.

In the beginning, he had relished the thrill of it, the exhilaration of pitting the speed of his draw against that of another. He had lived for the quick rush of fear and excitement as he put his life on the line. But now . . . hell, now he was just tired of it all.

The black slowed of its own accord after a few miles, and Longtree let the horse set its own pace.

Lost in thought, he paid little attention to the direction the stud was taking other than to note that they seemed to be drifting west.

Drifting, he mused. That was all he'd done in the last twelve years, just drift, like some rootless tumbleweed. Of course, for a man who had no ties, and no place to settle down even if he was of a mind to, there wasn't much else to do but drift.

Good whiskey, easy women, and bucking the tiger; those had been his main pursuits since he left home. Somewhere along the way, he had discovered he could draw and fire a gun in the blink of an eye. In addition to being shit fast, he was possessed of an uncanny knack to hit what he aimed at. He had been pushed into killing his first man. He had been young and impulsive at the time, quick to anger, quick to take offense when someone called him a low-down dirty halfbreed. Until that fateful night, he had never fired his Colt at anything more dangerous than jackrabbits and empty beer bottles. But that night, goaded into a showdown, he had drawn his gun and killed a man. He would never forget that night, the recoil of his Colt, the quick flash of muzzle fire, the acrid stink of gunpowder. The sickly-sweet, coppery smell of blood that had overpowered everything else.

His first reaction was that he was glad he wasn't the one lying facedown in the dirt. It was only later, after the first rush of adrenaline had passed, that the full impact of what he had done hit him.

He had killed a man only a little older than himself.

He had been arrested and spent the night in jail, only to be released when witnesses declared that Ridge had fired in self-defense. During that one night in jail, he had discovered that he had a powerful dislike for being locked up in small spaces.

He had seen the grief he had caused at the funeral three days later, seen it in the eyes of the young man's mother and father, in the tears that flowed down the cheeks of the boy's intended bride. He had heard the sorrow in the voices of those who had been the young man's friends.

Muttering an oath, Ridge thrust the memory from his mind. He had killed a dozen men since that first one, and in doing so, he had made quite a name for himself. His reputation followed him from town to town, as relentless as his shadow. There was no way to outride it, no way to get shed of it. It stuck to him like a bur to a saddle blanket. In time, he had learned to live with it.

It was near dark when he spotted the house, a sprawling two-story place located in a shallow valley. There were a couple of peeled-pole corrals filled with horses on one side and a big red barn on the other, along with a bunkhouse, cookhouse, and springhouse. Several tall trees shaded the front porch. A long plume of smoke spiraled from the chimney of the main house, and even as he watched, lights appeared in the windows.

The place looked downright prosperous. Prosperous enough to maybe give him a place to bunk down for the night.

Clucking to the black, he rode down the hill.

Chapter 2

"Rider coming in."

Dani Flynn looked up from where she was setting the table. "Should I set another place?"

Marty Flynn shook her head. "Looks like a stranger," she said, lifting the rifle from the rack above the front door. "And a dangerous one."

"Well," Dani said, "if you invite him to dinner, you might not have to shoot him."

Turning away from the window, Marty glanced at her sister, one dark brow arched. "If I shoot him, we won't have to invite him to dinner."

"Well, you'd better let Pa talk to him before you pull the trigger. We could use another hand, you know. Pa won't like it if you take a shot at this fella and then find out he was just looking for work."

Marty looked out the window once more. "This one doesn't look like a cowhand to me."

The stranger was in the yard now. Mounted on a handsome black horse, he wore a dark gray shirt, black trousers, expensive-looking boots, and a black hat with a snakeskin band. He sat there a moment, his head slowly turning from side to side as he looked the place over. He sat tall in the saddle, his hat pulled low, his hand resting on the butt of his gun.

She watched him dismount, noting the easy way he moved, the fact that he took the time to stroke his horse's neck before dropping the reins over the hitching post. Then the stranger turned toward the house, and she got her first look at his face.

It was a strong face, made up of clean lines and sharp angles. His brows were straight and black, his nose slightly crooked. His jaw was shadowed by a day's growth of bristles. Long black hair fell past his shoulders.

Dani went to look out the window, her eyes widening when she saw the stranger. Maybe her sister was right. He sure didn't look like any of the cowboys from around here. She couldn't put her finger on what it was that set him apart. Maybe it was the way he moved, loose-limbed and confident; maybe it was the fact that his clothes looked more expensive than those worn by the local cowboys. Whatever it was, she didn't like it.

Dani backed away from the window as he climbed the porch steps, sent a worried glance at Marty when the stranger knocked on the front door.

Holding the rifle loosely in the crook of her arm, Marty opened the door.

"Evenin'," said a deep voice. "I was wonderin' if you could put me up for the night."

Standing out of the stranger's sight, Dani watched Marty's gaze move over the man. Marty was a good judge of character, in both horses and in men.

After a long pause, Marty said, "I suppose you can bunk with the hands for the night."

"Obliged to ya."

"Tell Scanlan I said it was okay."

"And you'd be?"

"Martha Jean Flynn."

"Ridge Longtree." He touched a finger to the brim of his hat, turned, and descended the porch steps.

Looking out the window again, Marty watched the stranger take up his horse's reins and walk toward the bunkhouse. He had a long, easy stride. She noticed that his left hand stayed close to the butt of his gun.

"You didn't ask him if he was looking for a job," Dani remarked.

Marty closed the door, her expression thoughtful. "He's not a cowboy."

Dani didn't think so either, but she couldn't resist asking, "How do you know?"

"Didn't you see the way he wears that Colt? Like it's part of him? I'd bet my last pair of bloomers that he's some kind of fast gun."

Dani leaned forward, her eyes sparkling with curiosity. "Do you really think so?"

"Yes. And you stay away from him, you hear?"

"Don't worry. Anyway, he's leaving tomorrow."

"Yes," Marty said. "And it's a good thing. You'd better finish setting the table. Pa will be home soon."

With a nod, Dani returned to her task.

Walking to the fireplace, Marty put the rifle back in the rack. Pa had gone to town that morning to pick up the mail. Dani was expecting a dress she had ordered from the East. It was the first new dress she'd had in over a year, and Marty couldn't blame her for being excited. Dani set a store by pretty clothes and fancy things. Marty knew Dani was hoping to wear it the next time Cory came to call. Dani was also hoping for a letter from their mother, even though Marty knew a letter would never come.

Nettie Flynn had moved back to Boston seven years ago. She had left without a word, something Marty could neither understand nor forgive. Dani didn't understand it either. She had cried for Mama for weeks, had begged Marty to write their mother and ask if they could live with her, but Marty had flat-out refused. Marty loved the ranch, loved the West, and she wasn't about to go east. Finally, Marty had agreed to write their mother and ask if Dani could live with her. Dani had given the letter to her father and asked him to mail it for her. Weeks passed. Every time Pa came home from town with the mail, she had been certain he would have an answer to her letter. But her mother had never written back.

In the end, Marty had convinced Dani that Mama didn't want them anymore. Marty knew Dani didn't believe that, would never believe it. Marty couldn't help feeling sorry for her sister. She knew Dani often wondered what it would be like to live in the East. If Dani lived with their mother, her life would be much easier than it was now. She would be wearing dresses instead of pants and cotton shirts, pretty shoes instead of boots run down at the heel. But, as Marty had told her sister so often, there was nothing to be gained in daydreaming about things that would never come true.

Putting thoughts of her mother and sister aside, Marty found herself thinking about the stranger. Ridge Longtree. A curious name. He was a handsome man, in a rugged, weathered sort of way. He wore his hair longer than most of the men in these parts. She wondered if he preferred it that way, or if he was just in need of a haircut. Not that it mattered. Tomorrow, he'd be gone.

The desultory chatter inside the bunkhouse ceased as Ridge stepped through the doorway. Seven pairs of eyes swung in his direction, all giving him a quick once-over and reaching the same conclusion—he wasn't a cowhand.

Ridge nodded to the room in general. "I'm looking for Scanlan."

A tall, lanky man with bushy eyebrows and a shock of brown hair liberally streaked with gray stepped forward. "I'm Scanlan."

"The lady up at the house said I could bunk here for the night."

Scanlan jerked his chin toward a cot near the far side of the building. "You can use that one."

"Obliged."

The men went back to what they were doing, but Ridge was aware of their curious stares as he walked toward the empty bunk.

The bunkhouse was long and rectangular. Cots lined both sides of the room. A number of windows in the east and west walls provided cross-ventilation in the summer; a potbellied stove stood in the center of the floor. Pictures of women cut out of magazines were tacked to the walls here and there. A calendar advertising Pete's Hay and Feed hung from a nail near the door.

Ridge dropped his saddlebags on the floor at the foot of the bunk. Sitting down, he pulled off his boots, then stretched out on the cot, his arms folded behind his head, his hat pulled low over his eyes.

After a moment, a low hum of conversation filled the room. On the brink of sleep, Ridge wondered idly how much of it involved him.

Marty drew the curtain away from the window and stared out into the darkness. "What do you suppose is keeping Pa? I can't believe he'd be late on a night when he knows you're doing the cooking."

Dani smiled, pleased by her sister's offhand compliment. "I hope he's all right."

"I'm sure he's fine. Sunny probably came up lame, that's all. I've been telling Pa for over a year that he needs to put that old mare out to pasture."

Dani dropped the apron she'd been mending into the basket and stretched her shoulders and neck. "Sometimes I think he loves that old horse more than he loves us."

Marty let the curtain fall back into place. "I'm going to bed, and so should you. Maybe he just decided to spend the night in town."

"He wouldn't!" Dani exclaimed. "He wouldn't worry us like that, not at a time like this." She looked into her sister's eyes and saw her own anxiety mirrored there. "You're worried, too, aren't you?"

Marty nodded. "But there's no sense worrying until we know there's something to worry about. Come on; we might as well get some sleep."

Later, lying in bed, Marty wished she could take her own advice, but she couldn't shake the feeling that something was terribly wrong. Pa never stayed out this late. What if something had happened to him? What if Sunny had thrown him? What if that low-down dirty snake Victor Claunch had bushwhacked him? Claunch had been after their ranch ever since he had bought the neighboring spread. He had tried buying them out. He had tried scaring them out. He had tried damming the river. He had even poisoned some of their cattle. Of course, they couldn't prove any of it, but Marty knew Claunch was behind it. He had even tried courting her, but she had turned him down flat and threatened to geld him if he didn't leave her alone. She grinned into the darkness. She could do it, too, she thought smugly. She could rope and ride with the best of the cowhands.

Turning onto her side, she pillowed her cheek on her hand. Her last thought before sleep claimed her was of the stranger. He wasn't an ordinary cowhand, that was for sure. So who was he and what was he doing here? Was it just coincidence that he had turned up at the ranch on the same day that Pa had gone missing?

"Dani! Dani! Wake up!"

Marty's voice roused Dani from the delicious dream she'd been having. "Go 'way."

"Dani, get up."

Dani peered at the window, a frown creasing her brow. "It's not even morning yet," she said with a groan. "Go away."

"Pa's horse just came in."

Dani bolted upright. "His horse? Where's pa?"

"I don't know. There's blood on the saddle."

Dani leaped out of bed. Grabbing her robe, she flew down the stairs and out the front door. Her father's horse stood at the hitch rack. Suddenly reluctant, she paused a moment before descending the steps.

The door opened behind her as Marty emerged from the house, a lantern in her hand.

Dani stared at the ugly reddish-brown stain on her father's saddle, at the rust-colored drops that trailed down Sunny's coat. Heart pounding, Dani looked across the horse's back and met her sister's gaze. "Do you think he's . . . ?" She couldn't say the word.

"I don't know." Settling her hat on her head, Marty walked down the stairs. "I'm going to get Scanlan and Smitty and backtrack Pa's trail."

"I'm going with you."

"No."

Dani let out a huff of exasperation. Marty was six years older than she was and had been bossing her around ever since their mother had decided she'd had enough of ranch life and returned to the East. Most times, Dani let Marty get away with it just to keep peace in the family, but not now.

"I'm going, and you can't stop me!"

"Oh, all right, go get dressed while I saddle our horses."

Ridge stood in the doorway of the bunkhouse, one shoulder propped against the jamb while he watched the commotion at the barn. Several lanterns had been lit, both inside the barn and out. He could see a number of cowhands, most of them wearing their jeans over their longhandles, clustered around Martha Flynn and a horse. The men were gesturing at the animal, and they all seemed to be talking at once. Ridge wasn't much given to curiosity, but since he was awake. . . . With a shrug, he ambled over to see what was going on.

Martha Flynn was issuing orders. "Scanlan, you and Smitty come with me. . . ."

"Hold on," Scanlan said. "There's no need for you to be riding out in the middle of the night. We'll—"

"There's every need," Martha Flynn interjected, her voice cool. "He's my father, and I'm in charge when he's not here."

Ridge grinned inwardly. It was obvious from the Flynn woman's tone of voice that she was accustomed to giving orders and having them obeyed without question. It was equally obvious that Scanlan didn't like it one bit.

"As I was saying," Martha Flynn continued, "Scanlan, you and Smitty will come with me. Lon, I want you and Johnson to keep watch while we're gone."

"It was that son of a . . ." The man looked at Martha and cleared his throat. "It was Claunch who done this," he said. "You know it. I know it. We can't just let him get away with it."

"We don't know anything for certain right now," Martha Flynn said, "except that Pa's missing. The rest of you might as well go back to bed."

Murmuring among themselves, the cowhands who had been dismissed moved away, some going into the cookhouse for coffee, the others going back to the bunkhouse.

Ridge figured none of them would get much sleep. Aside from the fact that the boss was missing, it would be dawn in less than an hour.

Martha Flynn looked at the four men standing nearby. "Smitty, why don't you go saddle the horses. Oh, and saddle one for Dani."

"Yes, ma'am."

The other three men followed Smitty into the barn, leaving Ridge to wonder who Danny was. Her husband? A brother, perhaps? He rubbed his hand over his jaw. If she had male kin, why was she out here giving orders?

Martha Flynn looked up as Ridge Longtree drew closer. She glanced at the gun strapped to his thigh, her expression thoughtful.

"Trouble brewin'?" he asked.

"My father's horse came in without him. There's blood on the saddle." She glanced at his gun again.

"And you're wondering if I did it?"

"Did you?"

"You probably wouldn't believe me if I said no. I'll

be riding out first thing in the morning." He turned to walk away when her voice stopped him.

"Hey, Longtree, are you any good with that iron?"

Ridge swung around to face her. He regarded her for a moment, as if considering her reason for asking, and then shrugged. "I generally hit what I aim at."

"How would you like to work for me?"

"Doing what?" he asked, though he already had a pretty good idea.

"Whatever needs to be done."

"I thought you had me pegged as your old man's killer."

"I never said that."

Removing his hat, Ridge ran a hand through his hair, wondering if he wanted to get tangled up in Martha Flynn's troubles. She was a tall woman, with a passable figure and pretty features. Her hair, what he could see of it beneath her hat, was the reddish brown of autumn leaves. Her eyes were dark brown—hard, serious eyes that looked at him head-on and knew him for what he was. But there was a vulnerability there, too.

"Well?" Martha asked.

Ridge was about to accept her offer when the sound of hurrying footsteps caught his ear. Turning his head, he saw a girl running toward them. Tall and lithe, she ran with the effortless grace of a doe, her long blond braid flying behind her. As she drew closer, he saw that she wasn't a girl at all, but a young woman, probably no more than seventeen or eighteen, and pretty enough to take a man's breath away.

Cheeks flushed, she stopped beside the other woman. "I'm ready."

Martha Flynn nodded. "Just a minute, Dani. What do you say, Mr. Longtree?"

"Sure, I can do whatever needs doing." He glanced at Dani. Definitely not Marty Flynn's brother.

"Good," the Flynn woman said, extending her hand. "You're hired."

Ridge shook her hand. She had a firm, no-nonsense grip.

"Mr. Longtree, this is my sister, Danielle."

"Pleased to meet you, Miss Flynn."

"Please," she said with a shy smile, "call me Dani."

He nodded.

"Are you really a gunfighter?" Dani asked. "Like Wild Bill Hickok?"

"Not exactly," Ridge replied dryly. "Hickok is dead."

"Was he killed in a gunfight?" she asked, her eyes alight with morbid interest.

"No. He was shot in the back while playing cards in a saloon over in Deadwood."

"Who . . . ?"

"As fascinating as this is, we don't have time for these questions now, Dani," Martha interjected. "Longtree, why don't you saddle up and come with us?"

"Yes, ma'am."

Moments later, Ridge rode out of the yard behind the two women, the disgruntled foreman, and the cowhand called Smitty.

When she reached the road, Martha Flynn turned south. Since no one seemed to be searching the ground for tracks, Ridge figured she knew where she was going.

They rode for a mile or two with no one saying much of anything. The rising sun chased the night from the sky. Ridge spent a few minutes admiring the sunrise, then turned his attention to the two women.

They might be sisters, but they were as different as spring and autumn. As far as he could tell from what little he had seen and heard, being kin was the only thing they had in common. The young one, with her curly blond hair and green eyes, was easily the prettier of the two. The older one looked tough enough to chew lead and spit bullets; the younger one looked as warm and soft as one of the feather beds in Sally Moffet's house of ill repute.

He grinned inwardly. He had always liked autumn's colorful leaves more than spring's green, and feather beds made him sneeze.

They had gone close to five miles when the foreman reined his horse to a halt. The others drew rein behind him. Ridge stopped behind the others.

"What is it, Scanlan?" Martha Flynn asked.

The foreman gestured at the trail. "That there looks like a print from your dad's mare."

Martha Flynn leaned forward, her eyes narrowed as she looked where Scanlan indicated. And then she nodded. "I think you're right."

Dismounting, Ridge squatted on his heels and studied the ground for several minutes. Dropping his horse's reins, he walked ahead a few yards, studying the ground as he went, and then he turned and walked back toward the others.

He looked up at the foreman. "Do you recognize the tracks of the second horse?"

Scanlan shook his head. "No."

Ridge grunted softly. The second horse had a tendency to drag its left hind foot. It left a distinctive trail. Find the horse and he'd most likely find the killer.

"The way I see it, Flynn was on his way home when a second rider came up beside him back there a ways.

They rode side by side for a while, which leads me to believe Flynn knew the other man. They stopped here."

He frowned, his gaze moving over the ground again. The second man had dismounted. There was a pile of horse droppings near the side of the road. A little farther on there was a stretch of ground that looked like something heavy had been dragged across it. A body, perhaps? Looking closer, he saw a few reddish-brown stains that could only be blood.

Ridge picked up a handful of manure and sifted it through his fingers.

The signs were clear. Two men had stopped here. Only one had ridden away. The texture and color of the droppings indicated that Flynn's horse had waited where its rider had fallen for several hours before going home.

Ridge followed the bloodstains into the patchy grass that grew alongside the road. He could hear what sounded like a river ahead, and he kept walking, paying little attention to the others who were coming up behind him.

He found the body near the edge of the river. A thick cloud of blowflies took to the air as he approached.

The man was dead; there was no doubt of that. He had been shot in the back at close range and had somehow managed to drag himself to the river before he died. A search of the man's body turned up nothing but a ring of keys, a half-empty sack of Bull Durham, and papers for the makings.

The two women were off their horses now, running up to the man's body. The young one, Dani, threw herself down beside the body, sobbing, "Daddy, Daddy."

"Was your old man carrying any cash on him?" Ridge asked. "Anything of value?"

"He always carried a hundred dollars cash money," Martha Flynn replied. "And the pocket watch that Nettie gave him as a wedding present."

Ridge gained his feet. "Then I'd say he's been robbed."

Martha Flynn looked at him suspiciously for a moment, then nodded.

"You want to search me?" Ridge asked, his voice like cold steel.

Martha Flynn shook her head. She glanced at her sister and then looked back at Ridge, her expression implacable, her eyes as hard as flint.

"I think you know what needs doing."

Dani sat huddled in her father's favorite chair, a blanket draped across her legs. "I can't believe you hired that dreadful man."

"He's a blessing in disguise, if you ask me. He couldn't have shown up at a better time."

"He's a hired gun, isn't he?"

Marty blew out a sigh. "He is now."

"He looks like an Indian."

Marty shrugged. "So what?"

"So, we don't know anything about him."

"He can use his gun. I know that."

"How do you know?"

"Dani, all you have to do is look at him."

"How do you know that he isn't working for Claunch? For all you know, Longtree could have killed Daddy and taken his money and his watch."

Marty shook her head. She didn't know how to explain it, but she knew in the deepest part of her being that, whatever else Ridge Longtree might be, he wasn't the kind of man who would shoot another in the back and steal his belongings.

"I don't like it, Marty," Dani said, hearing the tremor in her voice and hating it. "And I don't like him. He scares me."

"Everything scares you."

Dani looked away. She couldn't deny it. She was afraid of crowds. She was afraid of guns. She was afraid of the dark. She was afraid of being left alone. . . . Her throat grew tight and tears burned her eyes. First her mother had left her, and now her father was gone, killed in cold blood.

Scanlan and Johnson had taken Pa's body into town. Tomorrow she would go with Marty to make arrangements for the funeral and speak to the sheriff. When that was done, she was going to insist that Marty send a wire to their mother to let Nettie know what had happened. She wondered if her mother would come home now.

Rising, she gathered the blanket around her shoulders and went out on the porch. She stood there a moment, then made her way to the corral that held her father's horse.

Sunny whinnied softly at her approach. Trotting up to the fence, the mare pushed her nose against Dani's chest.

Blinking back her tears, Dani scratched the mare's ears. "You're going to miss him, too, aren't you, girl?" she murmured.

The faint glow of a cigarette caught her eye. Glancing to the left, she saw the new man standing in the shadows watching her. He was a big man, with broad shoulders, a narrow waist, and slim hips.

He took a last puff on his cigarette, then dropped

it in the dirt and ground it out with the toe of his boot. Before she quite realized what he intended, he was moving toward her. Every instinct she possessed screamed at her to turn and run away, but she stood frozen to the spot, watching him walk toward her, his long legs quickly covering the ground between them.

"Evenin'."

She took a step back and clutched the blanket tighter, as if a flimsy piece of cloth would protect her. "Hello."

"I'm sorry about your old man."

"Thank you."

Ridge shoved his hands in his pants pockets. He wasn't used to making small talk with ladies. He hadn't spent much time with decent women lately, and the women he did spend time with weren't much interested in conversation. They weren't as young and innocent as this one, either. He wasn't sure why he had felt the need to see her up close, or why, seeing the tears in her eyes, he wanted to pull her into his arms. It was obvious she was on the verge of crying again, and just as obvious that she was scared to death of him.

She bowed her head, probably to hide the tears filling her eyes.

Muttering an oath, Ridge closed the distance between them and put his arms around her. She went stiff as a board the minute he touched her, and then, with a sob that went straight to his heart, she sagged against him and bawled like a baby.

He had been a long time without a woman, and his body reacted instinctively. For a moment, he almost forgot that she was grieving for her father and that she was a damn sight too young for him and as innocent as a newborn babe. With a shake of his head, he reminded himself that he was supposed to be offering her a shoulder to cry on and nothing more. And then he kissed her.

"Danielle Marie Flynn, what the hell is going on out here?"

At the sound of her sister's voice, Dani jerked out of his arms and backed away from him. "Nothing, Marty. I . . . he . . . we . . ."

"There was nothing going on," Ridge said. "She was crying for her old man and . . ." He shrugged. "She needed someone to comfort her and I was here."

"Is that what you were doing?" Martha asked. "Comforting her?"

"That's what I said."

Martha Flynn's gaze burned into him for a long moment, the warning plain in her frosty brown eyes. *Keep your hands off of my sister.* He heard the words as clearly as if she had shouted them.

Martha Flynn picked up the blanket that had fallen from Dani's shoulders, then took her sister by the hand. "Let's go."

Ridge watched the two of them walk toward the house. Marty and Dani. He grinned wryly, thinking that the boyish name Marty suited the older one far better than the staid name of Martha. But that was neither here nor there. If he was as smart as he thought he was, he would get on his horse and light out right now.

His gaze rested on the surprisingly enticing sway of Martha Flynn's hips. And then he grinned.

Sometimes, he just wasn't very smart.

Chapter 3

The rapid tattoo of rain falling on the roof of the bunkhouse woke Ridge early the following morning. He listened for a moment, then swore softly. He had intended to ride out this morning and take a second look at the tracks where the body had been found. A look out the window told him riding out now would most likely be a waste of time. Whatever tracks he might have found had probably been washed out by the rain.

Rising, he grabbed his hat and followed the smell of coffee to the cookhouse. There were only two cowhands inside, and they were heading out as Ridge went in, which suited him fine.

He poured himself a cup of coffee from the big pot sitting on the potbellied stove, then sat down on a bench at one of the long wooden tables. The coffee was black and strong enough to float a horseshoe, which was just the way he liked it. He sipped it appreciatively while he stared out the window at the rain. But it wasn't the dark sky or the rain he saw, but the face of the prickly-tempered Martha Flynn. He didn't know what there was about her that intrigued him so, but he'd been awake a good part of the night trying to figure it out.

With a shake of his head, he drained his cup and stood to get a refill. Maybe he'd just been too long without a woman, he thought sourly. Maybe at this point any woman would look good to him, but even as the thought crossed his mind, he shook his head. If that were true, it would be Dani Flynn keeping him awake nights—Dani with her huge green eyes, long golden hair, and innocent, untapped sensuality. She was a visual feast guaranteed to keep any red-blooded male on edge. Instead, it was Martha Flynn he found so appealing. There was something in her eyes that called to him, something that spoke of a soul-deep hurt.

Muttering an oath, he took a drink from his cup and swore again as the hot bitter brew burned his tongue. Damn! He'd better keep his mind on why he was here and stop getting himself tied up in knots over some woman who looked at him as if he were going to drag her little sister into the woods and eat her alive.

Ridge laughed out loud, the sound echoing off the cookhouse walls. Damn, if that wasn't a mighty tempting thought.

Emptying his cup, he left the cookhouse and ran toward the barn. Opening one of the big double doors, he stepped inside. The scent of hay and horses and the pungent odor of manure filled his nostrils as he moved deeper into the barn. His horse occupied a stall about midway down the aisle. The stallion poked its head over the door and whinnied softly at his approach.

"Hi, fella." Resting one hip against the edge of the stall, Ridge scratched the horse's ears.

He glanced around the barn. It was pleasant in there, listening to the rain on the roof and the sound of horses munching hay. He was about to leave when what sounded like a sob caught his attention.

Curious, he walked to the end of the aisle, then paused, listening. He had decided he was hearing things when it came again. Turning right, he followed the sound to the last stall in the back of the barn.

Peering over the side, he saw Marty Flynn sitting on a pile of hay, her hand covering her mouth. She looked up, her eyes widening when she saw him standing there. Last night she had looked as hard and unyielding as iron. This morning, with her hair falling in thick auburn waves around her shoulders and her cheeks damp with tears, she looked years younger. And every bit as vulnerable as her little sister.

"What are you doing in here?" he asked, though he had a pretty good idea.

She glared up at him. "Go away." She sniffed.

Instead, he walked around to the open stall door, removed his kerchief, and handed it to her. "Blow your nose."

Her eyes narrowed but she blew her nose, then stuffed his kerchief in the pocket of her trousers. "I'll wash it for you."

"Appreciate it."

"Now go away."

"Too late. What are you doing out here, anyway? Afraid to let your sister see you crying?"

He'd hit the nail on the head that time. Scrambling to her feet, she glared up at him again. "I'm not paying you to lollygag around the barn."

"Got someone you want me to kill?" he drawled. "Besides myself?"

Her lips twitched in what might have been a smile. "Not at the moment."

A tear trickled down her cheek.

Almost without conscious thought, Ridge wiped it away with the pad of his thumb. Her skin was warm and smooth.

She stared at him like a doe cornered by a timber wolf when he took a step toward her, her eyes wide and afraid. "What are you doing?"

Muttering, "Beats the hell out of me," he pulled her into his arms and kissed her.

At first she stood unmoving in his arms, her hands braced against his shoulders in an effort to push him away, and then, suddenly, her arms fell to her sides and she was kissing him back.

Ridge was pondering the possibility of laying her down in the hay and whiling away a pleasant hour or two when she twisted out of his arms and slapped him across the face. Hard.

"Don't you *ever* do that again," she warned, her voice as frosty as winter ice.

Ignoring her, he pulled her back into his arms and kissed her again, hard and quick, and then, before she could react, he turned and left the barn, whistling softly.

Outside, he lifted his hand and rubbed his cheek. She packed quite a wallop, he thought with a grin, but it had been worth it.

Marty stared after him, her fingertips pressed to her lips. Why had Longtree kissed her? Why had she let him? And why had she kissed him back? She had caught Dani in Longtree's arms last night, so why was he kissing her this morning? Making comparisons? Or was he in the habit of kissing every woman he met?

Marty blew out a sigh. It was obvious Mr. Ridge Longtree had been smitten with her little sister, just like every other man.

No matter where they went, men turned to stare at Dani, and who could blame them? Dani was beyond beautiful. She had a lovely willowy figure, big green eyes, skin that refused to tan, and an air of help-lessness that men seemed to find appealing. Next to Dani, Marty felt like an ungainly heifer.

Pulling Longtree's kerchief out of her pocket, she blew her nose again and then wiped her eyes. Longtree was right. She had come out to the barn because she didn't want Dani to see her crying. One of them had to be strong, and that responsibility had always fallen on Marty's shoulders. When Dani found a spider in her room, it was Marty who killed it. When Dani had nightmares, it was Marty who soothed her fears. When the men needed extra help with the branding or the castrating, Marty pitched in to help while Dani hid away in the house, unable to bear the stink of burning hide or the bawling of the calves. It wasn't that her sister was helpless. Dani kept the house clean, she did the cooking and the mending and all the other household chores, but there were times, especially at branding time or during the spring roundup when another pair of hands would have been a big help.

Marty knew it wasn't all Dani's fault. Pa had always made excuses for Dani—she was too young, she was too delicate, she was too impressionable to be exposed to the rough behavior and the coarse language of the cowboys. If she was going to be honest with herself, Marty knew she was as much to blame as Pa. She was just as guilty of coddling Dani as he was.

Taking a deep breath, Marty straightened her shirt, dusted off the seat of her jeans, and walked up to the house.

Dani was in the kitchen making breakfast. She

glanced over her shoulder when Marty entered the room. "Where were you?"

"Nowhere." Marty shrugged. "Just out in the barn."

"Breakfast is ready. I don't really feel much like eating, though."

"You've got to eat. Starving yourself won't bring Pa back."

"I know." Dani set two plates on the table. "Do you think Mama will come home?"

"This isn't her home anymore," Marty replied bitterly. "She didn't want to be here when Pa was alive. Why would she come now?"

Dani looked away, but not before Marty saw the tears in her eyes.

Marty blew out a breath. "I'm sorry, Dani."

She took a seat at the table. Maybe one of these days she would learn to think before she blurted out what was on her mind. She knew Dani still missed their mother, still hoped that someday Nettie would return to the ranch. There had been a time when those hopes had been Marty's as well, but no more. Where there had once been love in her heart for her mother, there was only bitterness now. Bitterness and anger for the hurt her mother had caused her father and Dani, especially Dani.

Dani filled their plates with scrambled eggs and ham, then bowed her head to pray. Marty dutifully bowed her head as well, but instead of listening to Dani's prayer, her mind filled with the memory of Ridge Longtree's kiss. She never should have hired that dreadful man, with his midnight blue eyes and insolent smile.

The worst of it was, she was going to have to ask him to ride along with them when they went into town. She had considered asking Scanlan or one of the hands to ride in with her, but she knew the men all had chores of their own to take care of. And, if she were completely honest with herself, she knew she would feel safer with Longtree than with anyone else.

"Marty? Marty!"

She glanced up, wondering how many times Dani had called her name. "What?"

"What time are we leaving?"

"Oh. About half an hour, I guess." Rising, she carried her dishes to the sink. "I'll meet you at the barn."

Grabbing her jacket off the hall tree, Marty left the house. She paused on the front porch and took a deep breath. She loved the way the land looked after a good rain. The sky was bright and clear, dotted with a few stray clouds. Everything looked and smelled fresh and clean.

Glancing at the bunkhouse, she summoned her courage. She wasn't looking forward to asking Longtree to go with them. The man made her nervous, made her think about things she had no business thinking about.

Putting a difficult task off never made it any easier, and, with that in mind, she descended the steps and walked toward the bunkhouse, her boots squishing in the mud.

She found Longtree sitting on his cot, a game of solitaire spread out in front of him. He was dressed pretty much as he had been the first time she saw him. His trousers were black wool and looked custom made. His shirt was dark blue, emphasizing the color of his eyes. His hat hung on a hook over his bed.

He looked up as she entered the room, one brow raised.

"We're going into town," she said brusquely. "I want you to ride along."

"All right."

"We'll be ready in about twenty minutes."

He nodded. "Yes, ma'am."

She should have turned and left then. She had said what she had to say but she stood rooted to the spot, held by his dark blue gaze, by the almost palpable attraction that hummed between them. It was a new sensation for her, and it left her feeling confused and uneasy. She didn't even like the man, so why did she have the sudden urge to close the door and shut out the rest of the world?

Her heart began to pound as he rose from the cot in a single fluid motion. He grabbed his hat and settled it on his head, then strode toward her, his long legs quickly covering the short distance between them until he was standing in front of her, forcing her to tilt her head back so she could see his face. She didn't like having to look up at him.

"What . . . what are you doing?" she asked, hating the breathless quality in her voice.

He thumbed his hat back on his head. "Going out to saddle my horse," he replied, his voice suddenly low and intimate. "What did you think I was going to do?"

Heat flooded her cheeks. "I . . . um . . . nothing."

He smiled down at her, one brow arched, a knowing look in his eyes, a look that caused her cheeks to burn even more.

His gaze moved over her face, lingering on her lips, before he stepped past her, his body lightly brushing hers. The mere touch of his arm and thigh against hers sent shivers down her spine.

Turning, she watched him stride toward the barn. He was a dangerous man to have around, she thought. Dangerous in more ways than one.

Marty slid a surreptitious glance at Ridge Longtree as he rode beside the buckboard on the way into town. He rode easily in the saddle, his hat pulled low, his hand resting on his thigh near the butt of his gun. A casual observer might think he was completely oblivious to what was going on around him, but she knew better. He was aware of everything around them. And she was acutely aware of him—of the way he sat in his saddle, the way he held the reins, the squint lines around his eyes. His eyes. At times they were as hard as flint and yet this morning . . . this morning his gaze had turned her insides to mush. Now just looking at him made her feel . . . shoot, she wasn't sure what she felt. Nervous? Excited? Apprehensive? No other man had ever affected her so strangely, or so strongly.

She'd had her share of suitors over the years. After all, the men far outnumbered the women in this part of the territory. But none of the men who had come courting had appealed to her. They were too old, too young, too foolish, or just too darned ugly. She had turned them down one and all, especially Victor Claunch. She grimaced at the mere thought of him. He was a tall, heavily built man with dark brown hair and cold hazel eyes. He was also the richest man in the territory and accustomed to having his own way— with everything. He was determined that the Flynn ranch would be his, and Marty was just as determined that it would never be his, even if she had to burn the place down lock, stock, and barrel!

Claunch. Even if she couldn't prove it, she was certain he had killed her father.

She glanced over at Longtree again. She had a feeling Longtree would shoot Claunch for her and never bat an eye if she just had the nerve to ask him, but if she did that, she'd be no better than Claunch.

*   *   *

Chimney Creek was a good-sized town. It had three
churches and twice that many saloons, a new school-
house, a fancy two-story hotel, a couple of restaurants
and dress shops, a general store, and a meat market.
The doctor's office was sandwiched between the bank
and the sheriff's office. The barbershop was at the
far end of the street. The barber also acted as the
town dentist.

McClain's Funeral Parlor was located across from
the newspaper office. Marty pulled up in front and set
the brake. Joe Alexander, the newspaper editor,
crossed the street as she alighted from the buckboard.
He was a short, rotund man, balding, with a fringe of
wispy gray hair, and watery blue eyes behind round
spectacles. He had been one of the town's first inhabit-
ants, along with Jim Eggers, who owned the hotel, and
Jonas Murray, who owned the stage line.

"Miss Flynn, I was sorry to hear about your father."

"Thank you, Mr. Alexander."

"He was a fine man."

"Yes, he was."

"If there's anything I can do, you just let me know."

"I will, thank you."

Turning away, the newspaperman tipped his hat to
Dani. He paused in the middle of the street when he
saw Longtree, a frown wrinkling his brow.

"What was that all about?" Marty asked when
Ridge joined them.

He shrugged. "Beats me."

"Do you know each other?"

"Not as I recall."

With a shrug, Marty stepped up on the boardwalk.

"I'll wait for you out here," Ridge said.

"All right. We won't be long."

Taking her sister by the hand, Marty opened the door to the funeral parlor and stepped inside.

Ridge stood on the boardwalk, his shoulder propped against one of the uprights that supported the roof overhang. Tugging his hat down, he stared after the newspaperman, wondering if the man had recognized him. Ridge had never been in Chimney Creek before, but there had been some flyers out on him in the past. It was possible one of them had made it here.

Dismissing the idea, he glanced up and down the street. It looked like a decent town. A number of men were gathered at the blacksmith shop across the way, their voices raised as they discussed the upcoming election.

Ridge blew out a sigh. It had been years since he had hired out his gun. After his last job, he'd vowed never to do it again, yet here he was, playing hired gun for a couple of females. He shook his head ruefully. Working for a woman was never a good idea. Working for two of them was probably worse, especially when one of them was as young and beautiful as Dani Flynn. It would be no trouble to seduce her, he mused. No trouble at all. A few compliments, a couple of kisses in the moonlight, and she would be his for the taking. Unfortunately, tender young virgins had never appealed to him. He liked women, not girls.

Women like Martha Flynn.

He pulled away from that thought like a jackrabbit from a rattlesnake. Marty Flynn was as thorny as a prickly pear. A man would have to be crazy to get involved with her. But there was nothing prickly about her kisses. Her lips were as soft and smooth as the petals of a wild rose.

He swore under his breath. He was here on business, nothing more. He'd find out who killed old man Flynn and then be on his way. Maybe he'd mosey on down to El Paso for a while, or head on over to Virginia City and renew acquaintances with that pretty little girl who worked at the mercantile. Hell, maybe he'd head south and spend the summer with the Apache. It had been a damn sight too long since he had paid a visit to his mother's people. Yet even as the thought of going home crossed his mind, he knew he wouldn't.

So how best to go about finding the old man's killer? The only real clue they had was that the killer rode a horse that had a tendency to drag its left hind foot. Not really much to go on, he thought, but it was all they had, that and the missing pocket watch.

He was still trying to figure out a plan of action when a ruckus over at the blacksmith's shop drew his attention. Glancing over his shoulder, Longtree saw that the discussion had gone from heated words to fisticuffs. Two men were rolling around in the street trading blows while another dozen or so looked on, whooping and hollering and making bets on which man would win. Ridge shook his head. The outcome was a foregone conclusion. The younger man was putting up a good fight, but he didn't have a chance.

Ridge was enjoying the show when Marty and Dani emerged from the funeral parlor.

Dani's eyes widened when she saw the scuffle.

Marty shook her head in disgust. "Come on, Dani; let's get out of here."

"Wait! Isn't that Cory?"

"Yes, the fool. Thinking he can take on Ben Watkins when the man outweighs him by a good forty pounds. Come on, let's get out of here."

Dani stared at the two men, her teeth worrying her lower lip as the two men continued to slug it out.

Ridge looked at Marty. "You want me to break it up?"

"You?"

"Sure."

"Do you think you can?"

His eyes filled with amusement. "Do you think I can't?" Without waiting for an answer, Ridge stepped out into the street. When the two men separated a moment, Ridge drew his Colt and fired into the dirt between them. "That's enough," he said curtly. "You're upsetting the women."

The two men turned to stare at him. "Mind your own business," the bigger of the two said, scowling.

"I am minding my business," Ridge replied, holstering his weapon. "I work for Miss Flynn, here, and your fighting was upsetting her little sister."

A few titters ran through the crowd of onlookers at the blacksmith's shop. The younger man—Cory, no doubt—flushed scarlet. The second man took a step forward. He was a big, bulky man, with hunched shoulders and bushy eyebrows.

"Ben, don't." The warning came from a tall, grizzled man wearing a pair of faded overalls. The muscles in his arms clearly proclaimed that he was the town blacksmith.

The man called Ben scowled over his shoulder. "Mind your own business, Hofstetter."

"Don't be a damn fool," the blacksmith warned softly. "He's a gunslinger."

Ben's eyes narrowed. He stared at Ridge for several moments; then, apparently deciding his friend was right, he turned and shuffled down the street.

"Here, now, what's going on here?"

Ridge swore under his breath as a man wearing a badge arrived on the scene. That was all he needed, he thought irritably, a run-in with the local law.

"Nothing, Sam," the blacksmith said jovially. "Couple of the boys got into a little scuffle, that's all. No harm done."

The lawman's gaze moved over the crowd at the blacksmith's shop, settled briefly on Ridge, then moved across the street to where Marty and Dani stood, looking on. He nodded to the women, then swung his attention back to Ridge.

"You're new in town, aren't you?" he asked.

Ridge nodded.

"Just passing through?"

Marty Flynn stepped off the boardwalk. "He's working for us, Sam."

The lawman regarded Ridge a moment more, then turned his attention to Marty. "I was sorry to hear about your father."

"Thank you. The funeral's set for tomorrow morning at ten."

"I'll be there."

"Do you have any idea who might have . . . have bushwhacked him?"

"No, I surely don't, but we'll keep looking." The marshal glanced at Ridge. "I didn't catch your name."

"I didn't give it."

Marty sent a warning glance at Ridge, and then smiled at the lawman. "Sam, this is Ridge Longtree. Mr. Longtree, this is Sam Bruckner."

The two men shook hands warily.

"You about ready to go, Miss Flynn?" Ridge asked.

"Yes, but first I need to send a wire. Good-bye, Sam."

Bruckner tipped his hat. "I'll see you tomorrow."

With a nod, Marty set off down the street toward the telegraph office. Dani smiled shyly at Cory, who was standing outside the blacksmith's shop dabbing at his bloody lip with his kerchief, and then hurried after her sister.

Conscious of the lawman's gaze on his back, Ridge followed the two women down the street.

Once again, he remained out on the boardwalk while they went inside. He didn't know whom they were sending the wire to, but figured it was most likely to a member of the family.

There were tears in Dani's eyes when she stepped out of the telegraph office. Ridge glanced at Marty, one brow raised inquisitively. She dismissed his unspoken question with a shake of her head, then took Dani by the hand and moved down the boardwalk to where she had left the buckboard.

Ridge lifted Dani onto the front seat, grinning inwardly as she smiled at him while murmuring her thanks.

He walked around the buckboard, intending to offer Marty a hand, but she waved him away and climbed up on her own.

With a rueful shake of his head, he swung into the saddle. "Where to now, ladies?"

"We might as well stop at the mercantile while we're here," Marty decided.

Ridge nodded. Most likely they wouldn't feel much like shopping tomorrow after the funeral.

The general store was located at the other end of town. Ridge was aware of several curious glances cast in his direction as he rode alongside the buckboard. Most of them came from men; one came from a fancy woman leaning over the balcony of one of the saloons.

Redheaded, her cheeks rouged and her lips painted, her full breasts barely covered by a gaudy silk kimono, she waved at Ridge.

"Hey, handsome," she called, "why don't you come see me sometime?"

"Sure enough, honey," he called back, only then remembering that the Flynn women were within hearing distance. Glancing sideways, he saw that Martha Flynn was watching him, her eyes narrowed, her expression sour.

Before he could say anything, she faced front again.

"Something bothering you, Miss Flynn?" he asked, unable to resist baiting her.

"Of course not," she replied coolly. Pulling back on the reins, she brought the buckboard to a halt in front of Grant's General Store. The sign read:

GRANT'S GENERAL STORE
Groceries
Dry Goods
Hardware
Best Selection This Side of the Missouri

Ignoring him, she climbed down from the seat and headed for the general store. "Come on, Dani," she said, glancing over her shoulder to make sure her sister was behind her. "We haven't got all day."

Chapter 4

Ridge stared after the two women. Dani Flynn might be as pretty as a spring day and as sweet as molasses, but Ridge had never had much of a sweet tooth, and the more he saw of Marty Flynn, the more he liked her, rough exterior and all.

Dismounting, he tossed his horse's reins over the hitching post and followed the women into the store. The smell of leather and coal oil mingled with the scents of pickles and cheese.

Figuring the women would be a while, Ridge strolled up and down the aisles. There were shelves filled with canned goods, bolts of calico and gingham, pots and pans, flatirons and horse harnesses. Moving on, he saw barrels filled with plump dill pickles, crackers, and sauerkraut. An assortment of soaps and laundry tubs were stacked in one corner. He saw sacks of potatoes and onions and apples as well as sacks of rice and beans and sugar.

One glass-topped counter held long bars of Brown's Mule plug chewing tobacco. The bars were creased along the top to make it easy for the proprietor to cut off the right amount. Red metal tags in the shape of a mule were stuck into each section. There were boxes of cigars. Sacks of Bull Durham came with free packs of papers.

Another counter held a variety of nostrums guaranteed to cure just about any ailment known to plague mankind, from John Bull's Worm Destroyer to Dr. Rose's Obesity Powders.

A table held an assortment of spectacles that were priced from four bits to a dollar a pair. As he passed by, Ridge saw a middle-aged gent trying on one pair after another until he found a pair that suited him.

There was also a shelf of veterinary supplies, including cures for scours, distemper, mange, and colic. Nearby were curry combs and brushes, calf ropes, picket pins, and saddle blankets. A couple of yellow rain slickers made a bright splash of color against one wall.

In a corner, he saw a jumble of washtubs, slop jars, cuspidors, milk pails, coffeepots, dustpans, teakettles, coffee grinders, and washbasins.

Moving on, he saw a display case filled with knives of every size and description, along with an assortment of fishhooks.

The back of the store held a rack of ladies' ready-to-wear dresses. Floor-to-ceiling shelves held an assortment of men's shirts, trousers, and longhandles.

By the time he made his way back to the front of the store, Marty and Dani were waiting at the front counter while their bill was tallied.

The man behind the counter kept up a running conversation while he added up their bill, talking about the upcoming church social and the new parson and the weather, until he figured out how much he was owed and handed Marty the bill. She looked it over carefully before she paid it.

"Here," Ridge said, stepping up to the counter, "let me help you with those."

For a moment, he thought she'd refuse his offer just to be ornery. Instead, she uttered a curt, "Thank you." It took all three of them to carry the supplies out to the buckboard.

They were about ready to go when the young man Ridge had seen fighting earlier came running toward them. He was a tall, lanky kid with wavy brown hair, mild brown eyes, and a sprinkling of freckles across the bridge of his nose.

Dani's eyes lit up as the young man approached the buckboard. He nodded at Marty, but it was Dani who held his attention.

"Cory, are you all right?" Dani asked anxiously.

The kid lifted a hand to his black eye. "Yeah, I'm fine. Don't worry about me. Listen, I heard about your father. . . ."

At the mention of her father, tears filled Dani's eyes.

"I'm sorry, Dani." Cory looked up at Marty, who was standing beside the buckboard, her fingers drumming impatiently on the wheel. "Miss Flynn, if there's anything I can do . . ."

"Thank you, Cory," Marty replied. "The funeral's tomorrow at ten. If you'll excuse us, we have a lot to do before then."

"Oh, right." He looked at Dani again. Ridge could tell the kid was itching to touch her but didn't dare, not with her sister standing there, watching his every move.

"I'll see you tomorrow, then," Cory said.

"Yes," Dani replied softly. "Tomorrow."

The trip back to the ranch was uneventful. Ridge

used the time to study the landscape. Two roads, one of them little more than an overgrown path, veered off the main trail. When asked, Marty told him that the first cutoff led to an abandoned homestead. The second led to the Circle V Bar C, Victor Claunch's spread.

Marty was certain Claunch had killed her old man.

Ridge shifted on the seat. He would have to arrange to meet Mr. Victor Claunch one day soon.

Judging from the crowd gathered at the grave site in the small family cemetery that morning, Ridge figured the whole town had turned out to pay their final respects to Seamus Flynn. Standing off by himself, Ridge let his gaze wander over the crowd. He recognized Dani's friend Cory, looking uncomfortable in a city suit and bowler hat. And there was Alexander, the newspaperman, and the lawman, Sam Bruckner. The blacksmith stood head and shoulders above everyone else.

Ridge shifted his gaze to the Flynn women. Both wore black. Dani wore a floppy-brimmed hat with a black veil. Her head was lowered, and Ridge knew she was weeping.

His gaze moved to Martha Flynn. She stood there with her head high and her eyes dry. It was the first time he had seen her in a dress. It fit well enough and looked good on her, but he thought pants and a shirt suited her far better.

She slipped her arm around her sister's shoulders as the parson began to speak, extolling the virtues of the late Seamus Patrick Flynn, who had single-handedly carved an empire out of the wilderness. Turning to the grieving daughters and the friends and neighbors of the deceased, he assured them that the dearly departed had gone to a far, far better place.

Tuning the parson out, Ridge let his glance move over the mourners once again. His eyes narrowed as they settled on a tall, well-dressed man standing on the far side of the casket. The man, who looked to be in his mid to late forties, had dark brown hair, hazel eyes, and a thin mustache just turning gray. He was bulky through the shoulders and his suit looked hand-tailored. A gold watch fob winked in the sunlight. The man wasn't paying any more attention to what the parson was saying than Ridge was. Instead, he was watching Marty Flynn.

Ridge would have bet his brand-new Winchester rifle that the man was none other than Victor Claunch.

Ridge blew out a breath of relief when the parson said the final amen. One by one, the mourners stopped to offer their condolences to Dani and Marty. Mr. Watch Fob was the last to offer his sympathy.

Ridge moved up behind Marty as the man took her hand in his.

"I'm sorry about your father, Martha. He was a good man."

"Yes, he was."

"If there's anything I can do for you in the next few days, you just let me know."

"Thank you, Mr. Claunch. I'm sure we'll be fine." It was clearly a dismissal.

Claunch knew it, too. A muscle twitched in his jaw. "I imagine you'll be moving back east with your mother now."

Ridge couldn't see Marty's face, but he saw her shoulders stiffen.

"We're not going anywhere," she said, her voice cool.

Ridge moved up to stand beside Marty. "Are you ready to go, Miss Flynn?"

Claunch looked at Ridge and then back at Marty. "Who's this?"

"A new hand. I hired him a few days ago."

Claunch's gaze moved over Ridge, lingering on the well-worn grips of his Colt. "What'd you hire him to do?" he asked brusquely. "He's sure as hell no cowboy."

"I hired him to kill varmints," Marty replied.

Claunch looked at Ridge again. "Is that right?"

Ridge nodded. "If you know of any varmints in these parts, you might warn them to stay the hell away from the Flynn place." He rested his hand on the butt of his gun. "I've got a real itchy trigger finger. Sometimes I shoot first and ask questions later."

Tension crackled between the two men as they sized each other up. Ridge noted the slight bulge under the man's jacket and wondered what kind of iron he carried, and if it was the same gun that had killed old man Flynn.

Knowing it would annoy the hell out of Claunch, Ridge took Marty's hand. "Shall we go?"

"Yes." Marty turned to her sister. "Come along, Danielle; it's time to go home."

The women were subdued on the short ride back to the ranch house. For once, Marty hadn't refused Ridge's assistance when he offered to help her onto the seat of the buckboard. He glanced at them now, their arms around each other. Dani had removed her hat, and he could see the tracks of her tears on her cheeks. Scanlan and the rest of the cowhands rode along behind the buckboard, careful to keep their voices low. Several carriages and buckboards brought up the rear, occupied by close friends of the Flynns'. Ridge knew it was customary for friends of the deceased to stop by with food and condolences and spend time with the family after the funeral. He had a feeling that Marty would just as soon be alone with her grief.

When they arrived at the house, he lifted Dani from the buckboard. She murmured her thanks, then hurried into the house. Turning back to the buckboard, he reached for Marty. She put her hands on his shoulders and he lifted her from the seat, letting her body slide down the length of his own as he set her on her feet. It was a good feeling, but this wasn't the time to pursue it. He took a step backward, putting some distance between them. He didn't want to give any of the cowboys any fat to chew, or add any grist to the gossip mill.

It was in his mind to make himself scarce until the Flynns' company departed, but Marty put an end to that right quick.

"I'd like you to come up to the house," she said.

"Why? You think there's gonna be trouble?"

"No. I'd just like for you to be there."

He wanted to refuse but he couldn't, not when she was looking at him like that. There were dark smudges under her eyes, making him wonder if she'd gotten any sleep the night before.

"All right. I'll be up after I take care of the horses."

"Thank you."

He watched her walk away, her shoulders slumped, until she reached the front door. She paused there a moment, then lifted her head and squared her shoulders. He knew she was pulling herself together so she could be strong for Dani.

Taking up the reins, he led the horses down to the barn, grateful to have a few minutes alone before he had to face the townspeople, who were arriving even now.

By the time he returned to the main house, the porch, the parlor, and the kitchen were overflowing with people standing in small groups. A long table had been set up against one wall. It was heaped with covered dishes, baskets of bread and rolls, some sliced meat and cheese, and a number of desserts.

Dani sat on the sofa, her face pale, an untouched plate of food on her lap. The boy, Cory, sat beside her. It was obvious from the look on the kid's face that he was in love. Marty moved from room to room, chatting quietly with her neighbors, thanking people for their condolences.

A small group of men stood clustered together in the dining room swapping stories about the deceased.

"He was a heck of a horse trader, Seamus was," one man was saying. "I remember he sold me the prettiest little filly I ever saw. Told me she was a top-rate trail horse. And she was, too, except for one thing: She was afraid of water. Never could get that horse to cross so much as a mud puddle, let alone ford a river. When I complained, old Seamus said if he'da knowed I wanted a horse that could swim, he woulda sold me a sea horse."

Quiet laughter filled the room.

"I remember one time . . ."

Moving away from the circle of storytellers, Ridge took a place near the front door, where he could see what was going on but wasn't in anyone's way. He was the first one to see Victor Claunch arrive. Ridge shook his head. If the man had, in fact, killed old man Flynn, then he had a hell of a lot of nerve to show his face here now.

Dismounting, Claunch tied his horse to the hitching post. Removing his hat, he shook off the trail dust, settled the hat back on his head, then walked up the porch steps and through the front door without knocking, as if he already owned the place.

A flicker of surprise showed in Claunch's eyes when he saw Ridge. "What are you doing here?" he demanded, his tone surly.

"I work here, remember?"

"Then perhaps you should be in the bunkhouse, with the other hands."

"Perhaps," Ridge said, his tone just this side of insolent, "but Miss Flynn invited me. Personally."

Claunch's eyes narrowed. "Just what is your relationship to Miss Flynn?"

"Maybe you'd better ask the lady yourself."

"Ask me what?" Marty said, coming up behind them.

Smiling indulgently, Claunch reached for Marty's hand. "There you are, my dear."

"Yes." She slipped her hands into the pockets of her skirt, thereby avoiding his touch. "What is it you wanted to ask me?"

"He wants to know what I'm doing here," Ridge explained.

"Mr. Longtree is here at my invitation," Marty informed Claunch coolly. "It is, after all, my house."

A muscle worked in Claunch's jaw at her rebuke. "I'd like to speak to you alone, Martha."

"I'm afraid that's impossible now." She gestured at the parlor. "As you can see, there are a number of other people here whom I must see to."

"Very well," he said stiffly. "I'll call on you in a day or so, if that's all right."

"Yes, of course," Marty said politely. "Now, if you'll excuse me."

Claunch nodded curtly.

With a glance at Ridge, Marty went back to her guests.

Claunch glared at Ridge. "Enjoy yourself while you can," he said brusquely. "You'll be out of a job as soon as Martha and I are married."

"From what I've seen, that could be a while."

Rage filled Claunch's eyes and mottled his cheeks. "We'll see about that!" He stalked out of the house, letting the front door slam behind him.

Chapter 5

Marty wandered aimlessly through the house, picking up a dish here, a glass there. The last of the mourners had gone home over two hours ago. Pleading a headache, Dani had gone to her room shortly after that, leaving Marty to clean up after their guests. In truth, she was glad to have something to do, anything that would keep her from thinking about her loss. She had always been closer to her father than to her mother, and now he was gone. . . .

She shrugged the thought away and concentrated on the compassion and openheartedness of their neighbors instead. It had been kind of their friends to come and express their condolences, to help them through the first bleak hours after the funeral. As always, at births or marriages or deaths, the women brought food.

She glanced at the painting of her mother and father that hung over the fireplace in her father's office, and suddenly the tears she had been holding back for so long flooded her eyes. With a choked cry, she ran out of the house, down the porch steps, and out into the darkness, where no one could hear her.

Pausing beneath a cottonwood tree, she dropped to

her knees. Wrapping her arms around her waist, she rocked back and forth sobbing, "Pa, oh, Pa!"

"Martha."

She glanced up at the sound of her name, and felt her heart skip a beat when she saw a dark shape materialize out of the shadows. She blinked at the apparition, wondering if it was her father's ghost, and then she realized it was Ridge Longtree.

"What are you doing out here?" She wiped her tears away, hoping he hadn't heard her crying. She hated weakness in anyone, most especially in herself.

"Do you want me to go?"

She started to say yes, and then sighed. "No."

He dropped down beside her. In the pale light of the moon, he could see the tears still trickling down her cheeks. With a wry grin, he offered her his kerchief.

She took it with a murmured, "Thank you."

"Anytime," he remarked, watching her dry her tears.

She managed a faint smile through her sniffles.

"Why do you hide your tears?" he asked.

"Dani's cried enough for both of us. One of us has to be strong."

"You think hiding your tears from your sister makes you stronger?"

"Yes. No. I don't know." Sparks danced in her eyes. "I just hate for anyone to see me crying. I always have." Ever since she had been a little girl, she'd gone off to cry alone, taking refuge in the loft or under the porch or out behind the springhouse.

"There's no shame in crying for a loved one."

She regarded him curiously, her own loss momentarily forgotten. "Did you lose someone you loved?"

Ridge nodded. Though it had happened years ago,

the wound was still fresh, still raw. And because he couldn't face returning home knowing she wasn't there, he had never gone back. Now, almost ten years later, he wasn't sure which hurt the most—the loss of his sister or the loss of his homeland. He gazed into the distance. The land where he had been born was in his blood. He had spent years running away, growing more bitter with every mile he had put between himself and the distant mountains where the Chiricahua made their home.

"Ridge?"

"What?" He drew his gaze from the distance and focused on the woman once again.

"I'm sorry for your loss."

"It was a long time ago."

"But you're not over it, are you?"

"No." And he never would be. "Come on," he said, rising. "I'll walk you back."

"All right." Ignoring his hand, she stood and took a step forward. A startled cry rose in her throat as she tripped over a rock and stumbled forward.

Instinctively, Ridge caught her in his arms.

"Let go of me."

"Hey, I could have let you fall."

"Thank you for catching me. Now let me go."

"You afraid of me, Martha Jean?"

"Of course not! I just don't like being held."

"I think it's just what you need."

"I don't care what you think," she said, trying to wriggle out of his arms. "Let me go!"

He ran his hand over her hair and down her back, soft and slow. "Easy, darlin'," he murmured, drawing her closer. He sensed more than saw her attempt to knee him. He turned sideways just in time, his arms tightening around her. "Hey, now, there's no need for that. I'm not gonna hurt you."

"Let me go, Longtree. Please let me go."

"Shh. You don't have to pretend with me. You don't have to be strong now. I know what you want, darlin'." And so saying, he lowered his head and kissed her.

At the touch of his lips on hers, she stopped struggling and melted into his embrace. His kiss was infinitely tender, demanding nothing in return. His hand moved up and down her back in long, slow strokes that were somehow soothing and sensual at the same time.

Lifting his head, he gazed into her eyes, and then he kissed her again. Marty's arms slipped around his waist. With a sigh, she closed her eyes and surrendered to his touch. He did indeed know what she wanted. There was nothing of tenderness in his kiss this time. His mouth claimed hers boldly. His tongue slid across the seam of her lips, demanding entrance. No man had ever kissed her like that before. At first she was shocked, and then, to her shame, curiosity overcame prudence and she parted her lips for him.

Shock rippled through her once again. Shock and pleasure, and a spiraling desire that started low in her belly and spread outward, like a wildfire fanned by the wind.

She clung to him, moaning softly, as he deepened the kiss. She didn't realize he had lowered her to the ground until she felt the dampness beneath her back. He cradled her head in one hand while the other began a slow exploration of her body.

Her eyes flew open at the touch of his hand on her breast. Startled, she slapped him and then scrambled to her feet, her arms crossed over her chest, her breath coming in ragged gasps, as if she had run a great distance.

He stared up at her, one hand rubbing his cheek. "Damn, woman, make up your mind."

She stared at him, her cheeks flushed with shame. He was a hired gun, a man she had known only a few days. What must he think of her? What would Dani think of her? Oh, Lord, what would her father think? She had buried him only that morning, and tonight she was rolling around in the dirt with a stranger.

Mortified, she turned and fled into the darkness.

Still absently rubbing his cheek, Ridge stared after Marty Flynn. He had kissed a lot of women in his day, but none of them compared to her. He had a feeling that once she let herself go, she would burn hotter and fly higher than a skyrocket on the Fourth of July. Not only that, but she'd likely burn up the man who taught her the pleasures of intimacy. Grinning ruefully, he knew he'd give his back teeth to be that man.

"Marty, where have you been? I've been looking everywhere for you." Dani looked at her sister and frowned. "Are you all right?"

"Of course I'm all right. What are you doing down here? I thought you went to bed."

"I did, but I couldn't sleep." Dani rose from the sofa, her eyes narrowed. "You've been crying."

"I have not."

"There's grass in your hair."

Marty stared at her sister defiantly. "So?"

Dani shrugged. "Your mouth is all swollen."

"Are you through taking inventory?"

"You were with him, weren't you?" Dani exclaimed in horror. "That gunslinger! Marty, how could you?"

"Dani—"

"Pa's not even cold in the ground yet."

"You kissed him, too," Marty said defensively.

"Not the night we buried Pa."

Marty sank down on the sofa, all the fight seeping out of her like water through a sieve. "I don't know how it happened. One minute he was comforting me, and the next we were . . ."

Dani's eyes grew wide. "You didn't let him . . . ?"

"No, of course not." But she had wanted to. Mercy, how she had wanted to.

"I think you should tell him to go away."

"No." Marty shook her head emphatically. "I need . . . that is . . . I mean, we need him here."

"For what?" Dani asked skeptically.

"To find out who killed Pa."

"We both know it was Claunch, even if there's no way to prove it."

Marty blew out a sigh. "Maybe it wasn't him."

Dani stared at her in disbelief. "How can you say that?"

"I don't know. I'm going to bed. Good night."

"Good night."

Upstairs in her room, Marty changed into her nightgown, then climbed into bed, only to lie there, her thoughts chasing themselves like a dog chasing its tail. What if Victor Claunch wasn't the one who had killed her father? And if it wasn't Claunch, then who? Try as she might, she couldn't think of anyone else in town who would have wanted her father dead. What if the murderer was just some passing cowboy? If that was true, they might never find the man responsible. And what was she going to do about Ridge Longtree? Maybe Dani was right. Maybe she should tell him to leave.

Rising, she went to the window, her restless gaze searching the darkness. A brief flare of light drew her gaze, and in its faint glow she saw a man standing near one of the corrals. It was Longtree. She knew it without a doubt. Clutching the neck of her nightgown, she stared down at him. What would have happened if she hadn't slapped him? Would he have continued to kiss and caress her until she was helpless to resist, until he had taken everything she had to offer? And where would that have left her? Unmarried and ruined for life.

But standing there, watching him, she couldn't help thinking it might have been worth it.

Dani sat at her bedroom window, the curtain drawn back ever so slightly. Ridge Longtree stood in the yard below. From time to time he took a drag on his cigarette. The faint glow cast red shadows on his face, giving him a devilish look. Fitting, she thought, and couldn't help wondering what had gone on between him and Marty. She couldn't help remembering how Ridge had kissed *her* only a few days ago. He had pretended he was comforting her, too, the way Marty said he was comforting her, but he was a liar. Nettie had told her men wanted only one thing from a woman, and that if a woman was smart, she didn't give anything away, especially her virginity, which could be given only once. It was, Nettie had said, the most precious gift a woman could give her husband.

She frowned, wondering why a woman had to be pure but a man didn't. She was pretty sure that Ridge Longtree had bedded plenty of women in his time, and she didn't intend to be one of them. And yet . . . She lifted her fingertips to her lips, remembering his kiss. It had been gentle, but it had made her yearn for things she didn't quite understand, things she had never felt when Cory kissed her. Did that make her wicked? Ridge Longtree was a dangerous man, a man who frightened her in ways she didn't comprehend.

A footstep in the next room drew her attention. So, she thought, Marty couldn't sleep, either. Was she standing at her window, staring down at Longtree?

With a sigh, Dani crawled back into bed and pulled the covers up to her chin. Once, she and Marty had spent hours wondering what went on behind Mama and Daddy's closed bedroom door. Being raised on a ranch, Dani and her sister knew what mating was. They had seen dogs and cats and horses mate. After watching a stallion cover a mare, Dani had declared she was never going to let any boy do that to her.

But she had been a lot younger then. She was a little older now, a little wiser. After all, she had once seen Cory swimming naked in the creek, although all she had seen was his bare behind. And that from a distance.

Sighing, she stared up at the ceiling and wished her mother was there to answer the questions she didn't dare ask Marty.

Chapter 6

Nettie Flynn stared blankly into the distance for several moments, then looked down at the telegram in her hand and read it again.

Pa was killed on the 5th by a person or persons unknown. Dani wants you to come home.
Martha.

Seamus was dead.
She read the words a third time, and a fourth.
Seamus was dead. The word seemed to echo through her mind—*dead, dead, dead*. A huge weight seemed to lift from her shoulders.
Seamus was dead. He couldn't hurt her anymore.
She read the telegram a fifth time, only then noticing that it said Dani wanted her home. Nothing to indicate that Martha wanted to see her. That wasn't surprising, but it hurt just the same.
She wondered if she would ever find the courage to tell her daughters why she had left them. They had grown up thinking she had deserted them without a qualm. Would they hate her all the more if she told them the truth? Even if they forgave her, they might still hate her for telling them the truth about their

father. Lord knew she would never forgive herself for leaving them. But she had been so young when it happened. So afraid of her husband's rage. Afraid of what her impressionable daughters would think if they found out.

She read the words again, her gaze lingering on the names of her daughters. Martha had just turned sixteen and Dani ten when Nettie left the ranch. They would be young women now. She had missed out on so much.

And now Seamus was dead.

Did she dare go back? How could she not?

She stared at the telegram again, wondering if she should send a wire and let Martha know she was coming. After a moment, she decided against it. Better to arrive unannounced than to risk having Martha tell her not to come.

With her mind made up, Nettie went into the bedroom and began to pack.

Chapter 7

Three days later, Marty sat in Randolph Ludlow's office, listening in disbelief as he read her father's will.

Unable to believe what she was hearing, Marty slammed her hands down on the arms of her chair. "He left the ranch to *her*? I don't believe it!"

"I'm afraid it's true, Miss Flynn." Randolph Ludlow tapped the paper on the desk in front of him. "You can read it for yourself, if you like."

"But . . . why?" Marty glanced at Dani, who was sitting beside her, as if her sister might have the answer, then looked back at the lawyer. "Why would he leave her the ranch? Nettie hated it, hated it so much she ran back to Boston."

"I'm afraid I couldn't say why. According to the terms of the will, she owns the house and the land, but all the stock and tack belong to you."

Marty stared at her father's lawyer in disbelief. Randolph Ludlow was short and compact, with thick gray hair, a handlebar mustache, and mild blue eyes. He returned her stare with unruffled patience, apparently accustomed to the outbursts of bereaved heirs.

"What about Dani?" Marty demanded. "Didn't he leave her anything?"

"Yes, of course. He left Danielle a sizable trust that she'll inherit when she turns twenty-one."

Dani's eyes widened in surprise, but she remained mute, as she had since they'd entered Ludlow's office.

Marty sat back in her chair, her mind reeling. Her father had left the ranch to Nettie. How could he? How could he, when he knew how much her mother hated it and how much she herself loved it?

"What if Nettie doesn't want the ranch?" Marty asked.

Ludlow shrugged. "Let's hope she does."

"But if she doesn't? Can she sell it?"

"Yes, I'm afraid so."

"But I want it!"

"You can always buy it from her."

"With what?" Marty fought back the useless urge to cry. Whatever had possessed her father to leave the ranch to Nettie, the stock to Marty, and the cash to Dani? She clenched her hands as anger washed through her. Hard on the heels of that anger came a sense of guilt for being angry with her father when he wasn't there to defend himself.

"Perhaps you could get a loan from the bank."

"Maybe." But she thought the chances of that were mighty slim. Even with the cattle as collateral, she didn't think Miles Jackson over at the bank would consider lending her enough money to buy the ranch.

"You could always sell the cattle," Ludlow suggested.

Marty shook her head. Cattle prices were down. Even if they were selling at top dollar, without the cattle, there was no way to make the ranch pay for itself. If she sold the cattle to buy the ranch, she wouldn't have any money left to restock it.

"Well," Ludlow said, spreading his hands, "perhaps

you're worrying for nothing. Your mother may not wish to sell."

"Thank you, Mr. Ludlow." Rising, Marty smoothed a wrinkle from the front of her skirt. "Come along, Dani."

Ludlow also rose. "I'm sorry you're upset." Rounding his desk, he offered Marty his hand, then shook hands with Dani. "Let me know if there's anything else I can do."

With a nod, Marty left the lawyer's office.

"You can use my money to buy the ranch," Dani said, coming up behind Marty.

"I could," Marty said, "but you won't get it for another four years."

"Well, I'm sure Mama would be willing to wait."

"I'm not," Marty replied curtly. Stepping off the boardwalk, she headed across the street to where they had left the buckboard, her thoughts growing darker with each passing moment.

"Marty! Look out!"

She glanced up at her sister's warning cry, felt her insides go cold when she saw a freight wagon bearing down on her. Before she could think to move, something crashed into her from behind and shoved her out of harm's way. She fell facedown in the dirt, scraping her hands and knees. Before she could recover, rough hands were turning her over. A pair of angry blue eyes moved over her from head to foot.

"You little fool!" Ridge Longtree admonished, lifting her from the ground and cradling her in his arms. "Didn't anybody teach you to watch where you're going?"

She blinked up at him as the back of the freight wagon rumbled past, trembling as she realized how close she had come to being trampled.

Dani came hurrying toward her. "Marty! Marty, are you all right?"

She nodded, too shaken to speak.

"Thank goodness you were here, Mr. Longtree," Dani said. "She might have been killed."

"She's all right," Ridge assured her. "Just a little spooked."

"You . . . you can put . . . put me down now."

"I like you fine right where you are." He whispered the words close to her ear so only she could hear them.

Marty stared up at him, her eyes widening.

For a moment, he thought she was going to slap him again.

"Please put me down," she begged. "People are watching."

Slowly, he set her on her feet.

She looked up and down the street, then walked as quickly as she could toward their buckboard.

"You're limping," Ridge observed.

"I scraped my knee in the dirt."

His hand on her shoulder brought her to a stop. "Let me see."

"Not here!" she exclaimed, conscious of watching eyes.

With a huff of annoyance, he let her go. Holding her head high, she made it to the buckboard, with Ridge at her elbow the whole way. He didn't ask her permission, merely lifted her off her feet and onto the seat. When she was settled, he lifted Dani up beside her.

"You two ready to go home?" he asked.

With a nod, Marty picked up the reins, wincing as the leather slid over her palms.

Ridge walked around the back of the buckboard to Marty's side. "Let me see your hands."

"I'm fine," she said through clenched teeth.

Eyes narrowed, he swung up beside her. "Let me see your hands." He bit off each word.

Glaring at him, she held out her hands, palms up. Muttering under his breath, Ridge passed the reins to Dani.

She shook her head, her eyes wide.

"Dani doesn't like driving the team," Marty said, reaching for the reins.

"We all have to do things we don't like once in a while," Ridge retorted.

Dani looked at Marty, a silent plea in her eyes. "Marty . . ."

Marty looked at Ridge, her jaw set. "I can do it."

"No," he said, "you can't."

Untying his horse from the hitching post, he secured the reins to the back of the buckboard. "Dani, get in the back."

She didn't argue. Looking relieved, she climbed over the back of the seat and dropped down into the bed of the wagon.

Climbing up beside Marty, Ridge took up the reins, released the brake, and clucked to the team.

As the horses trotted down the street, he slid a glance in Martha Flynn's direction. She sat beside him, her back rigid, her cupped hands resting on her thighs. Her black skirt was covered with dust, and the hem had been torn. Staring at her, he couldn't help wondering what the hell had upset her so badly that she had walked in front of a freight wagon.

With a shake of his head, he turned his attention to the road ahead. Even so, he was acutely aware of the woman sitting beside him. Her thigh occasionally brushed against his. Even above the smell of dust and leather and horse, he could detect the scent of the perfume she wore.

They were about a mile out of town when she said softly, "You saved my life. Thank you."

"Anytime." He looked at her again. "What made you do such a damn fool thing?"

"I just wasn't thinking about what I was doing, that's all."

"You were sure as hell thinking about something." He frowned. "You were coming out of Ludlow's law office, weren't you?"

"It's none of your business."

"Is that right?"

"Just because you saved my life doesn't give you the right to pry into my business."

She was getting prickly, Ridge thought with a wry grin. A sure sign that she was feeling better.

Silence fell between them again.

Ridge gazed out over the grassland that stretched away on both sides of the road. Cattle grazed on the lush grass. He spied a deer in the shadows. A hawk soared high overhead, wings spread wide as it drifted on the air currents until it abruptly changed direction, folded its wings, and swooped down on some unsuspecting rodent or rabbit.

Lifting his gaze, he stared at the mountains in the distance and felt an old stirring for home rise within him. It had been a long time since he had ridden up the narrow winding corridor that led to the entrance of the Apache stronghold, a place surrounded by rocky walls that were fifteen hundred feet high. It had been too long since he'd heard the sound of the drums and watched the devil dancers. Too long since he'd heard the harsh, guttural tongue of his mother's people. A lifetime.

As the silence stretched between them, Marty looked over at Ridge. He had a strong profile, prominent cheekbones, a nose that might have been broken, a determined jaw. "Where were you headed when you stopped at our place that first night?"

"Nowhere."

"Don't you have a home? People who miss you?"

"Not since I was a kid."

"Where did you grow up?"

He slid a glance in her direction. "In the Dragoon Mountains." The Apache sanctuary stood in splendid isolation, surrounded by alkali flats and desert. Since clouds of dust raised by approaching horses could be seen for forty miles, it was impossible for an enemy to approach them undetected. Water was available year-round, thanks to springs located inside the stronghold. The slopes were covered with piñon, mesquite, juniper, catclaw mimosa, yucca, and scrub oak.

"Indian country," she murmured, a note of awe evident in her tone.

He nodded. "You ever have any trouble with the tribes in this area?"

"Nothing serious. They steal a few cattle now and then, but Pa . . ." She took a deep breath and blew it out in a long sigh. "Pa said it was better to let them take a few head now and then than try to stop them. I guess he was right. The Apache raided a couple of the other ranches last year, but they left us alone."

Ridge grunted softly. "Your father was a wise man."

"Yes, he was."

She fell silent again, and he waited for the inevitable

question. It came a moment later. "Why don't you live with the Indians anymore?"

"Just because I work for you doesn't give you the right to pry into my personal business."

She didn't like having her own words thrown back at her. He could see it in the sudden taut line of her jaw, the quick flare of heat in her eyes.

Dani's laughter bubbled up from the back of the buckboard.

Marty glanced over her shoulder. "Hush up, you."

"Sorry," Dani replied, laughter still evident in her tone.

Marty looked at Ridge again. "I probably should have asked about this before I hired you, but you're not wanted anywhere, are you? By the law, I mean?"

"Are you sure you want to know? It might be better if you didn't."

"What do you mean?"

He shrugged. "If something happens later, you can always say you didn't know."

She pondered that for a few moments. "I think I'd better know now."

"All right. I'm wanted over in Dodge and in Abilene."

"What for?"

He looked at her, one brow arched. "What do you think?"

"Murder?"

"That's what it says on the poster."

"Are you . . . Did you . . . ?"

"It was self-defense both times. I didn't hang around to find out if a jury would agree."

"Why not?"

He looked at her as if she was one loaf short of a dozen. "I'm Apache. The men I killed weren't."

She didn't have to ask what he meant. Phil Sheridan wasn't the only one who thought that the only good Indians were dead Indians. Most of her friends and neighbors felt the same way. Even though the Apache did most of their raiding in Mexico, they raided the surrounding ranches from time to time, stealing cattle and horses. Last spring several ranchers had been wounded; one had been killed.

"I didn't have any luck in town," Ridge said after a time. "I asked around at the saloon and over at the smithy, but no one seems to know anything. As far as strangers in town, I seem to be the only one."

"I still think it's Claunch," Marty said.

"He seems to be well liked by the townspeople." Ridge had been in town the day before yesterday. Sitting in on a poker game, he had listened to the idle chatter of the other men at the card table. Victor Claunch had been mentioned from time to time. His neighbors considered him to be a fair man, worthy of their trust and their respect. He went to church on Sundays. He made sizable donations to the building fund for the new school.

Marty shrugged. "They see only what he wants them to see."

"I'll keep asking around and see if I can turn anything up."

Marty nodded, her thoughts returning to her conversation with Randolph Ludlow as they pulled onto the road that led to the ranch. Somehow, she had to convince her mother not to sell; if she couldn't convince Nettie to keep the ranch, she would have to find a way to buy her out, because she couldn't imagine living anywhere else. The ranch was home, the only one she had ever known, and nobody was going to make her leave. Nobody.

She grimaced as the ranch house came into view. Two horses were tied to the hitching post. She recognized them both. One belonged to Cory Mulvaney. The other belonged to Victor Claunch.

"Looks like you've got company," Ridge remarked, drawing the buckboard to a halt in front of the porch.

"Look, Cory's here!" Dani scrambled out of the back of the buckboard and ran up the front steps.

"At least she's happy to see the man who's come calling on her," Ridge said, watching Dani open the door and hurry inside.

Marty uttered a soft sound of agreement. For a moment, she thought about hiding out in the barn, but then it occurred to her that if she let Victor Claunch court her, she might find out once and for all if he had killed her father.

Swinging down from the buckboard, Ridge walked around the team and lifted Marty to the ground.

"Thank you."

He nodded, then glanced up at the house. "You want me to throw him out for you?"

"No." She brushed her skirt off as best she could, took a deep breath, and moved toward the porch. At the top of the steps, she turned to face him. "Thanks again for what you did this afternoon."

"Just don't let it happen twice."

She smiled at him, then opened the door and went inside.

Ridge stared after her. She was up to something, he thought. But what?

Curious, he followed her up the stairs and into the house.

Chapter 8

Victor Claunch rose from the overstuffed chair that flanked the sofa as Marty entered the parlor. It was all she could do to force a smile as he crossed the room toward her.

"Have you been waiting long?" she asked.

"Twenty minutes or so."

"At least you had company." Marty smiled over at Cory, who was sitting on the sofa. There was no sign of Dani. No doubt she had gone upstairs to freshen up.

"Yes," Victor replied, his tone clearly indicating he had little use for Cory Mulvaney.

"What brings you here, Mr. Claunch?" she asked.

"I'd like to speak to you." Victor glanced past her to where Ridge stood just inside the door. "Alone."

"I can't imagine you have anything to say to me that can't be said in front of Dani or Cory. Or Mr. Longtree."

"I can." Victor took her by the hand and started toward the front door. He paused in front of Longtree. "Don't follow us."

Ridge glanced at Marty. "Miss Flynn?"

"I'll be all right."

Claunch smirked at Ridge, and then followed Marty

out the door. He led her away from the house to a shady spot beneath an ancient pine.

"So," Marty said, "what did you want to tell me?"

"I know the timing isn't right, but I've waited long enough. I let you play your little games, but enough's enough. I need a wife. You need a man to help you with the ranch. It's time we got married."

She wondered how anxious he would be to marry her if he knew Seamus had left the ranch to Nettie. But if he knew that, he might not come around anymore, and she wanted to keep him coming around, at least until she knew whether or not he had killed her father.

"The timing isn't right," she said. "After all, I just buried my father a few days ago." Time, that was what she needed. Time to find an excuse to search Victor's house for her father's watch, time for Ridge to turn up the horse the killer had been riding.

"I'm not suggesting we wed immediately," Claunch said. "I just want things settled between us."

"I can't think of marriage right now," Marty said, wishing he would release her hand. "I can't think of anything but finding the man who killed my father."

"Bruckner said he was satisfied that your father was killed while being robbed. No doubt the man responsible has left the territory."

"Maybe. Maybe not." She forced a smile. "But any talk of marriage will have to wait untill I know for certain. Surely you can understand that?"

"Yes, of course. I have no problem with a long engagement." He patted her hand, looking pleased with himself. "It's settled then." And so saying, he pulled her into his arms and kissed her. It was all she could do to stand there and let him. Had it been any other man, it might have been a rather pleasant kiss. But this wasn't just any man. Even if Victor hadn't pulled the trigger, she was certain he was involved, if not downright responsible for her father's death.

When he released her, she clenched her hands to keep from wiping her mouth.

"I'm glad we've got that settled," he said.

She nodded.

"I'll see you at church on Sunday. Perhaps we'll make a day of it. What would you say to a picnic lunch?"

"That would be nice. What would you like to have?"

"I'll have Reyna take care of it." He kissed her again. "Why don't you get rid of that gunman?"

"I don't think so," she replied calmly. "Not just yet."

"Perhaps you're right," Claunch said. "I'll feel better knowing you've got some protection."

Frowning, Marty stared after Claunch. She had expected him to insist that she ask Ridge to leave. It confused her that he didn't. Had she misjudged him? But if he hadn't killed her father, who had?

She was still frowning when she returned to the house.

Opening the front door, she was disappointed, though not surprised, to see that Ridge was gone. She hadn't really expected him to hang around after she left with Victor, but she was disappointed just the same.

Then she saw her sister on the sofa and all thoughts of Ridge Longtree fled her mind.

"Danielle Flynn!" she exclaimed. "What are you doing?"

Dani and Cory jerked away from each other as if they'd been struck by lightning. It was a toss-up as to which of them was more embarrassed, Dani or Cory. They stared at her, both of them blushing hotly.

Cory stumbled to his feet. "Miss Flynn, I . . . I . . ." He glanced over his shoulder at Dani, then cleared his throat. "We're gonna get married!" he blurted, as if that made everything all right.

"Married?" Marty shook her head. "I don't think so."

Dani stood and slipped her hand into Cory's. "I love him, Marty."

"You're too young to get married, both of you."

"I'm seventeen!"

"And he's seventeen, and you're both too young."

Dani poked Cory in the side. "Say something."

"I'm almost eighteen," he said, squaring his shoulders. "I've got a job. I can support her."

"On what? That pittance you make working for Anderson?"

Cory nodded.

"Dani, you are not getting married," Marty said adamantly. "And I don't want to hear any more about it until you're at least eighteen."

"Why are you being so mean?"

"Why are you being so foolish?"

"Oh, I hate you!" Dani cried. "I really do! I wish Mama were here."

Marty bit back the angry words that rose in her throat. "Cory, I think you'd better go home."

He glanced at Dani, kissed her cheek quickly, and left the room. Marty thought he looked relieved.

"How could you?" Dani shouted. "How could you send him away like that? You treat me like a baby!"

"You're acting like one. Stop it."

With a sob, Dani ran out of the room and up the stairs.

Marty stared after her. Married, indeed! Neither

one of them had the sense God gave a goat. And yet it was easy to see that they were in love. What right did she have to stand in their way? Her mother had been married at seventeen. . . .

"And look how that turned out," she muttered sourly.

Ridge was sitting in the shade of the barn, glumly thinking that he was no closer to finding out who had killed Marty's old man than he had been when she first hired him, when he saw Cory mount his horse and ride out of the yard as if the devil were at his heels.

Taking a last drag on his cigarette, Ridge crushed it beneath the toe of his boot, then rose and ambled up toward the house, drawn by his curiosity at the kid's hasty retreat and a longing to see Marty Flynn. She was in his thoughts more and more these days. And in his dreams at night. No matter how often he told himself they had no future together, he couldn't get her out of his mind.

He found her in the kitchen, her hair tied back, a ruffled apron covering her dress. He knew immediately that the apron belonged to Dani.

"Everything all right?" he asked.

She looked up from the potatoes she was peeling. "Didn't anyone teach you to knock?"

"I did. No one answered."

"So you just walked in?"

"Do you want me to leave?"

"No."

"I saw the Mulvaney boy take off like he had a load of buckshot in his drawers."

Marty blew out a breath of exasperation. "They want to be get married."

"What's wrong with that?"

"What's wrong with it? She's only seventeen, that's what's wrong with it. And Cory . . ." She shook her head. "He hardly makes enough to support himself. How's he going to support Dani? And what if she gets pregnant?"

He rested one shoulder against the doorjamb. "Happens all the time."

She tossed him a sour look. "You're no help."

"What did Claunch have to say?" he asked, deciding to change the subject.

"We're engaged," she replied tartly.

"Looks like everyone wants to get married," Ridge drawled. He didn't like the idea of her marrying another man one damn bit.

"I don't. And we're not engaged. He just thinks we are. Honestly, the man refuses to take no for an answer." She squelched the little voice in the back of her mind whispering that all her financial troubles would be over if she married Victor Claunch.

"Why does he think you're engaged if you're not?"

"He asked me to marry him. I never said yes."

"Did you say no?"

"He didn't give me a chance." She picked up another potato and began to peel it. "I'm not so sure he killed my father."

"What changed your mind?"

"Well, for one thing, he didn't insist that I send you packing."

"Maybe he knew I wouldn't go."

"Wouldn't you?" The idea warmed her like a wool blanket on a cold winter night.

"How can I?" He closed the distance between them, his eyes hot and heavy-lidded.

"Why can't you?" She stared up at him, the knife and the half-peeled potato falling into the sink, unnoticed. Her heart began to pound with excitement. Anticipation ran through her like sweet honey. She swallowed hard, waiting, hoping.

His gaze caressed her face, lingering on her lips. "I haven't found the killer yet."

The heat of his eyes brought a flush to her cheeks. "Is that the only reason?"

"What do you think?" he asked, his voice low and husky.

Think? How could she think when he was looking at her like that, when she could feel the heat radiating from his body, when all she had to do was take one step toward him to be in his arms?

"Martha Jean, if you don't stop looking at me like that, I'm going to take you on the floor right here, right now."

She felt a rush of heat climb into her cheeks and with it the urge to throw her arms around him and beg him to do just that. She couldn't, of course. Not with the sun shining through the window. Not with the back door wide-open. Not with Dani upstairs. But she was tempted. Oh, Lord, she was tempted.

With an effort, she drew her gaze from his and took a step backward. "I think you'd better go."

"I think you're right."

She was glad that his voice sounded as ragged as her own.

He took a deep breath. "I'll go into town again tomorrow and do a little digging, see what I can turn up on Claunch and anybody else who might have had a motive for killing your old man."

She stared up at him. He might be talking about looking into her father's death, but it wasn't doing anything to ease the tension smoldering between them.

"Dammit, woman," he muttered gruffly.

She stared at him, her eyes widening, as he wrapped one arm around her waist and pulled her against him. He kissed her once, hard and quick, and then he was gone, leaving her standing there, her body tingling, every instinct urging her to run after him and make him finish what he had started.

Dani sat on the edge of her bed, listening to the grandfather clock chime the hour. She drummed her fingertips on the table beside her bed, wondering if her sister was ever going to stop pacing the floor.

Thinking she was going to scream in frustration if Marty didn't turn in soon, she pounded her fists on her pillow, her earlier anger at her sister returning with a vengeance. Darn Marty! Always spoiling her fun, always telling her what she could do and what she couldn't. It wasn't fair. Mama had gotten married when she was seventeen, so why couldn't she? She loved Cory, and he loved her. And she was old enough to get married if she wanted to. She knew how to cook and sew and keep house. Hadn't she been doing the cooking and the cleaning since she was a little girl? She could make jams and jellies with the best of them, and her apple pie had won the blue ribbon at the county fair four years running.

She hit the pillow again. She would make Cory a good wife.

The downstairs clock chimed again. Rising, Dani walked across the room and pressed her ear to the wall that separated her room from Marty's. She didn't hear anything. Had Marty finally gone to sleep?

She waited another twenty minutes, and when she didn't hear anything, she locked her door, put on her shoes, and then tiptoed toward the window.

* * *

Ridge was standing in the shadows near the barn, smoking a last cigarette before he turned in, when he saw Dani Flynn climb out of her bedroom window and shinny down the big old tree that grew alongside the house. She paused a moment, glancing right and left, then hiked up her skirt and took off running in the direction of the creek.

Ridge grinned into the darkness. It didn't take a Pinkerton agent to figure out where she was headed.

He glanced up at Marty's window, debating, for a moment whether to wake her and let her know what her little sister was up to, and then he shrugged. Dani Flynn wasn't the first love-struck girl to run off to meet her sweetheart in the middle of the night, and she wouldn't be the last.

Chapter 9

Cory looped his horse's reins over a shrub near the creek. He didn't much like sneaking around to meet Dani, but it was better than never being able to see her alone. He had been crazy about Dani Flynn for as long as he could remember. They had grown up together. He remembered teasing her when they were younger because that was the only way he knew to show her that he liked her. He had pulled on her braids, chased her home from school. Once, he'd put a big ol' bullfrog in the pocket of her coat. He grinned with the memory. Never in all his life had he heard a girl holler so loud.

Picking up a handful of rocks, he skipped them across the water, one after the other, then glanced up at the sky. She was late tonight. He hoped Martha hadn't caught Dani sneaking out of the house. Things were bad enough as they were.

He was bending down to pick up another rock when he heard a faint rustle in the undergrowth across the creek.

Straightening, he stared into the darkness that stretched away on the other side. Probably just an animal of some kind rooting around in the underbrush.

The sound of footsteps approaching from behind him sent his heart racing, and he whirled around, blew out a sigh of relief when he saw Dani walking toward him.

"Tarnation, girl," he muttered.

"What's wrong?"

"Nothing." He wrapped his arms around her. "You're late."

"Longtree was outside having a smoke. I had to go around the back way, then cut through the pasture."

"I'm glad you're here."

"Me, too." She rubbed up against him, her face lifting for his kiss.

Murmuring her name, he drew her close, his mouth covering hers.

She moaned softly and pressed herself against him. With a low groan, Cory broke the kiss.

Dani stared up at him, wondering why Cory's kisses didn't excite her the way Longtree's had, and then brushed the thought aside. She loved Cory, and if he didn't excite her . . . well, it was probably just because she knew him so well. They had grown up together, after all. "More."

Cory took a deep breath. "Dani, you're driving me crazy."

She ran her tongue over her lower lip. "Good."

He shook his head. It was getting harder and harder to resist her, but he had to be strong enough for both of them. It would be so easy to take what she offered, but he loved Dani and wanted to marry her. She said she didn't want to wait, but he couldn't defile her, couldn't take her innocence. Because he loved her, he knew he had to be strong enough for both of them. He knew what happened when a man couldn't control his lust. His older brother had gotten a girl in trouble.

Rather than marry Sherene, Rob had left town. Cory had never forgiven his brother for running off like that. Not only had Rob left Sherene to face the town's scorn alone, but he'd let his child be born a bastard. A few months later, Sherene had taken the baby and left town. It had just about broken his mother's heart. Cory couldn't forgive his brother for that, either.

"Cory."

Dani ran her hands over his arms, down his chest, over his belly, her fingers sliding seductively back and forth.

He cleared his throat. "I don't think we'd better meet down here anymore."

"Why not? I know you want me, Cory. You know I want you."

"I'll talk to your sister again. . . ."

"She won't listen! Let's run away. We could go to Bisbee and get married."

"Are you sure?"

"Yes!" She threw her arms around his neck and kissed him. "Let's do it, Cory, now. Tonight!"

It was a mighty tempting offer, and one he couldn't resist. He drew her closer, one hand stroking her hair. "Mrs. Cory Mulvaney."

"I like the sound of that," she said, smiling.

"Maybe we should wait until tomorrow night."

"Why?"

"We'll need some money, a change of clothes. I don't have any cash on me. You'll need a horse."

"I don't want to wait," Dani said, pouting prettily. She was tired of waiting. She wanted to know what all the mystery was about.

"It's just one more day." Cory stroked her cheek. "We can wait that long."

"I guess so." She looked up at him, her eyes shining in the moonlight. "But only if you kiss me again."

She didn't have to ask him twice.

Caught up in her nearness, lost in the smoldering heat of her kiss, Cory didn't pay any attention to the noise behind him until it was too late.

Chapter 10

Nettie Flynn alighted from the stagecoach. She had forgotten how much she disliked traveling by stage! Settling her hat on her head, she brushed the dust from her clothing as best she could. Lifting her skirts to avoid a mud puddle, Nettie made her way to the boardwalk to wait for the driver to unload her luggage.

She glanced up and down the street, noting that Chimney Creek had grown considerably in her absence. Of course, it was still just a cow town, with wide, dusty streets and the stink of cattle in the air. Still, she was pleased to note there were several decent-looking restaurants, and a new hotel. She might find herself staying there, she mused, depending on the welcome she received from her daughters.

A young boy in too-short pants and a faded blue shirt hurried toward her. "Help you with your bags, ma'am?" he asked politely. "Only two bits to carry them to the hotel."

"Why, thank you, young man. Those two are mine," she said, pointing at a large suitcase and a flowered carpetbag. "But I'm not staying at the hotel. How much to carry them to the livery barn?"

"No extra charge, ma'am."

She smiled. "And do you know someone who could drive me out to the Flynn ranch?"

"You're looking at him, ma'am."

"You?" Nettie exclaimed.

He nodded enthusiastically. "Yes, ma'am."

"How old are you?"

"Thirteen, ma'am."

"And what's your name?"

"Tommy Moorland."

"Very well, Mr. Moorland. Let's go."

She was following young Tommy across the street when she heard someone calling her name. Pausing, she glanced over her shoulder to see Randolph Ludlow hurrying after her.

He smiled as he approached her. "Mrs. Flynn, I thought that was you."

"Good morning, Mr. Ludlow."

"I'm sorry you had to come home to such sad news," Ludlow said.

"Thank you."

"I have a copy of Mr. Flynn's will for you. I was going to mail it to you. If you'll just wait a moment, I'll get it."

She nodded, wondering why she needed a copy. Surely, after all that had happened between the two of them, Seamus had left everything to the girls.

Mr. Ludlow returned a few minutes later. He handed her a large envelope that was addressed to her home in Boston. "If you have any questions, I'll be happy to answer them."

"Thank you, Mr. Ludlow."

"Welcome home, Mrs. Flynn."

She murmured her thanks once again, then stared down the street, bemused.

She looked down when Tommy tapped her on the arm. "Are you ready to go, ma'am?"

A short time later, they were on their way to the ranch. Nettie sat on the spring seat, the envelope clutched in her hands. She studied the boy sitting beside her, a capable driver in spite of his youth.

"Why aren't you in school, Tommy Moorland?"

He hunched his shoulders. "Can't make no money goin' to school."

"I see. Do you live in town?"

"Yes, ma'am."

"With your parents?"

"Just my ma. Pa run off when Nell was born."

She resisted the urge to brush a lock of hair from his brow, certain he wouldn't take kindly to such a gesture. "I'm sorry to hear that."

"We don't need him," Tommy said. "I'm man enough to take care of Ma and the girls."

"How many girls are there?"

"Six."

"You have six sisters? Are they all younger than you?"

"No, ma'am. Leticia's sixteen. She works over to the Red Dog Saloon. And Polly's fifteen. She works as a maid for Miss Ellen over to the boardinghouse."

Nettie stared at him, shocked that he had a sister who worked in a saloon.

"The rest of the girls are too young to work. They goes to school."

"And what does your mother do?"

"She takes in laundry and does ironing for the ladies in town."

"She's lucky to have you to look after her," Nettie said.

He looked straight ahead, but she saw the flush that

crept into his cheeks and reddened the tips of his ears. She had the feeling he hadn't too many compliments in his young life.

Unable to restrain her curiosity any longer, she opened the envelope and withdrew the last will and testament of Seamus Patrick Flynn.

She pressed a hand to her heart when she saw her name.

And to my wife, Nettie Flynn, I bequeath the Flynn Ranch, including the house and outbuildings, to do with as she sees fit, though it would please me greatly if she would stay and make it her home for the sake of our daughters.

"Oh, my," she murmured. "Oh, my!"

"Is something wrong, ma'am?" Tommy asked.

Nettie smiled at him. "No, nothing."

Taking a deep breath, she quickly read the rest of the document, unable to believe that Seamus had left her the ranch. What had he been thinking? Was this his way of trying to make amends for sending her away all those years ago? She had never truly liked living in the West. True, the sunrises and the sunsets had been breathtaking, and she had loved the endless sea of grass and the herds of wild horses, but she had missed the excitement of life in the East. She had missed the parties and fancy-dress balls, the fashionable shops, and having tea with her friends on Sunday afternoons. She had missed the comforts and conveniences she had taken for granted in Boston. Perversely, it wasn't until she returned to Boston, when she knew she would never see the ranch again, that she began to miss it. But, most of all, she had missed her children.

With a sigh, she gazed out over the prairie. She never should have married Seamus Flynn. It had been a mistake from the start, but he had been so handsome, so charming, she had been unable to resist him even when her father warned her that marrying Seamus would cause her nothing but grief. Even when her mother warned her that Seamus Flynn's drinking and fits of jealousy would not make for a tranquil marriage. Headstrong and foolish, Nettie had ignored her parents. So what if Seamus drank? So did her father. And it was flattering to think that Seamus loved her so desperately that he couldn't bear for her to look at another man, or have another man look at her.

If only she had listened to her parents before it was too late . . .

"We're here, ma'am."

"What?" With a shake of her head, she realized they had arrived at the ranch.

Ridge emerged from the cookhouse, a cup of coffee in his hand, in time to see a rickety, one-horse wagon pull into the yard. He paused just outside the cookhouse door. He had been on his way up to the house to talk to Martha Jean, but it looked like she was about to have company. Taking a drink of his coffee, he wondered who had come calling.

As the wagon came to a stop, he got a good look at the face of the woman alighting from the rig. Holy hell. Unless he missed his guess, the woman in the stylish traveling suit was none other than the widow Flynn. His gaze moved over her appreciatively. She wore her hair swept up under a ridiculous bonnet adorned with flowers and a long, curling feather. The fitted jacket and slim skirt she wore showed off a nicely rounded figure. She was a handsome woman, and she knew it, he thought. There was confidence in the way she carried herself. In her heyday, she must have turned heads everywhere she went, he thought, much like her younger daughter. Even now, the few men hanging around at the barn turned to stare at her.

Moving into the shade, he rested his shoulder against a corner of the cookhouse. His talk with Martha would have to wait.

Marty looked out the kitchen window, wondering who would be coming to call so early in the morning. Although it really wasn't that early. The hands were already out on the range, and she'd had breakfast. She guessed Dani was still angry about last night, since she hadn't come downstairs yet. No doubt she would stay in her bedroom all day, sulking.

Marty frowned as Tommy Moorland helped a woman alight from the carriage. Her attire was impeccable from the curling white feather in her bonnet to her short peach-colored jacket and striped taffeta skirt.

Marty leaned forward, her eyes narrowing. No, it couldn't be. But it was.

Nettie Flynn had finally come home.

Tommy trailed after Nettie, a bag in each hand.

Marty took a deep breath. She had imagined this moment a thousand times in the last seven years. Now that it was here, her first thought was to turn and run out the back door.

What could she say to this woman? This woman who now owned the ranch that Marty had called home for as long as she could remember. Like it or not, her mother had the power to keep the ranch or sell it to the highest bidder. Marty muttered an oath, one she had never dared speak aloud in front of her father. She never should have let Dani persuade her to send that wire. Not that it would have solved anything. If Nettie hadn't shown up, Randolph Ludlow would doubtless have sent her a copy of the will.

She waited, her heart in her throat, wondering if her mother would knock or just breeze into the house as if she had never left.

Her answer came a moment later, when there was a soft, ladylike knock on the door.

With a sigh of resignation, Marty left the kitchen to open the front door for the woman she had hoped never to see again.

For a timeless moment, Marty stared at her mother through the screen door, and her mother stared back.

Nettie spoke first. "Martha Jean," she murmured tremulously. "You're all grown-up."

Marty nodded, unable to speak, uncertain of what she was feeling. Nettie looked much the same as she remembered. Her hair was still a rich auburn color, though there were several strands of gray visible beneath her perky bonnet. There were a few fine lines at the corners of her eyes and mouth. She had gained a little weight, though it was not unattractive. Marty was certain that men still turned to stare when her mother passed by.

Nettie tilted her head to one side. "May I come in?"

"Why ask me?" Marty replied, unable to keep the bitterness from her tone. "It's *your* house now."

Turning away from the door, Marty went into the kitchen and poured herself a cup of black coffee, hating the way her hand trembled. She heard Nettie thank the Moorland boy for driving her out to the ranch, then the sound of the front door closing as Tommy left the house.

Nettie Flynn had come home.

She should go upstairs and wake Dani.

She glanced at the back door, tempted once again to turn tail and run away just as far and fast as she could.

"Martha Jean?"

Willing her hands to stop shaking, Marty turned around to face her mother.

"What bedroom should I use?" Nettie asked quietly.

"Why are you asking me? Like I said, the house is yours now. I guess you can have any room you want."

"That bitter tone is most unbecoming."

Marty squared her shoulders and lifted her chin. "Get used to it. As long as you're going upstairs, why don't you wake Dani? I'm sure *she'll* be happy to see you. Now, if you'll excuse me, I have chores that need doing."

Putting her cup in the sink, Marty grabbed her hat off the hook by the back door and left the house. It was all she could do to keep from running toward the barn. She needed to get away, at least for a little while. Needed to get used to the idea of Nettie being at the ranch again. Needed to start thinking of what she would do, where she would go, if Nettie sold the ranch.

Caught up in her own thoughts, she didn't see Ridge Longtree until it was too late.

"Whoa, girl!" he said as she barreled into him. "Where are you going in such an all-fired hurry?"

"Sorry, I didn't see you."

"Yeah, I guessed that." He held her at arm's length. "Are you all right?"

"No, I'm not. I may never be all right again."

"You wanna talk about it?"

"Yes. No. My mother's come back."

So he'd been right. Nettie Flynn had come home at last. He regarded Marty thoughtfully for a moment. "From the look on your face, I'd guess you don't want her here."

"Of course I don't want her here!" Shrugging out of his arms, she began to pace in front of the barn.

"All right, spit it out; what's got you so riled up?" Ridge crossed his arms over his chest. "It's got to be more than the fact that your mother's come home. Hell, you must have been expecting her. You wired her about your old man, didn't you?"

Marty nodded curtly. "All right, I'll tell you why I'm so upset! Daddy left *her* the ranch!"

"So?"

She stared at him in exasperation. "Don't you see? If she doesn't want it, she can sell it, just like that!"

"Didn't he leave you anything?"

"He left *me* the stock."

He nodded, understanding at last. "So if she decides to sell the ranch, you've got no place to graze the herd."

"Exactly."

"Maybe your old man figured it was a way to bring you and your mother back together."

Marty made a sound of disdain in her throat. "Then he was badly mistaken! I don't want to have anything to do with her. I just want her gone."

"Maybe she won't want to sell."

"Why would she want to stay?"

Ridge glanced past Marty. "Why don't you ask her?"

Marty turned to see her mother walking toward them, the hem of her skirt hiked up to keep it from dragging in the dirt.

"Martha Jean, here you are."

"What do you want?"

"Danielle isn't in her room. She isn't in the house at all."

Marty shrugged. Dani sometimes went riding early in the morning. "Cal!" she called to one of the hands that had just ridden in to get a fresh mount. "Did you see Dani this morning?"

"No, ma'am, but I noticed her horse was gone when I rode out after breakfast."

Marty frowned. Dani sometimes got up early, but never as early as the cowhands.

"Where do you think she's gone?" Nettie asked.

"I don't know." Marty looked at Ridge. "You haven't seen her either?"

"Not since late last night."

"When? Where? How late?"

"Sometime after eleven. I figured she was sneaking out to meet the Mulvaney kid."

Marty stared at him, her hands fisted on her hips. "And you didn't stop her?"

Ridge shrugged. "I wasn't hired to look after your sister."

"Did you see her come back?"

"No. I heard a noise out behind the barn a little later and I went to check it out. For all I know, she could have shinnied back up the tree while I was gone."

"Did you notice which way she went?"

He jerked a thumb over his shoulder. "She started off toward the creek. I'll go check it out, see what I can find."

"I'll come with you."

"Suit yourself."

"I'll wait up at the house," Nettie said.

Ridge waited for Marty to answer, and when she

didn't, he said, "That's a good idea, Mrs. Flynn. We'll walk you back." At Marty's frown of annoyance, he added, "I need to check your sister's tracks, make sure she didn't veer off in some other direction before she reached the water."

They left Nettie Flynn standing on the porch, one hand clutching an upright, an anxious expression on her face.

It only took a few moments for Ridge to pick up Dani's footprints. They were the only fresh tracks leading away from the side of the house toward the creek. Marty trailed behind him, stepping where he stepped.

Ten minutes later he hunkered down on his heels near the edge of the creek, easily reading what had happened in the scuffed footprints left in the damp ground along the shore.

"She met someone here, the Mulvaney boy, most likely. They were standing close." Ridge looked up at Marty and grinned. "Kissing, I reckon."

She made a face at him.

Ridge chuckled, then turned his attention to the ground once more. He studied the tracks another few minutes.

Rising, he shook his head. "They're long gone."

"Gone? Gone where?"

Ridge took a deep breath, wondering how she'd take the news. "They've been captured by Apache."

"What? I don't believe you. The Indians have never bothered us."

"See that? It's a moccasin print."

She looked where he pointed. The footprint was barely visible. If Ridge hadn't pointed it out to her, she never would have noticed it.

"I was coming up to the house to talk to you earlier,

before your mother arrived. I found some Indian sign out behind the barn last night. They were likely looking to help themselves to a couple of your horses. I reckon I scared them off."

"So they took Dani instead?"

"Looks that way."

"We've got to go after her."

Ridge stared across the creek. The last thing he wanted to do was go back home.

Marty frowned at his hesitation. "I know I'm not paying you to look after my sister," she said, and he heard the tears in her voice, "but . . ."

Muttering an oath, he drew her into his arms. "Hey, don't cry. I'll bring her back."

"Thank you," she said, sniffling. "She's all I've got."

He wanted to remind her that she still had a mother, and that she ought to spend time with her while she could, but he didn't think Martha was in the mood to hear that just now.

He gave her a squeeze, then let her go. "Come on, I need to get my gear together."

"I'm going with you."

"No, you're not."

"How soon will you be leaving?"

"Just as soon as I saddle up. But you're not going. You'll only slow me down. Besides, somebody should ride over and tell Mulvaney's folks what happened."

"You're right. I hadn't thought of that."

"Can you ask Cookie to pack me enough grub for three or four days?"

"Of course."

Nettie Flynn was waiting for them on the front porch.

"Try to be nice to her," Ridge said, giving Marty a little push toward the house.

Marty muttered something unintelligible under her breath as he turned and headed toward the barn.

"Did you find her?" Nettie asked anxiously.

"No. Mr. Longtree says Dani and Cory were captured by Apache."

Nettie clutched the porch rail, all the color draining from her face. For a moment, Marty thought her mother was going to faint.

"Captured?" Nettie repeated. "By Apache?"

"Yes. I'm going with Mr. Longtree to look for her."

"Oh, Martha Jean, do you think that's wise?"

"Probably not, but I can't just sit here and twiddle my thumbs. Anyway, she's my sister, not his."

"Martha Jean—"

"I've got to get ready. He won't wait."

Before her mother could argue further, Marty went upstairs to pack her trail gear.

Ridge checked the cinch on his saddle, slid his rifle into the boot, and took up the reins. Leading his horse from the barn, he glanced toward the cookhouse, wondering if Marty had talked to the cook about provisions. He was about to go find out when he saw her emerge from the building carrying two pairs of saddlebags slung over her shoulder.

"I asked Cookie to pack enough food for a week," she said.

"Obliged."

"There's some hardtack and jerky in there, too, in case it takes longer. Just let me get my horse."

"Hold on. I said you weren't going."

She glared at him, her chin jutting out in that obstinate way he was beginning to recognize. "And I said I was."

"Dammit, woman—"

"Don't swear at me!" She advanced toward him until they were standing toe-to-toe. "In case you've forgotten, Mr. Longtree, you're working for me, not the other way around."

"Yes, ma'am. But this isn't a pleasure ride. So you can fire me, or you can stay home. Either way, I'm riding out alone."

"You are the most obstinate man I've ever met."

"We're wasting time, Martha Jean."

"Oh! I think I hate you. I really do."

"Yes, ma'am."

She thrust a pair of saddlebags into his hand, turned on her heel, and stomped off toward the barn.

With a shake of his head, Ridge stared after her, admiring the sway of her hips, the way her ponytail swished back and forth. She was the damnedest woman he'd ever known.

After lashing the saddlebags behind the cantle, he swung into the saddle and rode out of the yard, aware of Martha Flynn's angry gaze on his back. If looks could kill, he'd be a dead man by now, he thought as he urged his horse into a lope. At the moment, Marty Flynn was least of his worries.

Marty paced up and down in front of the barn for ten minutes, mentally calling Ridge Longtree every nasty name she could think of. Stubborn, overbearing man! She was the boss here, not him, and if she wanted to go with him to look for Dani and Cory, then, by gosh, she would go! And not Ridge Longtree nor anyone else was going to stop her!

Slipping a bridle over her horse's head, she led it out of the stall. She dropped the saddle blanket in place, then smoothed it out the way her father had taught her so there wouldn't be any wrinkles to raise sores on the horse's back. The saddle came next, and she cinched it up tight.

Mouth set in a determined line, she tied her saddlebags behind the cantle, put her foot in the stirrup, and climbed into the saddle.

Leave her behind, would he? Not hardly!

She knew which way he was headed. It shouldn't be hard to find him.

"Martha Jean!" Her mother's voice stopped her.

"What do you want?" Marty asked, glancing over her shoulder.

"Where are you going?"

"I told you before. I'm going to go and look for Dani."

"I don't think you should go. It's too dangerous."

"I'm past caring what you think," Marty retorted.

Giving her horse a kick, she rode out of the yard, leaving her mother standing on the top step of the porch, staring after her.

Chapter 11

Dani had never been so scared in her whole life. Not that time when she was six and she got lost in the woods. Not the time she was eight and fell out of the loft in the barn and had the breath knocked out of her. Not even when Mama left without a word.

She stared at the Indians spread out on either side of her. They were the most fearsome-looking creatures she had ever seen. They had dark skin and thick black hair that fell to their waists. They wore breechcloths and thigh-high moccasins with turned-up toes. The paint smeared on their faces and chests made them seem even more frightening.

She glanced over at Cory, who was riding beside her. The Indians had tied his hands behind his back. Blood was crusted in his hair. There was a nasty lump on the side of his head where one of the Indians had struck him the night before.

She shuddered with the memory. One minute she had been wrapped in Cory's embrace, caught up in the forbidden thrill of his kiss; the next he had slumped forward, nearly knocking her off her feet. Before she could react, before she could loose the scream that rose in her throat, one of the Indians had covered her mouth with his hand and carried her, kicking and clawing, across the creek. Another Indian had taken up the reins to Cory's horse; a third Indian had settled Cory over his shoulder and splashed through the stream. The other five Indians had followed them, as silent as shadows.

On the far side of the creek, the Indian carrying Cory had dumped him facedown over the back of a horse, then tied Cory's hands and feet together beneath the animal's belly. She had been thrust onto another horse's back and an Indian had taken the reins.

They had ridden until well after dawn, then stopped for a short time to rest the horses. When Cory had regained consciousness, the Indians put him astride the horse and then tied his hands behind his back.

To her surprise, the Indians had removed her shoes and Cory's boots and given them moccasins to wear instead. It seemed an odd thing to do, but after she thought about it awhile, she realized it was probably so anyone following them wouldn't be able to distinguish their footprints from those of the Apache.

Less than thirty minutes later, they were riding again. Clinging to the saddle horn, she had looked over at Cory, hoping for reassurance; instead, she had seen her own fears mirrored in his eyes. After a while, fatigue had overcome her fears. She wasn't used to riding for long periods of time. Usually, when she went into town with Marty, they took the buckboard.

Dani groaned softly. Her back and shoulders ached, her thighs were sore, and she was thirsty, so thirsty. Sweat beaded across her brow, pooled between her breasts, glued her shirtwaist to her back. Considering all that Cory had been through, she feared he was probably feeling even worse.

Tears stung her eyes. When Marty found out that

Cory was also missing, she would likely assume they had run off together to get married. No one would come looking for them, at least not right away. By the time Marty and the Mulvaneys realized she and Cory were missing, it would be too late. They would be so deep in Indian country that no one would ever find them.

Dani lowered her head, blinking rapidly so Cory wouldn't see her tears, but, try as she might, once she started crying, she couldn't stop.

"Dani, honey, don't cry."

"I can't help it," she sobbed. "I'm so . . . so scared."

"I'm sure they won't hurt you," he said reassuringly.

But she heard the lie in his words. She knew about the Apache. She had overheard the cowboys talking on more than one occasion. The Indians were savages, heathens who killed indiscriminately. In the old days, they had covered people with honey and buried them up to their necks in anthills. They had staked captives out in the sun, tied wet rawhide around their heads, and left them to die in agony. The Apache were known to be tireless, merciless, relentless. And even though they were supposed to be at peace, the Indians still raided the nearby ranches from time to time.

And now she was their prisoner. A shiver ran down her spine. She was afraid to die, so afraid, and even more afraid that they wouldn't kill her.

Dani slid a surreptitious glance at the warrior riding beside her, felt her heart leap into her throat when she saw that he was watching her intently.

She quickly looked away. Why was he staring at her? What would the Apache do to her when they finally reached their destination? The answer that sprang to her mind was far more frightening than anything else she had contemplated.

In spite of herself, she looked over at the Indian again. He returned her gaze, his expression impassive. She tried to draw her gaze from his but instead found herself noticing that his eyes were black, his brows thick and straight. He wore some sort of amulet on a rawhide thong around his neck; there were yellow zig-zag marks painted on his cheeks and chest. His arms and legs were long and well muscled. The sun cast blue highlights in his hair.

Her eyes widened as he lifted one brow, a faint smile curving his lips. With a little huff, she stared straight ahead, shocked to realize that, for an Indian, he wasn't bad-looking, and even more mortified to think that he knew she thought so.

And still they continued on, stopping only once to water the horses at a slow-moving river.

She practically fell off her horse in her hurry to reach the water. Dropping to her hands and knees, she drank greedily, crying out in protest when some-one pulled her away from the water.

She glared at the Indian who had been riding beside her. "Let me go! I'm thirsty."

"The water is cold. You must not drink so fast. It will make you sick."

She jerked her arm from his grasp. "I don't need you to tell me what to do," she said, and then frowned in astonishment. "You speak English!"

He grunted. "Come. We go."

"What's your name?"

"I am Sanza. How are you called?"

"Dani."

"Da-ni." He nodded. "We go now."

"I'm still thirsty." Turning her back to him, she scooped water into her hands and drank and drank.

The water was cold and it tasted wonderful. And then, to her horror, her stomach cramped and she vomited.

Humiliated, she wiped her mouth on the hem of her skirt, gasped when the warrior lifted her to her feet.

It was then that she realized they hadn't given Cory anything to drink.

Indignant that the Indians would treat him so cruelly, she looked over at the warrior again. "My friend is thirsty."

The warrior dismissed her concern with a gesture of disdain.

"He needs a drink."

The Indian continued to ignore her.

"Listen, you . . . you . . . you heathen monster, I insist you give him something to drink right now!"

The warrior looked at her, a glint of humor in his dark eyes as he handed her a waterskin.

She refused to thank him. Taking the waterskin from his hand, she carried it to Cory and held it for him while he drank.

"Slowly," she warned.

Cory nodded. "Thanks, honey."

She placed her hand on his arm and gave it a squeeze, then offered him another drink.

Before she could ask Cory how he was feeling, the warrior took the waterskin from her hand, then led her away from the others to a sheltered spot behind some tangled underbrush. Making a vague gesture with one hand, he walked away a few feet and turned his back.

Dani glared at him, refusing to be grateful that he was allowing her some privacy. Turning her back to him, she lifted her skirt and relieved herself, embarrassed and ill at ease to be doing something so private out in the open with a savage standing only a few feet away.

When she was finished, the Indian led her back to the others. In spite of her protests, he lifted her onto the back of her horse.

A short time later, they were riding again.

Chapter 12

Ridge urged his mount across the creek and up the other side. Dismounting, he quartered back and forth on the other side, his narrowed gaze moving over the ground. It took only a few minutes to find the unshod tracks of Apache ponies, and the prints of several shod horses, which suggested that, in addition to the horses ridden by Dani and Cory, the Indians had stolen some stock from one of the other ranches in the area.

Ridge studied the tracks for several minutes. He had expected the Apache to head north, toward the mountains. Instead, they were headed away from the Dragoons. Of course, that didn't mean they wouldn't eventually circle back and head for the stronghold.

His people hadn't remained free all these years by making it easy for others to follow them. He knew he would never catch the Apache before they reached their destination, not with the head start that they had, although he figured Dani and the boy might slow them down a little.

He muttered an oath when he thought of Dani Flynn being held captive by the Apache. If he couldn't find her, she was in for a hell of a rough time. The boy, too.

Swinging into the saddle, he pushed the stallion as hard as he dared. It had been said that a white man would ride a horse until it dropped, and that an Apache warrior could get on that same horse, get another twenty miles out of it, and then eat it. And while Ridge admired that about his mother's people, he didn't want to find himself afoot out here, not now, not when Dani's life might be at stake.

He stopped once at a shallow water hole to rest and water his horse, and then he was in the saddle again. Time after time, his gaze was drawn toward the distant mountains. Memories he had buried long ago moved through the corridors of his mind, rising up like shadows through the hazy mists of time.

His first memories were tied up within the high walls of the Apache stronghold. It had been in the mountains that his father and his maternal grandfather had taught him how to be a warrior—to hunt and track, to navigate by the sun, the moon, and the stars, how to find food and water. It was there that he had learned to ride a horse, to use a bow and arrow. He remembered hunting birds and squirrels and rabbits. His grandfather had told him that each successful hunt would help him gain important warrior skills such as stealth and patience. He remembered his pride at his first kill. His mother had praised him for his skill. That night she had cooked the rabbit for him; a few days later she had presented him with the skin.

To be a warrior . . . For a male Apache there was no other goal in life, and Ridge had pursued it relentlessly. Training began almost in infancy. While still young, he had been given a bow and a handful of arrows to play with; when he grew older, he was taught to make his own weapons. The games he had played with the other boys had been games designed to instruct him in the art of war, to sharpen his senses, to hone his skills, to develop physical stamina.

The boys in the tribe swam in the river both summer and winter, even if there was ice on the water. They ran long distances without stopping, often to the top of a hill and back, sometimes with a mouthful of water to make sure they breathed through their nose and not their mouth. Sometimes they ran for miles over rough ground while carrying a heavy load on their back. They were made to go without sleep for long periods of time. In the winter, they rolled naked in the snow. No hardship was too great for a true Apache. At the end of a long period of training, the boys were required to spend two weeks alone in the wilderness, where they were to survive using the skills they had been taught.

To an Apache, anyone not of the blood was the enemy. Apache wealth was measured in stolen horses and cattle. A warrior who could kill the enemy without being wounded, who could steal from the Mexicans and the White Eyes without getting caught, was held in high esteem by the People.

Life had been good in the mountains. He remembered spending long evenings listening to the seasoned warriors talking about old fights, recounting old battles. They boasted of coup counted and brave deeds or told tales of Coyote, the trickster. There were ceremonial dances before and after the men went to war. There were social dances for the unmarried braves and maidens. There were always a number of older people at such occasions. They sat on the outside of the dance circle, talking and laughing and generally having a good time.

He recalled the long, lazy summers spent swimming in the river. Evenings spent gambling, wagering horses and blankets and weapons; winters spent playing the hoop-and-pole game. He was sure Miss Martha Flynn would be shocked to learn that it wasn't just the men who gambled, but the women and children also. There were contests and races and wrestling matches, games of skill with bow and arrow.

It had been a good life, and over too soon.

He rode until dark, then bedded down in a shallow draw. Lying there with his head pillowed on his saddle, his horse grazing nearby, he gazed up at the night sky, remembering. . . .

Remembering his father, a tall man with an easy laugh and large, capable hands, one who had made the stronghold his home even though the Apache weren't his people.

Remembering his mother, a slender woman with a quick temper and a ready smile. She had been a gifted storyteller, loved not only by her own children but by all the others in the village as well.

Remembering his sister. Pain twisted his heart when he thought of Neeta. She had been a beautiful little girl with large, dark eyes and graceful hands. But for him, she would be alive today. . . .

Guilt and self-hatred rose up within him. With an oath, he jerked his thoughts away from a past that could not be changed.

Curling his hands into tight fists, he closed his eyes, and took a deep breath.

Martha Jean's image drifted through his mind. He chased it, grabbed on to it like a lifeline, focused all his attention on the woman who hadn't been out of his thoughts since the first day he saw her.

Martha Jean Flynn, as soft as dandelion down one minute, as prickly as a cactus the next. She was the most annoying, intriguing, stubborn woman he had ever met, never happy unless she was getting her own way, a woman who didn't like taking no for an answer. . . .

Springing to his feet, Ridge swore under his breath, his gaze probing the darkness. How could he have been such a damn fool? What had made him think she would stay home just because he told her to?

Dammit! Every instinct he possessed told him she was out there somewhere, either bedded down for the night or trying to find his camp.

Hunkering down on his heels, he drummed his fingers on the ground. Should he go after her tonight, or wait until morning?

There was only one answer. Rising, he kicked dirt over the embers of his campfire.

Five minutes later, he was saddled and riding over his back trail.

Drawing her horse to a halt, Marty glanced into the darkness that surrounded her. She should have stopped riding at sunset, but she had kept pushing, thinking she would ride for just another mile or so, another half an hour, another few minutes.

Night had fallen quickly, and now she had lost the trail and she feared she had lost her way, as well.

Dismounting, she loosened the saddle cinch. There was nothing to do now but wait until morning and see if she could pick up the trail again. Damn. Pa had always claimed she had too much stubbornness and not enough sense. Pa. She took a deep breath, wishing he were there with her now. She wouldn't be afraid if he were there.

Marty stripped the rigging from her horse, spread her bedroll, then rummaged in her saddlebags for something to eat, glad that she hadn't stored all the

food in Longtree's pack. She ate some of Cookie's
buttermilk biscuits along with some canned meat and
sliced cheese for dinner, cursing softly when she realized that the coffee was in Longtree's saddlebags. She
could use a cup right about now. She grunted softly.
Even if she'd had the coffeepot, she knew she
wouldn't dare light a fire for fear of bringing every
Indian in the area down on her.

Ridge Longtree was Apache. She didn't know how
much Indian blood he had, but there was no mistaking
it. She might have asked him, but he didn't seem inclined to talk about it, or about his past.

She washed the last of the meat and cheese down
with water from her canteen, then she pulled off her
boots, removed her hat, and crawled into her bedroll,
only to lie there, wide-awake, wondering if Dani and
Cory were all right. She couldn't imagine her little
sister at the mercy of the Apache, a tribe that was
known far and wide for its cruelty. What would they
do to Dani? To Cory? Images of the two of them
being tortured crowded her mind. Even worse were
the horrible images of her sister being raped by
savages.

She stared up at the sky, her eyes damp with tears.
"I know I don't talk to You as often as I should, but
please let her be all right. I don't care if Nettie sells
the ranch. I don't care what happens to the cattle, but
please don't let them hurt Dani." She took a deep,
shuddering breath. "And please help me to find that
stubborn man."

"You found him."

Marty jackknifed into a sitting position, her hand
reaching for her gun, panic welling within her in those
few short moments before she recognized his voice.

She had often heard the expression "weak with relief," but she had never really known what it meant until now.

She watched Ridge dismount, a fluid outline in the darkness. And then he was hunkering down beside her bedroll.

"What the hell are you doing out here?" He bit off each word as he said it.

"Going with you to look for my sister."

"I thought I told you to stay home."

"I never said I would. And you keep forgetting one thing, Mr. Longtree. I. Am. The. Boss."

"Yes, ma'am. Of course, you realize that since I had to come looking for you, we're that much farther behind."

"How did you even know I was here?"

It was a good question. He wished he had a good answer.

"Well?" she coaxed.

He didn't want to admit he had been lying in his blankets thinking about her. But even that didn't explain how he had known she was out here. But he had known. "I'm going to look after my horse."

He unsaddled the stud, hobbled it, and turned it loose to graze. Removing his bedroll from behind the cantle, he spread it out alongside Martha Jean's. Close, but not too close.

Settling down on his blankets, he realized that just being within sight and smell of her was too close.

Drawing her legs up, Marty clasped her arms around her knees. "Will they hurt her?"

"No."

"How can you be so sure?"

"They're my people, Martha Jean."

"What *will* they do to her?"

He shrugged. "Female captives usually become slaves to the tribe."

"A slave! Will they . . . ?" She couldn't say the word out loud.

"Rape her?" He shook his head. "No warrior would force himself on a woman. Captives are kept as slaves. Sometimes they're traded to other tribes. Sometimes they're ransomed back to their own people. Sometimes they choose to marry one of the men."

"What about Cory?"

"I don't know." Males Cory's age weren't usually taken prisoner.

"He's just a boy!"

"Among my people, he's old enough to be a warrior."

"Tell me about your people."

"They're just men and women trying to get along. They get married, have kids, fight to protect what's theirs. Most of them are good people. Some aren't."

"I never knew Indians got married."

"What did you think they did?"

"I don't know. I guess I never really thought about it." She hesitated, grateful for the darkness. "Are you . . . ?"

"Married? Hell, no."

"Don't you want to have a home? And a family?"

"We can't always have what we want," he replied quietly.

Even though she couldn't see his face, she knew he was watching her. She could feel his gaze on her face, as warm and tangible as a caress.

"What . . ." She swallowed hard. "What do you want that you can't have?"

"You."

Marty's heart skipped a beat. It was suddenly hard

to breathe. Heat spiraled through her, rising from the deepest part of her, climbing up her neck into her cheeks. Once again, she was grateful for the cover of darkness.

She gasped as his arms went around her, and then all thought fled her mind as his mouth covered hers. Fleetingly, it occurred to her that she should protest, but that thought was quickly forgotten, burned away by the heat of his kisses, the feel of his arms around her. His scent filled her nostrils. His arousal fanned her own desire, and she pressed shamelessly against him, driven by a need she had never known before.

Without taking his mouth from hers, he eased her down until she was lying on her back on her blankets. His lips were warm and firm and relentless. He rolled her onto her side so they lay face-to-face. His hand slid down her back, molding her body to his, so that their bodies touched from shoulder to knee.

He groaned softly, as if he were in pain. Odd, she thought, when she was experiencing pleasure unlike anything she had ever dreamed of. Her heart beat wildly in her breast. Every nerve ending seemed vibrant and alive. Her skin felt hot, there were a million butterflies fluttering madly in her stomach.

Needing to touch him, she slid her hands beneath his shirt, let her fingertips run up and down his back. His muscles were tense, his skin as hot as hers.

He drew back a little. Though she couldn't see his expression in the dark, she could feel his gaze moving over her face. He muttered, "Damn, Martha . . ." And then he was kissing her again.

His hands began an exploration of their own, and she moaned with pleasure. No man had ever touched her so intimately. Had any other man dared to let his hands fondle her so brazenly, she would have slapped his face and demanded an apology. With Ridge, she was tempted to beg him for more. And then she realized she didn't have to beg. He was intent on taking what he wanted.

The heat of his callused hand sliding up the inside of her thigh shocked her. What was she doing, rolling around in the dirt with a man she hardly knew?

"Ridge, stop."

For a moment, she was afraid he wouldn't do as she asked, that he would take her by force.

For one wicked moment, she hoped he would.

And then he took a deep breath and let her go. "Change your mind?" he asked, his voice husky.

"Yes. No. I mean, I never intended—"

"You could have fooled me."

Heat flooded her cheeks. She couldn't blame him for what he was thinking. She had behaved shamelessly.

Rolling onto his back, he stared up at the sky, his breathing ragged.

Not knowing what else to say, she murmured, "I'm sorry."

"There's nothing for you to be sorry about. It was my fault. You can't blame a man for tryin'." He looked over at her, and even in the darkness she could feel his gaze on her face. "But I'm giving you fair warning here and now, Martha Flynn: I'll most likely try again."

Chapter 13

Dani slumped to the ground, her whole body trembling. Her thighs were sore, her back and shoulders aching. How did the Indians ride so long without resting? It was Sunday afternoon and they had been riding almost nonstop since Friday night. She had never been so utterly weary in her whole life. She hurt in places she never knew existed. And she was hungry, so hungry. In the last two days all she'd had to eat were a few hunks of dried meat and sips of lukewarm water. How did the Indians survive on such rough, meager fare?

She watched them now as they moved about, making camp, talking and laughing with each other. She had never imagined Indians having a sense of humor.

She glanced over at Cory. He fared no better than she did. Indeed, he fared far worse. And since the Indians kept his hands tied behind his back, it was left to her to make sure he had food and water.

With a sigh, she curled up and closed her eyes, feeling the sting of tears as her thoughts turned toward home. How long would it take for Marty to realize that Cory and Dani hadn't run off together? Would she ever see her sister again? What were the Indians going to do with them? She wished her father were still alive. He would find her, no matter how long it took.

Tears stung her eyes. She still couldn't believe he was dead, that she would never see him again, never hear him call her his "little sunflower girl" again. In spite of his quick temper and his gruff ways, she had known without a doubt that he loved her best of all.

Drawing the blanket up over her head, she gave way to the tears she could no longer hold back.

Dani woke with a start when something nudged her in the side. Looking up, she realized that it was morning. Streaks of red and gold and violet were just fading from the eastern sky. The warrior who had captured her was standing over her, an impatient look on his face.

When he saw she was awake, he thrust a hunk of meat into her hands.

Dani eyed it suspiciously, wondering what it was. She hesitated only a moment, then took a bite, grateful to have something to eat besides jerky. She ate half of it before she remembered that Cory was probably hungry, too.

Scooting closer to him, she tore off a strip of meat and fed it to him.

He swallowed it greedily, and she tore off another strip, feeding him until the meat was gone.

"Thanks, hon."

She nodded, too weary, too discouraged, to try to make conversation.

"It'll be all right," Cory said.

"No, it won't."

He didn't argue, and she knew then that he was just as worried and afraid as she was.

A short time later, the warrior jerked her to her

feet and lifted her onto the back of her horse. There was a rush of activity as the Indians broke camp and caught up their horses. Because of that, it took Dani several minutes to realize that the Indians were splitting into two groups. One group of warriors was heading south; the second, smaller bunch, of which Dani was a part, had veered off and were heading in the opposite direction.

Dani glanced over her shoulder, searching for Cory in the midst of the Indians. She spied him in the distance, noting that he was now mounted on an Indian pony.

A wordless cry of dismay rose in her throat when one of the warriors took up the reins to Cory's horse and started out after the group of Indians headed south, toward Mexico. Fear congealed in her heart. If they took Cory to Mexico, she would never see him again.

"No!" Yanking her horse to a halt, she turned it around. Hollering, "Cory, wait!" she started toward him.

"Dah!" The warrior who had been looking after her rode up beside her and grabbed the reins from her hand.

"Let me go! Cory! Cory!"

Cory turned to look at her, but with his hands bound behind his back, there was nothing he could do.

She didn't think she would ever forget the look of love and despair on his face.

Dani glared at the warrior beside her. "Where are they taking him?" she demanded. "Damn you, answer me!"

The warrior said nothing, only clucked to his horse and followed the five warriors trailing toward the distant mountains.

Dani glanced over her shoulder one last time. With tears streaming down her face, she watched Cory ride away until he was out of sight.

The Indians rode until dusk, then made camp in a shallow ravine. The warrior lifted her from her horse, caught her in his arms when her legs refused to hold her.

She went rigid in his embrace, her heart pounding with fear and trepidation. He was an Apache. The enemy. He smelled of horse and sage and sweat. She put her hands on his chest and shoved. It was like trying to move a mountain. His skin was warm beneath her palms—warm and covered with a fine sheen of perspiration.

She stared up at him and found him watching her, an amused expression in his dark eyes.

"Let me go!"

He didn't move, only continued to watch her.

"I know you understand me." She pounded her fists on his chest, trying to recall his name. Vanza? Danza? No. Sanza. That was it. "Sanza, let me go!"

Slowly, as though reluctant to do so, he released her.

"Where are they taking Cory?"

"To the stronghold."

"Where are you taking me?"

"To the stronghold."

"Then why did we split up?"

"We are being followed."

"Followed?" Hope surged within her. "Who is it?"

"White Eyes."

Dani pressed a hand to her heart. Could it be Marty? She shook her head. Not Marty, but perhaps she had sent Ridge Longtree to look for her. She smiled inwardly. If anyone could rescue them, Longtree could!

"What . . ." She hesitated, not sure she wanted to know the answer to the question that had been uppermost in her mind since the Indians captured them. "What are you going to do with me? With Cory? Why don't you let us go?"

His dark gaze met and held hers. "It was not my war party. Iron Lance was in charge of the raid. I rode with him because he is my close friend. Iron Lance's only son was killed by a white man. He took the boy to avenge the death of his son."

"Cory didn't do it!" she exclaimed, then stared at him, dread coiling tight in the pit of her stomach. "Are they going to . . . ?" She couldn't say the words aloud. To say it would make it so.

"The boy's fate rests with Iron Lance."

"Then tell him to let Cory go!" she cried. "He'll listen to you!"

"It is not for me to tell another what to do." His expression softened. "I do not know what Iron Lance plans for the boy. He may kill him. He may keep the boy as his own."

She had to believe that Iron Lance wouldn't kill Cory, that somehow she and Cory would find a way to escape from the Indians and return home together.

"What about me?" she asked. "Is Iron Lance going to decide what happens to me, too?"

Sanza's gaze rested on hers. "No. He would have left you behind."

Dani stared at him, her heart sinking with the realization that, but for this savage, she would be safe at home now, free of this horrible nightmare.

"What are you going to do with me?" she asked tremulously.

"I have not yet decided."

Feeling as though she might faint, Dani turned

away. Her legs felt weak as she made her way toward
a barren stretch of ground. Dropping to her knees,
she stared into the distance, grateful that Cory wasn't
there. At least he didn't know the fate that awaited
him.

She clasped her hands together to still their trembling.
She couldn't give up, not now. The warrior said they
were being followed. It had to be Ridge Longtree. It
just had to be. He was Indian. If anyone could save
them, he could.

She clung to the possibility, held it close that night
when she lay in her blankets, staring up at the sky.

The Apache lay in a circle around her, save for one
warrior who stood in the shadows, keeping watch.

Her warrior. Sanza. She wondered what his name
meant.

She studied his profile in the moonlight, wondering
at her fascination with this man who had taken her
away from all that she knew, all that was familiar. If
she were at home now, she would be sitting in the
parlor with Marty, perhaps reading aloud, or maybe
working on a piece of embroidery. Marty would be
curled up on the sofa, going over the monthly ex-
penses, or bringing the ranch accounts up-to-date.
Later, they would have hot chocolate, or, if Dani had
baked that day, they would have a piece of pie or
cake and talk about the day's events.

She swallowed the urge to cry and concentrated on
what the warrior had told her. They were being followed. It had to be Ridge Longtree coming to rescue
her. It just had to be.

Shivering, she drew the single blanket the warrior
had given her up to her chin. A small fire burned a
few feet away. She wished she had the nerve to scoot
a little closer, but that would put her closer to a couple

of the Indians, and she had no desire to get closer to any of them.

A movement to her left caught her eye. She watched the warrior move toward the waterskin hanging from a branch. Lifting it, he took a long swallow, then hung it on the branch again. He glanced in her direction, then added a few pieces of wood to the fire.

Had he noticed her shivering? She thrust the thought aside, refusing to believe that a heathen savage would care if she was warm or cold.

As though aware of her thoughts, he turned toward her. She shivered anew, but it had nothing to do with the cold. She didn't understand what she was feeling, didn't understand why his nearness made her feel fluttery inside, why his touch excited her. She had experienced similar longings with Cory, but they paled next to the way the warrior made her feel. It was a troubling realization.

Turning her back to the warrior, she stared into the darkness, refusing to think of copper-colored skin and black eyes that seemed to see into the very depths of her soul.

Sanza grinned as the white woman turned her back on him. Da-ni. She could pretend indifference, but there was no denying the tension that flowed between them whenever their eyes met, or the heat that flared between them when they touched. Among his people, she was of an age to be married. He had taken her with the idea of trading her to the Comancheros for guns. White women, especially young, untouched white women, brought a high price, but that no longer interested him. His captive was a gentle creature. She would never survive the brutality of the Comancheros and the idea that they might defile her or sell her into slavery among his enemies was abhorrent. Perhaps, when they reached the stronghold, he would keep her as his slave.

His gaze moved over her, lingering on her slender form, the fall of golden hair that tempted his touch. Her skin was pale and unblemished, her eyes the color of spring grass. He did not need a slave; nor did he want the women of the tribe to mistreat her or look at her with scorn in their eyes, as they would surely do if he made her a slave in his lodge.

He frowned a moment, and then smiled into the darkness as he solved the problem.

He would not keep her as a slave; instead, he would take her for his wife.

Tomorrow he would take her to a place he knew, a place where they could be alone.

Chapter 14

Nettie Flynn couldn't help staring at the man who stood framed in the doorway. Victor Claunch. It had been years since she had last seen him, yet he looked much the same as she remembered—tall and strong, rich and powerful. The years had been kind to him. His hair was still thick and brown, with no trace of gray. Only the faint lines at the corners of his eyes and mouth betrayed the passage of time.

"Nettie." It was obvious that he was just as surprised to see her as she was to see him.

"Hello, Victor."

They stared at each other. He was apparently as much at a loss for words as she was. Victor Claunch had kissed her once. It had been on New Year's Eve. Victor had been a little drunk, and when he found her alone in the kitchen, he had insisted on claiming a kiss. And because she had also been a little drunk, and a little curious, she had kissed him back. Just one kiss, but she had never forgotten it. And then, to her utter amazement, he had whispered that he loved her. His words had shocked her. Knowing how he felt, she had made it a point to never be alone with him again, not only because of what he had said, but because she was a married woman and had no business being attracted to another man. Neither of them had ever mentioned that incident. No doubt he had forgotten all about it long ago.

"When did you get back?" he asked.

"I've just arrived."

His gaze moved over her, lingering on her face, her lips. It had been years since she blushed, but she felt her cheeks grow warm. Was it possible he was remembering that night in the kitchen?

"I'm sorry for your loss," he said, obviously groping for words. "Seamus was a good man."

She hesitated a moment before answering, "Yes, he was."

"I don't mean to disturb you at such a time, but I was wondering . . . is Martha Jean at home? We were supposed to go on a picnic this afternoon."

"A picnic?"

He nodded. "I thought it might do her good to get away from the ranch, think about something else, if you know what I mean."

"Yes." Victor and Martha? How long had this been going on? "I'm afraid Martha isn't home. She must have forgotten you were coming." Nettie hesitated, wondering if she should tell him about Dani and Cory, and then decided against it. There was nothing he could do to help, and she didn't want to talk about it. Not now, not with him. "I'm sorry, I don't know when she'll be back. Can I help you?"

"I don't think so," Victor said. His gaze rested heavily on her face, making her uncomfortable.

A look that Nettie couldn't read flashed through his eyes, disturbing her still more. He shifted from one foot to the other, suddenly reminding her of a tiger about to pounce. And then he smiled. "It was good to see you again, Nettie. Tell Martha I'll call on her later in the week."

"Yes, I will."

"Good day to you then." Turning, he went down the stairs, whistling cheerfully.

Later that night, Nettie wandered through the house, pausing now and then to look out one window or another, even though she knew it was far too soon for Martha and the cowboy to have returned with Danielle. She refused to consider the possibility that they wouldn't find her youngest daughter. The alternative was unthinkable, as was the possibility that Martha might be hurt or killed while searching for her sister. She thrust the prospect aside. She would not so much as entertain the notion.

Mr. Mulvaney had come calling on her the evening Martha Jean had gone off to look for Danielle and Cory. Apparently Martha had sent one of the hired hands over to let the Mulvaneys know that Danielle and Cory had been captured by Apaches. She had told Mr. Mulvaney what little she knew. He had left shortly thereafter, telling her that he intended to round up some of his men and go after his son. She had wished him well, thinking that the more people there were out looking for Danielle and Cory, the more chance there was of finding them, which made her wonder why she hadn't enlisted Victor's aid when she had the chance.

She stood in the doorway of the parlor. The house seemed larger than she remembered, but little had changed. The same large leather sofa and chair were in the parlor. The bear rug she had always hated still covered the floor. A pair of antlers hung over the mantel. There was a gun rack in one corner, a book-shelf in another. The piano she had brought with her from the East stood against one wall. How many times had she closed her eyes in her room in Boston and imagined her daughters in this setting?

She tied the sash of her robe tighter, then added a few sticks of wood to the fire in the hearth. Gazing into the flames, she wondered if Martha Jean was any safer with Ridge Longtree than Danielle was with the Indians. Nettie had spent enough time out West to know a hard case when she saw one, and Longtree had trouble written all over him. He wasn't a cowboy; she knew that.

Dropping onto the sofa in front of the fireplace, she leaned back and closed her eyes. The house was quiet, so quiet, with only the crackle of the flames and the chiming of the hall clock to break the silence.

She couldn't remember a time when the house had been so still. When the girls were little, the air had been filled with the sounds of their voices—their laughter, their tears. Christmases had been especially wonderful. She had played the piano for the girls while they sang Christmas carols. Seamus had often joined in, his deep voice a little off-key. She remembered the winter nights when the girls had put on puppet shows, remembered sitting in the big chair, doing the mend-ing, while Martha read stories to Danielle. Sometimes their childish voices had been raised in anger, though those occasions had been mercifully rare.

She pictured the girls in her mind as they had been the last time she saw them. Martha had always been her father's daughter, happier to be outside with the cowboys and the cattle than indoors. It had been a battle trying to teach that girl to do housework. To her chagrin, it was something Nettie had never accomplished. Martha had always been happier castrating cattle than cooking, more adept at mending harnesses than mending linens. She had preferred pants to dresses, boots and chaps to frills and fashion. She had considered embroidery a waste of time, and reading something for those who were infirm or bedridden. Nettie had despaired of ever finding her a husband.

Danielle had been her sister's opposite in every way. From the beginning, she had been Nettie's shadow, eager to learn how to cook and keep house. She had a fine hand with a needle, could prepare simple dinners by the time she was eight. She loved pretty clothes and shoes, spent hours in front of the mirror, trying out different hairstyles. She loved to read.

With a sigh, Nettie pictured the girls in her mind's eye as they were today. Both were lovely, but while Danielle's beauty was blatantly obvious, one had to look harder to see Martha's. She shunned makeup, wore her hair in an unflattering braid down her back, dressed in pants and shirts more suited to the cowboys than a young woman.

How she had missed her girls! Every day and every night since she had left the ranch, she had wondered what they were doing, if they were happy, if they missed her. Mostly she wondered how Seamus had explained her unexpected departure.

"Damn you, Seamus," she murmured, but there was no rancor in her voice. Her anger had dissipated years ago, overpowered by a sense of hopelessness. She had made one mistake, and Seamus had tried to make her pay for it for the rest of her life. Granted, it had been a mistake that would be hard for any man to forgive, but surely her punishment had outweighed the crime, all things considered.

Too restless to sit still, Nettie rose to pace the floor

in front of the hearth, then went to the front window. Drawing back the curtains, she peered into the darkness, her thoughts and prayers going out to Martha and Danielle.

"Please," she murmured. "Please bring them safely home to me."

Chapter 15

Ridge eased back on the reins, slowing the black to a trot, then a walk. A short time later he reined his horse to a halt. Dismounting, he studied the ground in an ever-widening circle, searching for signs of Cory and Dani. All he saw were horse tracks and moccasin prints. He frowned a moment, then muttered an oath when he realized what the Indians had done.

"What is it?" Marty asked, coming up behind him. They had been on the trail for five days now. It had been slow going. Sometimes the tracks were almost invisible. One night a cloudburst washed out the trail, which cost them valuable time the next day while Ridge scouted the area until he picked it up again. "What's wrong?"

"They've taken Cory's boots and Dani's shoes."

"What do you mean? Dani's barefooted?"

"No, they've put moccasins on her and the boy. See here." He gestured at two sets of moccasin prints that were a little smaller than the others. "One set probably belongs to Dani."

"What about the other one? Cory's feet are bigger than that."

"There could be a novice riding with the war party.

A young warrior," Ridge explained. "Or one of the warriors could be a woman."

"A woman?"

"It's not uncommon. Lozen is a warrior woman."

"I don't believe you. You're just saying that."

"No, it's true. From the time she was a little girl, she made it clear to everyone that she wanted to be a warrior like her brother, Victorio. She dresses like a warrior and she fights like one." He grinned. "I'd rather tangle with a mountain lion than a woman warrior with her dander up. I heard once that when she was going out on a war party with her brother, she made the warriors promise that if her brother was killed in battle, they would eat his body rather than let it fall into the hands of their enemies."

Marty grimaced at the morbid images his words painted in her mind. "Is she still alive?"

"Last I heard. Besides being a hell of a fighter, she's also a medicine woman who has a unique gift for being able to find the enemy. I've heard it said she finds some quiet place to pray and that while she prays, she holds her arms outstretched with her palms turned toward the sky. She turns in a slow circle until her palms tingle and then she knows from what direction they're coming."

"That's incredible."

"It is that. Handy, too."

Marty gestured at the ground. "You can still follow their trail, can't you?"

"Yeah." Ridge moved through the deserted camp, checking the droppings left by the horses, stirring the cold ashes of the fire. "They're still a good day and a half ahead of us."

"But we'll find them? We'll catch them?"

"Sooner or later." Ridge followed the tracks with

his eyes. The Indians were still trailing south, toward the Dragoons. For Cory's sake, it had better be sooner, but he didn't mention that to Marty.

Taking up his horse's reins, Ridge swung into the saddle. He had been afraid having Marty along would slow him down, but that hadn't been the case so far. She didn't complain about the long hours in the saddle, bedding down on the ground, or the rough fare. When he said no fire, she didn't argue. Best of all, she made the best camp coffee he had ever tasted, even better than his own.

"I've been boiling coffee over a campfire most of my life," she said when he remarked on it. "I've always helped out with the cutting and the branding, and I always went on roundups with . . ." She took a deep breath. "With Pa and the hands."

Ridge grunted softly. In her own way, Martha Jean was as much a warrior woman as Lozen or Dahteste. "Why did your mother go back east?"

"Pa said it was because she hated it here."

"Why didn't you and Dani go with her?"

"We didn't have a chance. We woke up one day and Nettie was gone. No note, no good-bye. She just left."

He noted again that she always called her mother by her given name. "And she never sent for you?"

"No. When Dani found out Nettie was gone, she wanted to go and stay with her. Pa said if it was all right with Nettie, Dani could go. She wrote to Nettie that night, but Nettie never answered her letter."

"How do you know she got it?"

Marty shrugged. "Dani wrote Nettie every few weeks. Surely one of her letters would have gotten through."

"Would you have gone with your mother, if you'd had the chance?"

"No. I love it here; I always have. And I couldn't have left Pa. I couldn't have left him here, alone. Not after Nettie ran out on him."

She stared into the distance. She couldn't believe her father was dead. He had been a harsh man, but he had always had a tender spot for her. He had been proud of her ability to rope and ride, and often said there wasn't a man on the ranch who could sit a horse as well as she did. She had basked in his approval. And now he was gone. She wished she could have told him she loved him one more time.

With a nod, Ridge touched his heels to his horse's flanks.

Blinking back her tears, Marty followed him. She gazed at the surrounding countryside. She had never been this far away from the ranch before, at least not on horseback. She had tried to convince her father to take her along on trail drives, but he had adamantly refused. Roundups were one thing, he'd said, but trail drives were out of the question. No matter how she'd argued or begged, he had never relented. He had been willing to let her spend a few days in the company of the cowhands during roundup, eating trail grub and sleeping under the stars. Trail drives lasted a month or more, and as far as he had been concerned, that was just too far, too long. Besides, he'd argued, he couldn't expect the men to mind their manners and their language for weeks at a time, and he didn't want her showing up back home knowing more bad words than she knew when she left.

They rode for hours, going deeper and deeper into Indian country. Once again, Marty's thoughts turned to her sister. Poor Dani. She must be terrified. She hadn't gone on trail rides, wasn't used to sleeping outdoors or eating food cooked over a campfire. She was used to the comforts of home, of sleeping on a soft bed and bathing every day. She hated getting her hands dirty, refused to wear the same dress more than two days in a row.

Why had the Indians taken her sister? She shied away from the obvious answer. Apache men were still men, and Dani was young and beautiful. What other reason did they need? And where did that leave Cory? Again, she shied away from the answer that quickly came to mind. Everyone knew the Apache were a brutal, merciless people. She had heard lurid stories of Apache prisoners who had been tied to wagon wheels and used for target practice, of prisoners buried up to their necks, then covered with honey and left for the ants. She had never heard any tales of Apache showing mercy or pity. Instead, she had grown up on tales of their treachery. . . .

So why was she putting her trust in Ridge Longtree? He was half Apache. She didn't doubt for a minute that he could be as cruel and ruthless as the rest.

She looked at him now, riding easy in the saddle, his hat pulled low to shade his face, one hand resting idly on the butt of his Colt. A casual observer might think he was hardly aware of his surroundings, might even think he was dozing in the saddle. But she knew otherwise, wouldn't be surprised if he knew exactly how many jackrabbits they had passed in the last hour and if they were male or female.

She looked down at the ground again, needing to see the trail. Those faint, barely visible hoofprints were her only link to Dani, her one and only hope of getting her sister back.

And still they rode on. After a time, the silence

wore on her nerves. "So what brought you to our ranch?" she asked, unable to endure the quiet another minute.

"Just geography, I guess."

"Geography?"

"I was headin' west and your place was in the way."

"I see. How far west were you planning to go?"

"San Francisco, California."

"Really? I've never been there."

"Me, either." He looked over at her and grinned. "I reckon it'll still be there after I find your sister and take care of Claunch."

"Claunch." She spat the name as if it tasted bad.

"Just why do you think he's the one who killed your old man?"

Marty stood up in the stirrups to stretch her back and shoulders, then settled into the saddle again. "He's made no secret of the fact that he wants our ranch. He's been trying to buy us out for the last five years."

"That doesn't make him a murderer, just persistent."

"Why do you think he's innocent?"

Ridge shrugged. "I didn't say that. I just wondered why you're so certain he's guilty."

Marty frowned. She didn't have any real evidence against Victor Claunch other than her dislike for the man. She wasn't even sure why she disliked him so thoroughly, except that his very presence annoyed her. And if he wasn't guilty, then who was? Claunch was the only person she knew who had a motive. And it seemed awfully suspicious that every time her father had turned down one of Claunch's offers to buy them out, something had gone wrong at the ranch. A river dried up. One of the outbuildings caught fire. A couple hundred head of cattle took sick and died. It couldn't be coincidence every time.

Thoughts of Claunch and the ranch brought her mother to mind, and she wondered what Nettie was doing. Had she put the home place up for sale?

Her thoughts scattered as she and Longrree crossed a shallow stream. The Dragoon Mountains loomed ahead, high, rocky cliffs that rose in jagged splendor against the vast blue vault of the sky. Although it seemed as if they were thousands of miles from civilization, there were a number of towns within a few days' ride. She had even been to a few of them with her father, towns like Benson and Bisbee and Tombstone.

They made camp at dusk. Marty kept glancing over her shoulder as she dug a shallow pit and gathered wood for the fire, half expecting to see an Apache war party sneaking up on them. She told herself they should be safe enough. After all, Ridge was part Indian. Of course, that didn't mean *she* was safe.

She filled the battered coffeepot with water, her gaze drawn toward where Longtree was looking after the horses. She enjoyed watching him. He spoke softly to the horses as he removed the saddles and blankets, his movements swift and sure. She shivered as he ran his hands down her mare's neck, all too easily imagining those large, capable hands moving over her own body. He looked up just then. His gaze brought a rush of heat to her cheeks. She told herself it was silly of her to feel embarrassed. There was no way he could possibly know what she was thinking. Or was there?

A slow smile spread over his lips as he ran his hand over her mare's neck again. Discomfited, Marty turned her attention back to the coffeepot, surreptitiously watching Longtree again. He spent a few minutes scratching his stud's ears before he hobbled both of the horses for the night.

When he started toward the campsite, she busied herself with fixing the evening meal. Even when she wasn't watching him, she seemed to know exactly where he was, could feel his gaze following her every move. It made her body tingle with an awareness she had never known before she met him. She grinned inwardly. Lozen tingled when the enemy was near, Marty mused, but she tingled whenever Ridge was close by.

She felt that awareness now as he sat down behind her. And because she was trying to ignore him instead of concentrating on what she was doing, she accidentally sliced her thumb on the lid of the tin can she was trying to open.

Gasping in pain and surprise, she dropped the can, oblivious to the peaches and juice that scattered on the ground. She stared at the bright red blood oozing from the cut at the base of her thumb.

He was beside her in an instant. "What happened?"

She held her hand out, palm up, so he could see.

Removing his kerchief, he soaked it in water from the canteen and wiped the blood from her hand. He quickly rinsed the cloth, wet it again, then wrapped it tightly around her thumb and held her hand in his. "You need to be more careful."

She nodded, her gaze drawn to his.

"Does it hurt?"

"No." She was too caught up in his nearness, in the touch of his hand, callused and warm, on hers, to feel anything else. "Is it very deep?"

"No. You were lucky." His gaze searched hers, settling on her mouth for stretched seconds before meeting her eyes again.

She licked her lips, unnerved by his nearness, by

the desire rising in the deep blue depths of his eyes. His eyes burned hotter as his gaze followed the tip of her tongue sliding over her lips.

"Dammit, Martha Jean, do you know what you're doing to me?" he muttered, and before she could say yes or no, he pulled her into his arms and kissed her.

Her eyelids fluttered down, and she was lost in the searing heat of his mouth on hers. His free hand traveled restlessly up her spine, slid slowly down her back, his touch giving birth to little shivers of pleasure. She sucked in a deep breath as his hand settled on her hip and pulled her closer, letting her feel the need rising within him.

He swore softly as she pressed against him. "Martha?"

She looked up at him, her lips swollen from his kisses, her eyes cloudy with passion.

"Have you ever done this before?"

She stared at him blankly. "Done what?"

"Have you ever been with a man before?"

"No." Her hand cupped his nape, drawing his head down. "Kiss me."

He drew in a long, shuddering breath and let it out in a sigh of exasperation. He'd never deflowered a virgin in his life, and, as tempting as this particular flower was, he wasn't going to start now.

Placing his hands on her shoulders, he put her away from him and strode into the darkness, softly cursing the ache her nearness had aroused in him.

What was he going to do about Martha Jean Flynn? Back at the ranch, he could have found a dozen ways to elude her. But there was no way to avoid her out here. He couldn't ride off and leave her behind, couldn't pretend she wasn't there, not when he was aware of her presence every minute of the day. And worse, every minute of the night. Like now.

From the shadows, he watched her finish preparing the evening meal, noting the way she moved, the way she repeatedly brushed a stubborn lock of hair from her forehead, the way the light from the campfire caressed her face, the way her breasts strained against her shirt. Damn and double damn! Watching her wasn't doing anything to ease the ache in his jeans.

And it only got worse later that night while he watched her brush out her hair. It was a curiously sensual thing, watching her drag the bristles through her hair, which shimmered like auburn silk in the light of the fire. He longed to take the brush from her grasp and run his hands through the heavy fall of her hair, to bury his face in its softness, to lay her down on her bedroll and bury himself deep within her.

As though sensing his thoughts, she glanced over her shoulder. Feeling his gaze, she froze, the brush in midair. Like a rabbit cornered by a mountain lion, she didn't move, only stared at him, watchful and waiting. The tension hummed between them. She wanted him, wanted him as much as he wanted her.

Hands clenched, he stared back at her. She was here and he wanted her.

He took a step toward her, his earlier good intentions overpowered by the primal need burning through him.

She watched him a moment, her eyes wide and scared, and then she tossed her brush aside, dove into her bedroll, and pulled the covers up over her head.

Ridge sat down on his own blankets and fished the makings out of his shirt pocket, grinning ruefully as he rolled a cigarette.

In the morning, she refused to meet his gaze. With a shake of his head, Ridge led the horses to water, then checked their feet and saddled them while Martha Jean prepared breakfast. He thought she was going to jump out of her skin when he sat down beside her to eat.

"Dammit, girl, take it easy," he said. "I'm not gonna bite you."

"I'm sorry," she muttered, her cheeks a bright red.

"You're not making this any easier." He sipped his coffee. "There's nothing to be ashamed of, you know."

"Isn't there? I wasn't brought up to roll around in the dirt with a man I hardly know."

"You know me, honey. You knew me the minute I rode into the yard."

She looked at him then, and he saw the truth of his words in her eyes.

"I want you," he said quietly. "You want me. There's no shame in it."

She stared at him, mute. He couldn't blame her. For all that she had been raised on a ranch surrounded by men, he doubted if anyone had ever spoken to her so bluntly. He wondered if Nettie had talked to her oldest daughter about intimacy between a man and a woman.

"Do you want me to take you back to the ranch?"

"No."

"Are you sure? There's no telling how long we'll be out here."

She nodded, well aware of what he wasn't saying. They could be spending many more nights together, just the two of them. But she couldn't let him take her back home. It would waste too much time. Time Dani might not have.

"What I said before still goes. I'm a stubborn man, and likely to try again."

The flush in her cheeks grew brighter.

"But if you say no, I'll respect your wishes."

She nodded and they finished the meal in silence.

Marty quickly packed up the last of their gear. A short time later, they were riding again. She hung back a little, still embarrassed by what had happened between them the night before and his reference to it this morning. Part of her embarrassment came from her ignorance. She was twenty-three years old, yet she knew very little about what went on between men and women other than what she had overheard from the ranch hands. None of the hands were married, though, and all their experience seemed to be with saloon girls.

When they had been younger, she and Dani had often talked about it, wondering what all the fuss was about. They had watched horses breed, which had led to some interesting speculation about male anatomy which, Marty was thankful, had been put to rest when Marty accidentally saw one of the hands with his trousers down. Neither Marty or Dani had felt comfortable taking their questions to Pa. She had a feeling Longtree could tell her everything she wanted to know, and then some.

They rode at a quick walk, with Ridge stopping every so often to check the trail. "I'm surprised that the Indians don't make any effort to hide their tracks," she remarked.

"This close to home, I guess they're feeling pretty safe," Ridge remarked.

Marty nodded. For all that she loved the wide open spaces, she liked them a little closer to home. Sage and cactus and mesquite stretched as far as the eye could see, and looming over it all was the rocky face of the Dragoon Mountains.

It was shortly after noon when Ridge pulled his horse

to a halt. Dismounting, he hunkered down on his heels, his gaze sweeping back and forth.

"What is it?" Marty asked. She glanced at the ground, wondering what he saw there that she did not.

"They've split up again."

She frowned. "Split up? Why would they do that?"

"I don't know."

He studied the ground again. He ran his hand over a clump of grass, broke apart a pile of horse droppings. Rising, he walked a few steps one way, then turned and walked in the opposite direction.

Marty tapped the end of one rein on the pommel, her unease growing as he continued to study the ground. He stopped now and then, his brow furrowed. "Well?"

"You see this? The ground is all chewed up."

Marty nodded. It looked like the Indians had ridden their horses back and forth over the same stretch of ground. Any footprints that might have been there had been completely obliterated.

"Two of the riders broke off from the others and headed that way." He pointed away from the mountains. "The question is, which two?"

"Can't you tell?"

"No."

"Why would they separate?"

"Beats the hell out of me. Both horses are barefoot. A couple of the warriors might have decided to go hunting before they returned to the stronghold. Maybe they're taking some of the stuff they stole on the raid to trade for guns and whiskey. Who the hell knows?"

His irritation worried her. He was always so calm and in control.

"What are we going to do now?" she asked.

"I guess that's up to you." He gestured at the larger

set of hoofprints. "It stands to reason that they'd take Cory and Dani to the stronghold, and that's where these tracks are headed."

"So you think we should stay with the larger group?"

"Being a gambling man, I've got to go with the odds. And the odds are, Dani's with the larger group."

"But you're not sure?"

"Nothing's sure in this life."

"Maybe those tracks belong to Cory and Dani."

"No."

"How can you be sure?"

" 'Cause nobody's chasing them. These two went off on their own and nobody cared enough to try to stop them."

"Let's go after the big group then."

With a nod, Ridge swung into the saddle. He would have bet his last clean shirt that Dani was still with the larger group, and yet . . .

Shrugging his doubts aside, he clucked to the stud. With luck, they could make another ten or fifteen miles before dark.

Chapter 16

"Where are we going?" It was the fifth time in the last two hours that Dani had asked the question.

And the fifth time that the warrior refused to answer.

He really was the most exasperating man she had ever known! With a sigh, Dani stretched her back and shoulders. She was tired, so tired. Tired of riding from dawn till dusk. Tired of eating jerky and drinking lukewarm water. Tired of sleeping on the hard ground. Tired of wearing the same dress, of feeling gritty and grimy and not being able to bathe or brush her hair.

She glared at the Indian's back. Most of all, she was tired of that insufferable man's company. She wondered why they had left the other warriors. Foolish as it seemed, she had felt safer when the other warriors had been with them.

She blinked back the tears stinging her eyes. What was the point in crying when there was no one to see her, no one to care? *He* certainly didn't care. Again, she wondered why he never seemed to get tired or hungry or thirsty. She remembered hearing the men on the ranch talk about the Apache. The cowhands claimed the Indians weren't human. She was beginning to think they were right!

Sniffing, she dashed the tears from her eyes. She wanted to go home. And she would. Tonight, when he was asleep, she would run away. Even if she didn't make it home, at least she would get away from him. The thought no sooner crossed her mind than she was beset by doubts. What if she couldn't find her way home? What if she couldn't find water? What if she were captured by some other Indians, ones who were cruel? Even though she didn't want to be with *him*, at least he treated her well enough.

With a shake of her head, she cast her doubts aside. If Marty were in this situation, she would do *something*, even if it were the wrong thing! And so would she.

As usual, they made camp at dusk. Dani sat on a blanket while Sanza set up their camp. Then, to her astonishment, he tied her hands and feet together, took his bow and arrow, and walked away from their campsite.

Dani stared after him, unable to believe he had gone off and left her alone and unprotected out in the middle of nowhere. Where was he going? How long would he be gone? She stared at the setting sun. It would be full dark soon. Surely he didn't mean to leave her here, alone, in the dark?

She shifted her position on the ground, tugging against the strip of rawhide that bound her wrists.

She watched the sun drop lower in the sky. She had always loved sunsets, and this one was beautiful. She shivered as the sky turned red, reminding her of blood. If Sanza didn't come back for her, she would never see another sunset. Never see Marty again.

Overcome with despair, she peered into the darkness, listening for his footsteps. How long had he been gone? It seemed like hours.

Her shoulders began to ache.

Her nose itched.

She glanced at the waterskin and licked her lips.

What if he was never coming back?

She dismissed that thought as soon as it crossed her mind. Of course he would come back, she thought, overcome with a wave of self-pity; his horse was still here.

She sniffed back her tears. She wouldn't cry! And tonight, when he was asleep, she would run away.

Just when she was beginning to think that he had indeed, abandoned her, he suddenly materialized out of the darkness.

Wordlessly, he untied her hands and feet, grinning as she rubbed vigorously at her nose.

He held up a pair of rabbits. "Can you skin these?"

Horrified, Dani shook her head. She did most of the cooking at home, but she'd never had to kill the cattle or the sheep or the pigs. Or the chickens. Especially not the chickens! She would never forget the first time she had seen her father behead a chicken, or the way the headless chicken had run around. She thrust the gruesome memory aside. She wouldn't have skinned those rabbits even if she had the stomach for it, she thought rebelliously. He had kidnapped her, and he could darn well take care of her!

With a grunt, the warrior drew his knife. Dani turned away, trying not to listen as he skinned the furry little animals. In minutes, he had them cleaned and spitted over a small fire. The juice made little popping sounds when it fell onto the hot coals. The rich aroma of roasting meat made her stomach growl.

They ate in silence, tension crackling between them.

As soon as she finished eating, Dani rubbed her hands on the grass to remove the grease, then wrapped up in the blanket the warrior had given her. Soon, she thought, soon she would be on her way back home.

Sanza sat cross-legged in front of the fire, his gaze straying time and again to the woman. Perhaps he was making a mistake in keeping her. She could not skin game; he doubted if she could cook over a fire, or walk long distances. He was certain she did not know how to find wild fruits and vegetables, and equally certain she did not know how to tan a hide or make jerky or ash cakes. And yet she had eyes the color of new grass and skin as soft and smooth as doeskin. His body ached just thinking of her, lying only a short distance away. Perhaps she did not know how to live in a wickiup or do the other things the Apache women did, but she could learn.

When the fire burned low, he checked on the horses one last time, then rolled into his blankets.

He was almost asleep when he heard the white girl stir. At first he thought she was answering a call of nature, but then he heard her moving toward the horses. No doubt she thought she was being quiet, yet he heard the crunch of a leaf, the snap of a twig. He listened as she whispered to her horse, heard her soft grunt as she pulled herself onto the animal's bare back and rode away, leading his horse.

Foolish woman! Did she think a white woman could sneak away from an Apache warrior, or that she could survive out on the prairie on her own?

He waited until she was out of sight, then pulled on his moccasins and followed her.

As soon as the faint glow of the campfire was out of sight, the night seemed to close in on her. There was nothing to see in any direction, only the dark shapes of shrubs and trees that somehow seemed ominous in the faint light of the moon.

It occurred to her that predators roamed the night, animals that could be far more dangerous than the warrior she had left behind.

He would be furious when he woke in the morning to find that, not only was she gone, but that she had taken his horses as well.

She gazed up at the stars. Years ago her father had taken her on a roundup. One night he had told her the names of the constellations and taught her how to use them to find her way home. She wished now that she had paid more attention, that she could remember what he had told her. Tears burned at the back of her eyes. Marty would know. Marty remembered everything. She was never afraid of anything; she always knew what to do. She could rope and ride almost as well as the men. She knew how to keep the books and how to pay the bills. If need be, she could run the ranch single-handedly.

Dani sniffed. She tried to tell herself that a man wanted a wife who could cook and clean and sew, but those talents suddenly seemed woefully lacking. Knowing how to bake a pie wouldn't help her now. She needed to know how to follow the stars, not a recipe.

What would Marty do?

She would keep going, Dani thought, and that was what she was going to do. Hopefully riding away from Sanza would take her back the way they had come and she would find her way home.

Sanza trotted effortlessly in the wake of the horses. Apache could run for miles, if necessary. It was something he had done since childhood, his endurance and stamina growing as he grew. From boyhood he had participated in training and games that were intended to sharpen his senses and increase his stamina and fortitude. No matter the weather, he had run long distances before sunrise.

The young would-be warriors were encouraged to take care of their health and their body and to be self-confident and self-reliant. He had learned to hunt, mostly birds and small animals, until he had acquired the stealth and patience to hunt larger game. He still recalled his first kill—a squirrel. His grandfather had told him to eat the squirrel's heart, whole and raw. It was good medicine, he had said, for a boy to eat the heart of his first kill.

Once he had become adept at hunting game, he was ready to hunt the enemy. That, too, required skill and training. Novice warriors were required to go on four raids. They were not allowed to fight but were there to observe and to learn from the seasoned warriors. They prepared the food, looked after the horses, and did whatever they were told by their elders. They were to be constantly alert and vigilant, and to stand guard at night. If a young warrior behaved improperly or displayed traits that were undesirable, such as dishonesty or cowardice, or refused to be disciplined, he would be considered unreliable and would be treated as such from then on.

On each of the four raids, the novice warrior wore a ceremonial hat for protection. He was not to speak except in the language of the warpath. He could drink water only through a tube and was allowed to eat only cold food. If he performed well on these four raids, he was accepted as a warrior, and as such he could smoke, marry, and enjoy all the privileges of a warrior.

There were young men who refused to fight, and young men who were considered unfit for warfare. Such men were treated with contempt. A true Apache warrior was relentless, a master at stealth, surprise, and flight. Sanza had learned to disguise himself with dirt and desert plants, to lie motionless so that an unwary traveler would never suspect he was in danger until it was too late. He could travel on foot from fifty to seventy-five miles a day, if necessary, and find food and water along the way.

Like all Apache, he excelled at tracking. An overturned rock, the way a twig had been bent or broken, horse manure dropped along the trail, all told tales. Following a white woman across the open prairie, even after dark, was no challenge at all.

Curious to see how long she would ride before she realized she was lost, Sanza continued to follow her until, after two hours, she pulled her horse to a halt.

From his place in the shadows, he watched her. She sat there, unmoving, for several moments. Even in the darkness he could see her shoulders shaking. It was the sound of her tears that urged him forward, had him reaching up to pull her from the back of the horse and into his arms.

"Let me go! Let me go!" she shrieked, her puny fists pummeling his chest. Then, with a strangled sob, she collapsed against him, her tears falling like warm rain on his skin.

He held her in his arms, one hand lightly stroking her back. He had never had a woman. He could feel her every breath, the warmth of her skin. His hand strayed to her hair, exploring its softness. She not only looked different from the women of his tribe; she smelled different. And she was his.

Awareness speared through him. He had already

decided to make her his wife. At the time, it had been to keep his people from mistreating her. Now, for the first time, he realized that, as his wife, she would be his to do with as he pleased. He could take her to his bed, seek pleasure in the warmth of her body.

As though reading his mind, she gave a little cry and jerked out of his grasp. It was only then that he realized his body had betrayed his thoughts.

She stared at him, her green eyes wild and frightened in the moonlight.

"Da-ni," he said quietly, "I will not hurt you."

"I don't believe you!"

He held out his hand. "Come. We will go back to camp."

"No! I want to go home!"

He took a step forward.

She took a step backward.

His eyes narrowed. "You must do as I say, Da-ni."

She was torn between the desire to oppose him and fear of what the consequences might be. Just because he hadn't punished her for running away didn't mean he wouldn't beat her for being disobedient.

He took another step toward her, anger cooling his ardor. "Let us go. Now."

Shoulders slumped, she surrendered with a sigh, hating herself for her cowardice. Knowing that Marty would have fought back only made it worse.

She gasped when Sanza's hands went around her waist and lifted her onto the back of her horse. He handed her the reins, then swung up on the back of the second animal. His gaze met hers; then he turned his horse and headed back the way she had come.

She hesitated for a moment, wishing she had the nerve to run away again. But what good would it do? If he could so easily catch her when he was on foot, she certainly wouldn't be able to escape him when he had a horse.

With a sigh of resignation, she lifted the reins, tapped her heels against the horse's flanks, and followed Sanza back to their campsite.

Chapter 17

Marty's eyelids flew open and she sat up, one hand pressed against her heart. Frantic, she glanced around, then blew out a sigh of relief. It had been only a dream, after all. But it had been so real, especially the blood . . . her sister's blood.

It was the worst nightmare she'd ever had. After days of tracking Dani and Cory, Ridge had found them. Cory had been used for target practice. Dani had been horribly mutilated. And scalped. She had seen her sister's long blond hair dangling from an Apache lance.

Marty buried her face in her hands, a silent prayer rising in her heart. *Please let her be all right . . . please . . . please . . . please.*

She lifted her head and looked up when she realized she was no longer alone.

Ridge stood beside her, a frown creasing his brow. "You all right?"

"Yes, fine."

"Uh-huh." He hunkered down on his heels, his hands wrapped around a tin cup of strong black coffee. "What's wrong?"

"Nothing. I . . . I just had a bad dream, that's all." With a nod, he offered her the cup.

She murmured her thanks as she took it from his hand and sipped it gratefully. It was hot and bitter, just what she needed.

"Want to tell me about it?" he asked.

"I dreamed that we found Dani and Cory. They were both . . ." She took a deep breath, reminding herself that it had been only a dream. "They were dead. Mutilated. Scalped."

She looked at him, her eyes begging for reassurance.

"Have any of your dreams ever come true?"

"No."

"Then I wouldn't let this one upset you."

"But this one could come true, couldn't it?"

There was no use lying to her, and while he doubted his people would kill Dani, he couldn't promise that Cory's life would be spared.

She didn't misread his silence. "Do you think they're still alive?"

"There's no way of knowing, but since we haven't . . ." He swore under his breath.

"Haven't what?" she whispered.

He had never believed in sugarcoating the truth. In his experience, telling a lie to soften an ugly truth usually did more harm than good in the long run.

"Tell me," she urged.

"Since we haven't found their bodies, there's a good chance they're still alive. And if that's true, there's a good chance we'll find them in time."

She handed him the cup, then flung the covers aside. She pulled on her boots and stood up. "Let's go. We're wasting time."

"I'll saddle the horses while you fix breakfast."

"I'm not hungry. And I can saddle my own horse. Let's go."

He understood her anxiety, and he didn't waste time

arguing with her. They could eat later. It took less than ten minutes to pack their gear, douse the campfire, and saddle the horses.

Marty tried not to think of her nightmare as they rode deeper into Apache territory, but she couldn't shake the awful images from her mind. She would never forgive herself if anything happened to Dani and Cory. If she hadn't been so openly opposed to their marriage, Dani wouldn't have had to sneak out of the house in the middle of the night to meet Cory and they wouldn't have been captured by Indians. Any harm that came to Cory or her sister would be all her fault. How would she ever be able to live with that on her conscience?

She looked over at Ridge. As always, he rode easy in the saddle, but she knew he was aware of everything around them. She could sense his tension, see the wariness in his eyes as he glanced from side to side. Time and again he checked their back trail, lifting his head to peruse the distant mountains. She felt safe with him, and yet he was only one man. If they were attacked . . . She thought again of all the horrible stories she had heard about what happened to Apache prisoners, how they were tied up and burned alive, or staked out in the desert with strips of wet rawhide tied around their heads and left in the sun. When the rawhide dried, it grew tighter and tighter, until . . .

She shook the gruesome image from her mind. There was nothing to be gained by dwelling on what would happen to them, to her, if they were attacked by Indians. Instead, she glanced at the surrounding countryside. Like the Apache, it could be a hard, cruel land, and yet there was a kind of raw beauty in the desert and in the jagged mountains that loomed ever closer. It called to something wild and untamed deep within her.

She was watching an eagle soaring on the air currents high above when a rising dust cloud caught her eye. And then a dozen braves materialized over the edge of a gully and thundered toward them, brandishing lances and rifles.

Marty stared at them in horror. Before she could think or cry out, the air was filled with the sound of gunfire.

Ridge hollered, "Grab your rifle and hit the dirt!"

Shaking with fear, she pulled her rifle from the boot, dismounted, and dropped down on her stomach beside him. Her horse bolted, head high, reins trailing.

Ridge fired a shot and the Indians pulled up out of range, then began riding in a circle around them, yelling what sounded like curses.

"Can you use that rifle?" Ridge asked.

"Of course."

"All right. I'll cover your back; you cover mine."

She nodded and he scrambled around so that they were lying side by side, firing in opposite directions.

She stared at the Indians, knowing that all the savages had to do was wait them out. They had no food, no water.

"Why are they shooting at us?" Marty asked. "Aren't they your people?"

"I haven't been home in years. I doubt if any of these warriors even know me."

"Can't you tell them who you are?"

"I'm not sure they'll stop shooting long enough to listen."

Marty was afraid he was right.

The next few minutes were the worst of her life. The Indians taunted them, riding around them to draw their fire. She had to admire their horsemanship. Hanging over the far side of their horses, the Apache galloped toward them. Protected by the bodies of their horses, the Indians loosed arrows at them until Ridge shot one of the horses. The Indian rolled free and then shot an arrow into the air. Marty frowned, wondering at such odd behavior.

Then the arrow came down. Ridge grunted as it pierced his side.

Marty stared at him in horror, everything else momentarily forgotten.

In seconds, the Indians were on her. One grabbed her rifle. Another jerked her to her feet.

Ridge rolled onto his back, his rifle coming up, but he didn't dare shoot for fear of hitting her. An Indian came up beside him and struck him alongside the head with the butt of his rifle.

The warrior reversed his rifle in his hand and sighted down the barrel.

Marty screamed, struggling to free herself from the warrior who held her.

Before the first warrior could fire, a second warrior wearing a white feather in his hair pushed the rifle aside. He said something in a harsh, guttural tongue as he knelt beside Ridge. Marty held her breath. Had that been recognition she had seen in the Apache's eyes when he looked at Ridge?

The warrior with the white feather in his hair spoke to the warriors closest to him, then turned his attention to Ridge. Grasping the arrow in the middle of the shaft, he broke it in two and tossed the feathered end away. Then, removing the red sash from around his waist, he wrapped it tightly around Ridge's middle. After tying off the ends, the warrior rose to his feet and again spoke to the warriors gathered around him.

He sounded angry. If only she knew what he was saying!

Her heart sank as a horse was brought forward. Two burly warriors lifted Ridge and placed him face-down over the horse's back. Oh, Lord, was he dead?

A mounted warrior took the reins to her horse. The warrior wearing the white feather vaulted onto the back of his pony, then caught up the reins to the horse that was carrying Ridge. Without a word, the war party turned back the way they had come.

Marty glanced at the Indians, wondering if they were Apache. Wondering if they were the ones who had taken Dani and Cory. If they were Apache, why had they shot Ridge? He was one of them.

She stared at his back, willing him to move, praying that he was still alive. Her gaze was drawn to the blood smeared across the horse's withers. The sight of blood had never bothered her before. She castrated cattle. She helped with the calving. She had treated gunshot wounds and even a rattlesnake bite without turning a hair. She had dug a piece of glass out of Dani's foot, looked after one of the cowboys who had been gored by a bull, but the sight of Ridge's blood made her sick to her stomach.

They rode all that day. Gradually the prairie fell away and they began to climb a narrow trail cut into the side of a rock-strewn mountain.

As they climbed higher, Marty's fear for Ridge's life quickly turned to fear for her own. It was obvious the Indians were taking her and Ridge to their stronghold. Marty had heard bits and pieces about the Apache rancheria hidden high in the mountains. It was said that the stronghold was almost impregnable, and that a small number of Apache could hold off a much larger force.

What would the Indians do with her once they reached the stronghold? What would Ridge's fate be, assuming he was still alive? What if Dani and Cory were there?

She clung to that hope as the trail continued on, winding higher and higher. Finally, after what seemed like an eternity, they reached a narrow entrance guarded by a single warrior. Marty glanced over her shoulder, amazed at the view. From this vantage point, the warrior could see for many miles into the valley below. A few well-armed warriors could easily defend the stronghold from attack.

Marty clenched her hands to still their trembling as they rounded a curve in the trail and the Apache camp came into view. Her breath caught in her throat when she saw the brush-covered wickiups spread before her. Men and women could be seen moving about, engaged in various activities. Children and dogs ran everywhere. A vast herd of horses grazed alongside a winding stream beyond the village.

Men and women ran forward to meet the returning warriors, the women obviously searching for their men.

The warrior leading Ridge's horse moved through the throng, pausing when he came to a large wickiup. The Indian leading Marty's horse followed him. When they stopped, he lifted her from her horse, then rode away, leaving her standing there.

The warrior she had come to think of as White Feather dismounted and rapped on the door of the wickiup.

Biting down on her lower lip, she glanced at Ridge, then at White Feather, and then back at Ridge.

She was about to go to Ridge's side when an old man stepped out of the wickiup. Body bent, his long hair almost white, he glanced at her briefly, then turned his attention to White Feather. The two men spoke rapidly for several minutes; then the warrior lifted Ridge from the back of the horse and carried him into the wickiup. The ancient warrior followed.

Marty stood there for several minutes, not knowing what she should do. No one seemed particularly interested in her, although she seemed to be the object of a good many curious looks, especially from a handful of boys standing nearby.

Tapping her foot, she stared at the wickiup. What were they doing in there? Did she dare go inside? She wished the boys would go away.

Feeling uncomfortable, and anxious to know what they were doing to Ridge, she took her courage in hand and ducked into the wickiup.

It took several moments for her eyes to adjust to the dim light. From what she could see, the wickiup was made from a round framework of long poles driven into the ground. The poles were laced together at the top with what looked like strands of yucca. Bundles of grass were laid out over the frame. She had seen from the outside that animal hides were laid over the grass. The door was also made out of hide.

There were buckskin bags in various sizes hanging from the lodge poles, as well as a bow and a quiver of arrows. Besides those weapons, she saw a war club, a lance, and a shield. She saw a few clay pots, water gourds, and utensils to one side of the doorway. A small fire burned in the center of the lodge, its smoke curling upward to be drawn through a small hole in the roof.

Ridge was lying on a pile of furs located to one side of the wickiup. Someone had removed the bloody sash and undressed him. There was no sign of either the sash or his bloody shirt; his trousers and gun belt were in a pile in the back of the lodge. A blanket covered him from his hips down. Even in the dim interior of the wickiup, she could see the blood glistening on his skin, leaking from a ragged hole in his side. She pressed her hand to her mouth, her stomach churning.

The warrior who had carried Ridge inside spoke to the old man, then left the wickiup.

The old warrior ignored her. He moved about the lodge as if she weren't even there, pouring a bit of this and a little of that into a cup that seemed to be made of some kind of animal horn, buffalo perhaps. Chanting softly, he mixed it all together, then sprinkled it into the fire. Sparks rose from the coals like fireflies. Sweet-scented smoke filled the air. Using a large feather, the old warrior drew the smoke over Ridge, chanting all the while.

Marty took a step forward. A fine sheen of sweat dotted Ridge's brow and chest.

Glancing over his shoulder, the old warrior motioned for her to come closer.

She hesitated a moment, then went to stand beside him.

"Is he your man?" the old warrior asked.

Marty stared at him, startled that he spoke English. Should she say yes? Or no?

The old warrior nodded, apparently taking her silence for assent. "You must hold him still while I remove the arrowhead," he said.

Taking a deep breath, she knelt beside Ridge and placed her hands on his shoulders. She turned her head away, her stomach roiling, when she saw the long, narrow-bladed knife in the old warrior's hand.

Closing her eyes, she prayed it would be over quickly.

Ridge groaned, his body writhing in agony as the old warrior cut the arrowhead out of his flesh.

"It'll be all right," she murmured. "Don't move. Please don't move."

He stilled at the sound of her voice, his head turning toward her. "Martha Jean?"

"I'm here."

He opened his eyes, eyes that were dark with pain.

She took a hasty look at the old warrior, swallowing the bile that rose in her throat as he withdrew the arrowhead from Ridge's side. Blood flowed from the ugly wound.

Still chanting softly, the old warrior washed the wound and patted it dry. After smearing some greasy concoction over it, he wrapped a length of clean cloth around Ridge's midsection, then helped him to sit up, supported by a willow backrest.

The old warrior rose and went to a pot suspended on a tripod over the coals. He ladled what looked like broth into a bowl and handed it to Marty, along with a spoon made of horn.

"He must eat," the old warrior said, and then left the wickiup.

Marty sat cross-legged beside Ridge. Dipping the spoon into the bowl, she offered it to him.

He scowled at her. In spite of his sour look, she could see that he was hurting terribly. She could see it in his eyes, in the fine white lines etched around his mouth. His breathing was shallow, as if every breath caused him pain.

She lifted one brow. "You heard what the old man said. You've got to eat."

"I'm not hungry."

"I know you're not feeling well," she said patiently.

"Just take a few sips for now. It might make you feel better."

"Who do you think you are, my mother?"

Marty blew out a sigh of exasperation. What was it about men? They were all such big babies when they were sick. She decided to try one more time. She took a taste and smiled.

"Come on, Ridge, it's really good."

"Then you eat it."

The man would try the patience of a saint! "Listen, Longtree, you've got to eat if you want to get your strength back."

"Dammit, Marty—"

Before he finished speaking, she dumped the spoon's contents into his mouth.

His scowl deepened. "What are you trying to do, choke me to death?"

"You need to eat," she said sweetly, and dipped the spoon in the bowl again.

"I'm not an infant. I don't need you telling me what to do."

"Then stop acting like a baby and eat this."

"Dammit, I've been feeding myself for years and—"

She thrust the spoon into his mouth again. This time he did choke.

Setting the bowl aside, she patted him on the back.

As soon as he could breathe, he swore a vile oath, one even the cowboys hadn't dared use in her presence.

Marty shot to her feet and stood glaring down at him. "Eat. Don't eat. I don't care what you do," she exclaimed, and, turning on her heel, she stomped out of the wickiup.

Once outside, she came to an abrupt halt. What now? She didn't dare go storming off. For one thing, she wasn't sure the Indians would let her. For another, she was afraid to go too far for fear she would get lost. With an exasperated sigh, she sat down in the shade at the side of the wickiup.

All around her, she could see women working and caring for their children. She saw several little boys running a race, while others tussled on the ground like puppies. She frowned when she saw a handful of boys throwing rocks at each other. A strange game, if indeed it was a game. Off in the distance, she saw some older boys practicing with bows and arrows.

She saw little girls at play, as well. Three of them were making houses out of sticks and stones, and dolls from bits of buckskin. They looked her way from time to time, their dark eyes wide with curiosity.

The children, both boys and girls, wore only enough for modesty's sake.

Across the way, she saw several men hunkered down playing some sort of game. She studied them covertly. Most of them were nearly naked, wearing little more than a breechcloth to cover their loins and moccasins that reached midthigh. Some of the men wore their moccasins pushed down below their knees. Most wore headbands made of flannel or cotton. One or two wore blue cavalry shirts. One wore a forage cap.

She watched a couple of women as they stirred something in a large, odd-looking pot. The women wore long skirts of deerskin and loose-fitting cotton blouses. Their moccasins were different from those worn by the men, coming only a little above the ankle.

All too aware of the glances sent her way, both curious and distrustful, she rose, brushed the dirt from her skirt, and went back into the wickiup.

Ridge was still sitting up, though his eyes were

closed. As far as she could tell, he hadn't touched the broth.

She tiptoed across the floor, not wanting to wake him if he was asleep. She stood beside him and studied him. Was it the poor lighting, or did he look pale? His breathing was shallow, his brow dotted with perspiration.

Biting down on her lower lip, she placed her hand on his brow.

His eyelids fluttered open. "I'm still not hungry," he muttered.

"You've got a fever."

He grunted softly. "I feel like hell."

"I'm not surprised."

She poked around the lodge until she found a scrap of cloth and a waterskin. She eased him down on the furs, careful to keep the blanket in place.

After wetting the rag, she tore it in half. She folded one piece and laid it across his brow, then sponged off his arms and upper body with the other half. She paused when she came to the edge of the blanket. He caught his breath, waiting to see if she would remove it. She didn't. Instead, she folded the bottom up, covering his loins with another layer of cloth, then dragged the cool rag over his legs. If he hadn't been hurting so much, he would have teased her about being so modest.

In quiet amusement, he watched her through heavy-lidded eyes as she wet the rag again, and then again. The cool cloth felt like heaven against his fevered skin.

It was his last thought before sleep claimed him.

Chapter 18

Nettie Flynn blinked in surprise when she saw Victor Claunch framed in the doorway. What was he doing here again? she wondered, and then she recalled that he had mentioned that he would come calling on Martha Jean later in the week.

"Hello, Victor."

"Nettie."

"I'm afraid Martha isn't here."

"That's all right. I'm really here to see you."

"Oh?" She couldn't imagine why he would want to see her. With a sigh, she realized he was waiting for her to invite him inside. Taking a deep breath, she opened the screen door. "Where are my manners? Won't you come in?"

She stepped back, allowing him entrance to the parlor. "Would you care for a cup of coffee?"

He smiled at her. "I never turned down a good cup of coffee in my life," he said, following her into the room. "Or a bad one, for that matter."

She gestured at the sofa. "Please sit down. I won't be but a moment."

In the kitchen, she clasped her hands together and took a deep breath. It had been a long time since she had been alone with a man. In the East, she lived in a rented room in a respectable boardinghouse. Ever conscious of her reputation, she had been careful never to be alone in the company of male callers. Many men had expressed interest. Most had been honorable, but none had lingered once they learned she was a married woman.

Her hands were shaking as she filled the coffeepot with water, pulled two cups from the shelf, and placed them on the silver tray her mother had given her on her wedding day. She stared at it a moment, remembering how happy she had been that day, and how quickly that had changed. With an effort, she shook the memory from her mind.

She added the sugar bowl and creamer to the tray, along with a pair of teaspoons. For a fleeting moment, she wished she had some tea cakes or cookies to go with the coffee, and then decided she was glad she didn't. Perhaps he would just drink his coffee and go home. The memory of his kiss, and the way she had responded to it, still shamed her after all these years.

When everything was ready, she drew a deep, calming breath, picked up the tray, and returned to the parlor.

Victor rose when she entered the room. "Here," he said, "let me help you with that."

Taking the tray from her hands, he placed it on the table between the sofa and the easy chair, waited until she was seated before resuming his own.

"Sugar?" she asked.

"No, thank you."

"Cream?"

"No."

She handed him a cup. "I don't know how you can drink it like that," she remarked, adding a spoonful of sugar and a generous amount of cream to her own cup.

He smiled at her. "I like my coffee the way it comes from the pot, and my whiskey the way it comes from the bottle."

She returned his smile. "I don't really like coffee," she confessed.

"Then why drink it?"

"I couldn't find any tea."

His gaze met hers. "I like a woman who makes do with what she has."

Speechless, Nettie stared at him over the rim of her coffee cup. Was he flirting with her? "Victor . . ."

"We were friends once, Nettie." He put his cup down and leaned forward. "I know this is sudden and highly improper, what with your husband not even cold in the ground, but . . . hear me out, Nettie. I don't know how you felt about Seamus, but it's been over between the two of you for a good many years. I've never been a patient man—"

"Victor, please." She stared at him, wishing she had never let him in the house. Surely he wasn't about to say what she thought he was.

"Let me finish before I lose my nerve."

She lifted one brow. The man had enough nerve to fill the Grand Canyon.

"I've never forgotten that New Year's kiss, and I've never forgotten you. Tarnation, what I'm trying to say is, I'd like to court you, if you wouldn't mind."

Completely taken aback, she could only stare at him. She had never forgotten that kiss, either. On many a lonely night, she had wondered what her life would have been like if Victor had been her husband.

"I see I've shocked you."

"Indeed, you have."

"I didn't mean to, but like I said, I've never been a patient man. When I see something I want, I most generally go after it, the consequences be damned."

She didn't know what to say to that, and so she said nothing.

Victor drained his cup, then gained his feet. "Think about what I said."

She also rose. "Yes, I will." She doubted if she would be able to think of anything else. A proposal, at her age?

She followed him to the door. Victor Claunch had always been a powerful man. He had never made any secret of the fact that he wanted to add the Flynn spread to his own. He and Seamus had had more than one dustup about it in the past.

Standing in the doorway, she watched him ride away. And all the while she wondered if it was really her that he wanted, or if she was just a means of getting his hands on the ranch he had coveted for so long?

Victor Claunch grinned as he left the Flynn place behind. He would have given his back teeth to know what had happened between Seamus and Nettie that had sent her packing all those years ago.

He had always had a secret hankerin' for pretty Nettie Mae Flynn. He remembered the first time he had seen her. It had been at a party at the Dinsdale ranch. She had been a new bride then, as pretty as a prairie flower on a spring day. She'd been wearing a dress the color of daffodils and a floppy-brimmed white hat. She'd been laughing at something her husband had said. It was the first time in Victor's life that he had ever envied another man.

And then there had been that night in Nettie's kitchen. He had never forgotten the sweetness of that kiss. Nettie. She was the reason he had never married.

Victor grunted softly as he urged his horse into a canter. It had been in his mind to make Martha Flynn his wife. She was a pretty enough woman, though not the looker her younger sister was. But he was looking for a wife, not a daughter, and though there were only a few years difference between the two Flynn girls, Martha Flynn was a woman, while Danielle was still a child. Of course, thinking that Martha was her father's heir had been the deciding factor.

But now Seamus Flynn was dead, and his widow had returned to Chimney Creek. Victor rubbed a hand over his jaw, wondering why he hadn't considered the possibility of Nettie's return sooner. He should have known Flynn's death would bring her back as nothing else could. But it had been Randolph Ludlow who had given Victor the best news of all. Contrary to what Victor had thought, Seamus had not left the ranch to his oldest daughter, but to his widow.

And she was here now, as pretty and desirable as she had ever been. He smiled, pleased that Fate had brought her back to him. If he played his cards right, a single "I do" would grant him the two things he had coveted his whole life. The fact that he had already asked Martha Jean to marry him didn't worry him a bit. It would be a simple matter to tell her he had changed his mind. Given a choice, he thought Nettie Flynn would make him a better wife, one who would be infinitely more malleable than her daughter.

Winning Nettie's affection shouldn't be too hard. He had always felt as though there was an unspoken attraction between them. And unless he was wrong, it was still there.

Chapter 19

Dani glanced at her surroundings as Sanza turned the horses loose and began making camp. Two days of hard riding had brought them to this place, a small canyon sheltered by towering walls. Thick grass grew in scattered clumps. There were a few stunted trees watered by a shallow spring, and animal tracks of some kind near the water.

"Why are we here?" she asked.

"It is a good place."

"A good place for what?" She looked around again, wondering what it could possibly be good for, or how he had found it. He had no map to follow, yet he seemed to know every water hole and spring, every canyon and crevice, every rock and mountain. Since he had kidnapped her, they had never lacked for food or water.

"A place to stay."

"Here?" She glanced around in disbelief. "We're going to stay here? Why? For how long?"

"For as long as I say."

"I want to go home." She spoke the words automatically, even though she knew it was a waste of breath. He wasn't going to let her go. Still, even though she was no longer afraid he was going to kill her, she had no idea what it was he planned to do with her. It was that uncertainty that frightened her. Had he brought her here to torture her? Or worse, rape her?

She glanced back at the entrance to the canyon, wondering what her chances were of sneaking away in the middle of the night. She hadn't had much success the last time, she thought glumly. Still, one failure wouldn't stop Marty. But she wasn't Marty, had never had Marty's courage. And what if trying to run away again made the Indian mad? What if he decided keeping her alive was too much trouble? He might decide to kill her and take her scalp, or leave her out there, alone and at the mercy of wild animals and the elements.

"Woman, gather wood for the fire."

"Who, me?"

He nodded in a way that defied argument. With a little *hmph* of pique, she walked toward the trees, muttering under her breath.

Sanza watched her walk away, noting the sway of her slender hips, the way her full skirt swished around her ankles, the way the sunlight shone on her hair. He had never seen a woman with hair that color. He itched to run his hands through it, to feel the long strands curl around his fingers. As always, looking at her stirred his desire, made him long to feel his body sheathed within hers, to touch her in the way a man touched a woman. Perhaps tonight . . . He thrust the thought from his mind. He did not want to take her by force. Rape was unknown among his people.

Drawing his gaze from the woman, he set about setting up camp. There was much to teach her before he took her home. Tomorrow, her lessons would begin.

* * *

Dani stared at the Indian, her hands fisted on her hips. "I don't know how to skin a deer."

He nodded patiently. "That is why you must learn."

"Why? Why do I need to know?"

"It is women's work."

"Well, it might be women's work for an Apache, but *I'm* not an Apache!" She had never skinned an animal in her life, and she wasn't about to start now.

Sanza picked up his knife and made the first cut.

Dani's eyes widened. One hand flew to cover her mouth as the blade pierced hide and flesh.

"If you want to eat, Da-ni, you must do your share of the work."

"Then I won't eat." And so saying, she turned her back to him. After a moment, she pressed her hands over her ears to shut out the sound of the knife cutting through the deer's carcass.

He sent her to draw water from the stream while he finished butchering the deer, sent her for wood while he cut some of the meat into long, thin strips to be dried over the fire.

Butchering was hot, dirty work. When she returned from the stream, he reached for the waterskin, frowning when she recoiled.

"You still fear me?" he asked. "Why?"

"Why? Because you're an Indian. A savage."

"Savage?" He studied her for a moment. "Is that what you think I am?"

"Aren't you? Look at you. Your hands are covered with blood." Her gaze moved over him, lingering on his broad shoulders and chest. She hated the way she itched to reach out and touch his copper-hued skin, to run her fingers over his sun-warmed flesh. "You're practically nak . . ." Heat flooded her cheeks. Why did he have to be so tall, so handsome? She shook the thought away. "Savage! You kidnapped me and . . ." Tears burned her eyes. "And Cory."

Cory. How could she have forgotten about Cory? She hadn't thought of him in hours. For all she knew he could be dead now, tortured to death by Sanza's friends. For all she knew that very fate might lie in store for her, as well. Giving in to her despair, she sank down on the ground and buried her face in her hands.

Her tears came harder, faster. She wept for Cory. She wept for herself. She wept because she was homesick, because she missed Marty, because her father was dead, and her mother was thousands of miles away.

After a moment, Sanza washed the blood from his hands, then drew the woman to her feet and wrapped her in his arms. She struggled a moment; then, with a long shuddering sigh, she collapsed against him, wailing softly.

He stroked her back, thinking how delicate she was, how good she felt in his arms. Her tears were warm against his chest, her hair soft where it brushed his hand. He lifted a long golden strand, watched it curl around his finger. He knew now why none of the maidens in the village had appealed to him. He had been waiting for this woman-child. Once, in a vision, he had seen a small golden dove soaring above the jagged cliffs of the Dragoon Mountains. A ray of sunshine had rested on the dove, momentarily gilding her feathers with gold. In his vision, the dove had fallen to the valley floor and been rescued by an eagle. At the time, he had not known what the vision meant. Even the tribal shaman had been uncertain. But Sanza knew what it meant now. His totem was the eagle. And Da-ni was the golden dove in his vision.

"Da-ni," he said quietly, "do not weep. I may be a savage, as you say, but you have no reason to fear me. I will not hurt you."

She sniffed, her tears subsiding. "I want to go home." She looked up at him. "Please take me home. I don't belong here."

"Ask anything else of me," he said. "And I will do it. But I cannot take you home."

"Why not? Who's going to stop you?"

"No one."

"Then take me home!"

"Is that what you want?"

She started to say yes, of course it was, but somehow the words wouldn't come. Instead, she gazed deep into his eyes, felt her heart skip a beat when she saw the desire burning in their dark depths. It frightened her to know that he wanted her; it was even more frightening to know that she wanted him, too.

His arms held her loosely, yet she was aware of their strength, just as she was acutely aware of his body, long and lean, pressed against her own. He smelled faintly of sweat and horse and dust. It should have repelled her, but it didn't. She curled her hands into fists to keep from running her fingertips over his chest and shoulders.

A tremor ran through his arms.

She found it suddenly hard to breathe.

He drew her closer, flattening her breasts against the hard wall of his chest.

She stopped fighting the urge to touch him and let her hands explore the width of his shoulders, the thick muscles in his arms.

His hands cupped her buttocks, drawing her up against him, letting her feel the heat of his desire.

With a soft cry, she drew his head down and pressed

her lips to his. When he didn't respond, she looked up at him. "What's wrong? Don't you want to kiss me?"

"What is kiss?"

"Don't you know?"

He shook his head, his gaze fixed on her lips. "Show me."

Heart pounding, she stood on tiptoe and pressed her lips to his once more. A moment later, he was kissing her back.

He was, she thought, a quick study.

She gasped when he swung her into his arms and carried her swiftly to his blankets. He lowered her gently to the ground, then stretched out beside her and gathered her into his arms.

She stared at him, her emotions in turmoil, her body trembling. "I guess you like kissing."

He nodded solemnly. Then, with one hand cupping the back of her head, he kissed her again. And again.

He might be a savage, she thought, her mind whirling, but he sure didn't kiss like one.

She felt a rush of panic as he rose over her, his dark eyes burning with desire. She gasped as his hands moved over her body, touching her in places no man had ever touched before.

Filled with sudden panic, she put her hands against his chest. "No!" It was like trying to move a mountain. "Please stop!"

A low groan rose in his throat as he rolled away from her.

Dani sat up. Breathing heavily, she stared at him, wondering how she could be both relieved and sorry that he had done as she asked.

Sanza rose, his chest heaving, his hands clenched at his sides. "I am sorry," he muttered in a gruff voice, and stalked away.

Drawing her legs up her arms and wrapping around her knees, she stared after him. She had never been kissed like that before, never felt such a strong stirring of desire. Cory's kisses had never inflamed her in such a way—never. . . . She bit down on her lip. How could she have let Sanza hold her and kiss her like that when Cory's life was in danger, when, even now, he could be dead, killed by Sanza's people?

Dropping her head down on her knees, she began to cry.

Chapter 20

Ridge woke to the scents and sounds of his childhood. For a moment he lay there with his eyes closed, letting the memories of the past wash over him. He heard his mother's laughter as she played with his little sister, the deep voice of his grandfather telling one of Coyote's tales. He saw his sister trailing at his heels, always begging him to take her with him. It didn't matter if he was going hunting or riding or swimming; she had always wanted to go along. And because he had loved her, he had taken her with him whenever he could. And when she was forced to stay behind, she had always come running to meet him when he returned, hurling herself into his arms.

Thinking of her filled him with pain, and he opened his eyes, banishing the images.

The scent of hoddentin lingered in the wickiup. Made from tule, hoddentin was carried by every Apache male. Medicine men used it in healing. A small amount was placed on the breast or the brow of the sick. It was scattered on the path before a man who was sick or wounded. It was thrown toward the sun at planting time to ensure a good harvest or when a war party left the stronghold. It was sprinkled on the bodies of the dead. It was placed on the tongue of a warrior who was suffering from exhaustion.

He knew the medicine man had used it on him last night.

He groaned softly as he pushed himself into a sitting position. His side hurt like hell. Pressing his hand against the wound, he glanced around the wickiup. There was no sign of Nochalo or Marty.

He was wondering if he had the strength to get to his feet when the door flap opened and Marty stepped inside.

"You're awake," she exclaimed softly. "How are you feeling?"

"Better." Just looking at her made him feel good. "How long have I been out?"

"Since yesterday."

"How are you doing?" he asked. "Are my people treating you all right?"

"I'm fine." She sat down beside him, a bowl in her hands. "One of the women fixed this for you."

Ridge nodded. "Have you seen any sign of Dani or Cory?"

Marty's eyes filled with worry at the mention of her sister's name. "No."

"That doesn't mean they're not here," Ridge said in an effort to reassure her. "Have you eaten?"

"Yes. Here." She handed him the bowl and a spoon. "You must be hungry."

"Yeah, thanks." The bowl held thick beef broth, and he wondered idly whose cattle the Apache had stolen.

Marty sat beside him looking apprehensive, her brow furrowed. He knew she was thinking about Dani, wondering if her sister and Cory were still alive. Ridge didn't hold much hope for Cory, but he was pretty sure Dani was all right. If she was here, she was likely being held as a slave in one of the wickiups.

He drained the last of the broth from the bowl and set it down, then threw the covers aside.

"What are you doing?" Marty asked, averting her gaze.

"Getting up."

"Do you think you should?" She glanced at the strip of cloth swathed around his middle. It looked very white against the bronze of his skin.

"It's not a matter of should," he said, gaining his feet. "It's a matter of need."

"Oh." There was no mistaking what he meant.

She was glad to see that someone—Nochalo, most likely—had provided him with a breechcloth while she'd been gone. Rising, she followed Ridge out of the wickiup.

He went off a ways to ensure his privacy.

Marty stood outside the wickiup, feeling as out of place as a heathen at a prayer meeting. The sun was high in the sky. All around her, men, women, and children were engaged in various activities. The Indians had paid her little attention save to look at her with varying degrees of curiosity or mistrust, but there had been recognition in the eyes of some of the men and women when they saw Ridge.

He returned a few minutes later.

Some of the women smiled at him, a welcome in their eyes. Men came to greet him, grasping him by the forearm, speaking to him in his native tongue.

She watched the play of emotions on his face as he spoke to his people. He seemed as happy to see them as they were to see him, and she wondered how long he had been away from this place. It had obviously been a long time. Why had he gone away? And why had he stayed away?

Gradually, the Indians returned to their own wicki-ups, leaving Marty and Ridge alone.

"Come on," Ridge said, taking her by the hand.

"Where are we going?"

"Not far."

He led her away from the village, down a narrow, twisting path that led to a small verdant valley where horses grazed.

He sat down on a large, flat rock, one hand pressed against his side, and she sat down beside him.

He stared out at the horse herd for a long time. What was he thinking about? Why had he brought her here?

"Ridge?"

Slowly, he turned to face her. From his expression, she wondered if he had forgotten she was there.

He drew in a deep breath, grimacing as the movement sent pain skittering through his side. "Dani's not here."

"How do you know?" Marty asked. "Where is she? Is she . . . ?"

"A warrior called Sanza has taken her."

She frowned at him. "What do you mean, taken her? Taken her where?"

"I don't know."

"But she's alive?" she asked breathlessly.

Ridge nodded. "As far as I know."

She breathed a heartfelt sigh of relief. "Thank God! Why did . . ." She frowned as she searched her memory for the unfamiliar name. "Why did Sanza take her?"

"Beats the hell out of me," Ridge replied, but he

had a pretty good idea. Dani was young, beautiful, and innocent, a prize no warrior would hesitate to claim. She could be traded for whiskey, sold to the Comancheros for rifles, or kept as a slave.

"What about Cory?"

He didn't answer, only sat there watching her through eyes as dark and fathomless as a midnight sky.

"He's dead, isn't he?" she asked, her voice raw.

Ridge nodded. "He tried to escape in the middle of the night. One of the sentries killed him. If he hadn't run, he'd still be alive."

She nodded. Poor Cory, to have died so young, and so needlessly. She wondered if Dani knew of his death. Dani and Cory had practically grown up together. Their families had always been close. How would she ever be able to face his parents again, knowing they would always blame Dani for his death?

"So," she said, "what do we do now?"

"Wait for Sanza to come home, I reckon."

"Are you sure he's coming back?"

Ridge shrugged. "As sure as I can be."

Marty looked out over the horse herd. Needing something to think of besides Cory's death and her sister's fate, she turned her thoughts toward home, wondering what Nettie intended to do with the ranch. Did she plan to stay, or sell the place out from under them? Marty wasn't sure which would be worse, sharing the ranch with Nettie, or being forced to leave.

And what of Victor Claunch? If he wasn't the one who had killed her father, then who had, and why? To her way of thinking, Claunch was the only man who had a motive. But none of that seemed important now, not when Dani's life might be in danger. Poor Dani. She had little experience living in the outdoors, had only spent a couple nights sleeping on the ground.

How was her sister faring, out there in the wilderness, at the mercy of an Apache warrior?

She slid a glance at Ridge. "He won't . . . you don't think he'd . . . abuse her, do you?"

Ridge grunted softly. "No. He won't rape her."

Marty flinched at the word. "How can you be so sure?"

"You'll just have to trust me on this one."

Trust him? To her surprise, she found that she did, indeed, trust Ridge Longtree. No matter that he was a hired gun. No matter that he was wanted by the law. She knew she could trust him, not only with her life, but with her sister's as well.

"How long has it been since you've been back here?" she asked.

"Ten years."

"Why did you leave?"

His eyes went hard and flat. A muscle twitched in his jaw. "My father was a white man. I'm not sure how he met my mother, but he left his people to live here, with hers. I was born the year after they were married. The Apache adopted my father into the tribe and he became one of us. I was seven when my sister was born."

He paused, his gaze fixed on the mountaintop across the valley. "She was a beautiful baby. As soon as she could crawl, she started following me everywhere I went. The other boys teased me unmercifully, but I didn't care. I thought she'd stop trailing after me when she got older, but she didn't."

He smiled, a sad wistful smile. "She wanted to go everywhere with me. I took her when I could. Even when I didn't want to, I couldn't refuse her.

"It got worse when our mother died. I guess I was about fourteen then, and Neeta was almost seven. It was hard on her, losing our mother. It was harder on my father, partly because my parents had been in love and partly because my sister looked so much like our mother. Every time my old man looked at Neeta, he was reminded of what he had lost."

Ridge blew out a sigh that seemed to come from the depths of his soul. "As much as Neeta loved our father, I was the one she came to when she was hurt or when she was afraid. She crawled into my bedroll when she woke up crying at night.

"I was almost seventeen when I decided I wanted to go and see what the white world looked like. My old man didn't want me to go. He said no good would come of it, but I was old enough then to do what I wanted, and I was determined to go. Neeta wanted to go with me, of course. She begged and cried, but the old man said no, and that was the end of it.

"I left a couple days later. Neeta clung to me, begging me to take her. The old man and I disagreed about a lot of things, but I knew he was right about this. I told her she couldn't go with me. I promised I'd bring her a present, and she seemed happy with that."

Ridge shook his head. "I should have known she'd follow me. She'd followed after me her whole life. I'd made camp for the night and I was about to turn in when she came walking in, a big smile on her face. She was so pleased with herself that I couldn't be angry with her, and even though I knew we were both going to be in a pile of trouble when I got her back home, I was glad to see her."

He paused and Marty swallowed hard, wondering if she wanted to hear the rest.

"I took her to town and we had a good time. It wasn't really a town, just a wide spot in the road with a trading post and a saloon. I had some furs to trade, and I bought her a handful of ribbons for her hair and a rag doll and a sack of candy. I bought some tobacco for the old man, sort of a peace offering, I guess. I had a few dollars left over and I thought I'd give that to him, too. Apaches don't spank their kids, but I knew I was in for a hell of a whipping when I got home.

"It was late afternoon when we left the trading post. We were making camp when two men rode up. I knew they were trouble, but I thought I could take care of it. They were just a couple of saddle tramps, after all, and I was a warrior."

He slammed his fist against the rock, then lifted his hand and stared at his bloody knuckles.

"They'd come to rob me of the few dollars I had left. I should have given them the money. That was all they wanted, just the money. But I was too proud to give it to them. I was an Apache warrior! No white man was going to take what was mine."

He shook his head. When he looked at her, his eyes were filled with torment. "Why didn't I just let them take the damn money?"

She looked at him, wishing she had an answer, wishing she could erase the haunted look from his eyes, wipe the pain from his heart and soul.

"I don't remember how it happened, but suddenly the two men were off their horses and coming at me. I didn't have a gun, just a knife and my bow. One of the men struck me with his quirt, and then his partner drew a gun. The next thing I knew, we were all three of us on the ground, grappling for the gun.

"I could hear Neeta crying in the background and suddenly the money didn't matter. Nothing mattered but getting her out of there. I elbowed one of the men in the crotch, kicked the other one in the face, and rolled free. I grabbed Neeta and put her on the back of the nearest horse. I smacked the horse on the rump and it took off running, and then I swung up on one of the other ones and rode after her."

He stared down at the blood oozing from his knuckles. "There were three gunshots. One of them grazed my thigh." He drew in a deep breath, held it for a long time, then blew it out in a long, shuddering sigh. "The other two hit her in the back. When I got to her, she was dead."

Marty felt the sting of tears in her eyes as she placed her hand on his. "It wasn't your fault."

"Of course it was. She'd be alive today if it weren't for me." He looked at Marty, his dark blue eyes glittering savagely. "I knew the men would come after us because I still had the money. I left Neeta where she'd fallen and I found a place to hide, and I waited.

"I didn't have to wait long. When they saw Neeta's body, they dismounted. I killed them both, and they were a long time dying, but she was still dead. I left the bastards where they fell. I wrapped Neeta's body in a blanket and took her home.

"My father was waiting for us. He listened to what I had to say, and then he looked at me and said I was no longer his son. I left the stronghold that night. I haven't been back since."

"Does your father still live here?"

"No. Nochalo told me the old man took off shortly after I did."

"I'm so sorry, Ridge. But it wasn't your fault that those men tried to rob you. None of it was your fault."

His tortured gaze burned into her. "Then why do I feel so damned guilty?"

"That's only natural. You were there. She died and you didn't. Of course you feel guilty. But it wasn't your fault. You weren't responsible for what those men did."

"Dammit, don't you think I've told myself that over and over again? But it doesn't help."

She pulled a handkerchief from her pocket and wrapped it around his bloodied knuckles. "You have to forgive yourself, Ridge. You'll never be at peace with yourself or with the past until you do."

Chapter 21

Nettie sat in front of the fire in the parlor, a cup of tea cooling on the table beside her. Lost in thought, she stared at the flames flickering in the hearth. It had been over a week since Martha and that man, Longtree, had left the ranch to search for Danielle and Cory. Had they found them yet? Surely she would know, in some deep part of her being, if anything had happened to her younger daughter.

She spent a few minutes thinking about Ridge Longtree. Though she had barely met the man and hardly spoken to him, she knew he was a bad one. It was etched in the harsh lines of his face, in the catlike way he noticed everything around him, in the set of his shoulders, the way his hand was never far from the butt of his gun. The West was filled with men of his ilk. Men who didn't care if they lived or died, who sold their gun to the highest bidder. They did what they were hired to do and then they moved on without a backward glance. What was a man like that doing here? Seamus must have hired him, but why?

It seemed like months had passed since she had stood on the porch and watched Martha and Longtree ride away. It was easy to keep herself occupied during the day. She scrubbed the floors, waxed the furniture, washed the windows and all the bedding, polished the silver, beat the carpets, did the mending and the ironing. She baked every day, only to give most of it to the cowboys. After all, how much bread, cake, or corn muffins could one woman eat?

Yesterday she had gone up to the attic, where she had spent hours looking through old boxes and trunks, smiling wistfully as she went through the dresses and pinafores her daughters had once worn, holding the dolls they had once played with. Danielle's doll looked almost as good as it had when she opened it one Christmas morning. The dress on Marty's doll was torn; the doll itself was missing one eye.

Marty's rocking horse stood in one corner, covered with dust, one ear still bearing the marks of Marty's baby teeth.

Nettie sighed. She'd had no trouble filling the daylight hours. It was only at night, when the shadows grew long and the melancholy howling of coyotes filled the air, that she realized how lonely—and alone—she was.

Last night, with tears in her eyes, she had gone through Seamus's belongings. She had packed his clothing into a large box and asked Smitty to put it up in the attic for her. While sorting through her husband's personal effects, she found the diamond stickpin she had given him on their first anniversary, and the photograph of herself and Martha that she had given to him for Christmas the year Martha was born. Oddly, the pocket watch she had given him for a wedding present had been missing. She wondered if he had thrown it out or given it away. Seamus's wedding ring had been there, a plain gold band. Hers lay beside it. She remembered the night she had taken it off. . . .

She had waited at the top of the second-floor land-ing, watching her husband try, unsuccessfully, to tiptoe quietly up the stairs.

"You've been drinking again, haven't you?" She had sniffed the air, her nostrils filling with the scent of a cheap perfume that was all too familiar. "And you've been with her."

Seamus's head jerked up. At any other time, she might have found his surprised expression comical. But not now. Not this time.

"Haven't you?" she accused, her voice rising.

He had lifted one shoulder in a careless shrug. "Would it do me any good to deny it, wife?"

"Why, Seamus? Why?" She wanted to scream at him, to rake her nails down his face, to beat her fists against his chest, but, mindful of Martha sleeping just down the hall, she held her ground and kept her voice to an angry whisper. "I love you, Seamus Flynn! I've never denied you my bed or your right to be there. Why do you feel the need to go elsewhere?" She blinked the tears from her eyes. "Why?"

Weaving slightly, he shrugged again. "I'm a man."

"You're an animal!"

"Is that what you think?" He leered at her. "Shall I show you otherwise?"

She backed away from him, one hand pressed to her heart, as he took the stairs two at a time. With a cry, she turned and ran down the hall to their bedroom. She almost made it, but he was too fast. When she tried to slam the door in his face, he wedged his foot into the doorway, and then he was in the room, his eyes hot as he closed and locked the door. . . .

Later, sobbing into her pillow, she had taken off her wedding ring and thrown it across the room. She had never slept with her husband again. Danielle had been conceived that night. . . .

Thrusting the memories from her mind, she pulled her robe tighter as she glanced around the room. It was a comfortable room. A man's room. The sofa and chairs were large and covered with dark leather. The tables were of solid mahogany. Seamus's Winchester still hung over the massive stone fireplace. The hide of a bear he had killed with that rifle still covered the floor in front of the hearth, the same rack of antlers hung on the wall over a low table that held a number of decanters and crystal glasses.

Though the furniture was the same, there was little to show that she had once lived in this house. The few trinkets and the gilt-edged mirror she had brought with her from the East were nowhere to be seen. The doilies she had crocheted during her first long winter on the ranch were missing. So was the quilt she had made when she was pregnant with Danielle. She wondered who had removed her things. Had Martha Jean discarded them, or had Seamus thrown them out, the way he had thrown his wife out?

She stared at the photograph on the mantel. It showed a young Seamus holding a daughter on each knee.

"Damn you, Seamus," she murmured. "We could have been so happy together if you hadn't gone chasing after every skirt in town."

But that was over and done with now, and there was no way to rectify the mistakes of the past. She could only go forward, and hope it wasn't too late to make a new beginning with her daughters.

Chapter 22

Dani soon discovered that Sanza was a man of his word. When she didn't work, she didn't eat. It was all she could do to keep from vomiting the first time she skinned a rabbit, and yet she found a grim satisfaction in her accomplishment. Marty would have been proud of her! Sanza brought her birds to pluck and clean, and finally a deer to butcher. She didn't think she would ever be able to do it without gagging. She knew Marty would have done it without flinching, and so she clenched her teeth and pretended to be Marty. When she finished, Dani again felt a rush of satisfaction she had never felt before, and with it a newfound confidence in herself.

Sanza taught her how to tan the deer's hide, how to make ash cakes and jerky, how to start a fire and keep it going.

One morning, shortly after breakfast, he told her he was going hunting alone.

"You're going to leave me here?" she asked.

He nodded, his dark eyes thoughtful. "Will you be here when I return?"

She looked at him as if he had gone mad. "Where would I go?"

"I will have your promise that you will not run away," he said.

"I promise."

"It is good." His hand lightly stroked her cheek, sending shivers of delight coursing all the way down to her toes.

She fought back her fears when she saw him ride away, taking her horse with him. As a pack animal, she wondered, or to ensure that she didn't try to escape?

There was little to do while he was gone. She moved through their camp, straightening the blankets, rearranging their few cooking utensils, her gaze constantly searching for his return. If something happened to him, she would die out here, lost and alone.

Sitting in the shade, she wondered why she hadn't told Sanza she wanted to go home when he had asked. It was, after all, what she wanted, yet the thought of leaving him left her feeling desolate.

She couldn't hide her relief or her elation when he returned late that afternoon.

She tried not to notice the way his muscles rippled beneath his copper-hued skin when he moved, tried to ignore the way her heart skipped a beat whenever he looked her way. She resented the way her body yearned for him whenever he was near, the way her pulse raced whenever their bodies touched.

She knew that he was just as aware of her as she was of him. She saw the desire ignite in his eyes whenever he looked at her. And he looked at her often.

She had lost track of time. Her days were filled with tasks she had once found repulsive but that now filled her with a sense of accomplishment. She had never worked so hard in her life. She was exhausted when she sought her bed at night, but she was unable to sleep. Instead, she tossed and turned, and when sleep finally came, her dreams were filled with erotic images of the man who slept across the fire from her.

How could she want him so badly when she was supposed to be in love with Cory? Guilt seared her soul. She often went hours, sometimes a full day, without even thinking of him. Was it possible she had never truly loved him? Was that why his kisses had never excited her, why she had never yearned for him the way a woman yearned for the man she loved?

Now, curled up in her blankets, she tried to summon Cory's image, but to no avail. Every time she closed her eyes, Sanza's image filled her mind—deep black eyes, long black hair, corded muscles beneath smooth copper skin, strong shoulders, a broad chest, full, sensual lips. . . .

Thinking of his mouth on hers made her heart beat faster. Heat flowed through her, pooling deep in the core of her being, making her toss restlessly as she imagined him kissing her again, his hands caressing her. Her hands caressing him . . .

She sat up, one hand pressed to her heart. It was wrong, she thought frantically, wrong to feel this way about him. He was an Apache, her enemy. He had kidnapped her . . . and yet he had treated her kindly. He could have beaten her when she ran away, or just let her go. She would probably have died of thirst, or exposure, or exhaustion long before she found her way home, if she ever did.

She glanced across the fire, startled to find Sanza sitting up and staring back at her. She couldn't see his expression in the darkness, but she felt the weight of his gaze on her face.

"I . . . I couldn't sleep," she stammered.

He nodded. "For me it is the same."

"Oh? Why can't you sleep?"

He didn't answer right away. Rising, he tossed a few pieces of wood on the fire. He stood there, staring into the flames for stretched seconds. Flames licked at the new wood, casting reddish-orange shadows on Sanza's face and in his hair. He looked dark and forbidding and all too desirable standing there. Her heart seemed to turn over in her chest, and she was sorely tempted to go to him, to press herself against his back, to wrap her arms around his waist and hold him close.

As if divining her thoughts, he turned to look at her. Dani's breath caught in her throat as his gaze locked with hers. As though mesmerized, she stared back at him, unable to move, unable to think. His gaze moved over her, so strong, so intense, it was almost tangible. She shivered as she imagined his hands touching her in place of his gaze.

She grew still as he walked around the fire, closing the distance between them.

"Da-ni."

She looked up at him, speechless, her blood pounding in her ears.

Slowly he dropped to his knees in front of her. "Da-ni."

"Wh-what?"

"Will you be my woman?"

She stared at him, wondering if she had heard right. Be his woman? What did he mean by that? Surely not what she was thinking. Surely not what she wanted so desperately.

"Have you no answer?"

"I don't know what to say. I don't know what you mean."

A faint smile touched his lips. "Did I not speak clearly?"

"Are you asking me to . . . to sleep with you?"

"Sleep?" He considered that a moment, a frown furrowing his brow.

"You know . . ." Heat flooded her cheeks. "Sleep. Together."

"Ah. That would be part of it."

"Part of it?"

"I want you to share my wickiup. Be my woman. Bear my children."

She opened her mouth, but no words came out. He was asking her to be his wife! How could she marry him? She was promised to Cory.

"I know you want me in the way a woman wants a man," Sanza said, his voice thick. "I have seen the way you look at me."

Dani shook her head, as if to refute his words. "You're an Indian. We can't get married. Who would marry us?" She shook her head again. "No. No, I can't. Besides, I have a boyfriend."

Sanza frowned at her. "You cannot be my woman because you have a friend who is a boy?"

"He's not *just* a friend. We're going to be married."

Sanza's lips flattened and something dark and dangerous moved through his eyes. "No one else will have you, Da-ni. You will be mine."

"Oh, I will, will I?" she exclaimed belligerently. "What if I don't want to be yours?"

Lifting his hand, he ran his fingertips down her arm. Shivers of delight trailed in their wake. Slowly, ever so slowly, he leaned toward her until they were less than a breath apart.

"Do you not?" he asked softly.

And then he kissed her.

Every other thought fled her mind. It didn't matter that he was an Apache and she was white. It didn't matter that he lived in a brush hut and she was accustomed to a big house. She forgot about Marty and Cory, forgot everything but his mouth on hers.

She clutched his shoulders to steady herself, reveling in the strength beneath her fingertips, in the heat of his skin, the way he quivered at her touch.

"Sanza . . ."

His eyes burned into hers. "Be my woman, Da-ni."

How could she refuse when he was looking at her like that, when her whole body yearned for his touch?

"How do your people get married?"

"When a warrior wishes to take a wife, he speaks to his family and requests their permission. When that is done, he sends his father or his brother to speak to the girl's parents. When that is done, the warrior sends gifts to the girl and her family, and then he offers horses for her. In the night, the warrior takes as many horses as he can afford and ties them in front of the girl's wickiup. The number of horses he offers expresses his wealth and his love for the girl he desires. If the girl feeds and waters the horses, it means she has accepted his offer. She is allowed four days to decide."

He smiled faintly. "Most girls do not care for the animals on the first day. If the animals remain uncared for by the fourth day, the warrior knows he has been rejected.

"If he is accepted, there is a wedding feast that lasts for three days. During this time, the warrior and his woman are not allowed to speak to each other, but on the third night they run away from the feast to a temporary wickiup located not far from the main camp."

"For their honeymoon," Dani murmured, blushing.

"Six or seven days later, the couple returns to the

camp." He looked deep into her eyes. "Be my woman, Da-ni."

"Aren't you going to bring me horses?"

"I have many horses at the stronghold," he said, puffing out his chest. "They are yours. Will you accept them?"

"If I say yes, does that mean we're married?"

He nodded solemnly. "This will be our special place. When I take you to the stronghold, you will be my woman."

"What about your people? They'll hate me."

"No. They will accept you and treat you with respect."

Dani bit down on her lower lip. How could she make such a momentous decision on her own? What would Marty do? What would Marty say? How could she marry an Indian? She had always dreamed of getting married in church in a long dress with her family at her side. And what about Cory? How could she ever face him again? What could she possibly say?

She looked into Sanza's eyes and felt her heart melt. She had tried to hate him, but to no avail. He made her feel exciting and alive. She knew he would take care of her, protect her. With Sanza, she would never have to be afraid of anything, and yet . . .

As though sensing her doubts, Sanza drew her into his arms and kissed her again.

And her decision was made.

"Yes," she murmured. "Oh, yes."

Gently, he pushed her down on her blankets, his big body stretching out beside hers, a faint tremor in his arms as he drew her body against his. She could feel the evidence of his desire pressing into her belly. It aroused her even as it filled her with trepidation. She had never been with a man before, never done more than share a few kisses with Cory, and one unexpected kiss from Ridge Longtree, before Sanza entered her life.

She stared at him, her heart slamming against her ribs. "I don't know how . . . I've never . . . never been with a man."

Sanza looked down at her, his dark eyes filled with patience and love. Tenderly, he brushed a wisp of hair from her cheek. "I have never lain with a woman," he said. "We will find the path together."

She nodded, pleased that he was as ignorant as she.

His hands moved over her slowly and she shivered at his touch, pleased and surprised at her body's response to his caress. Was she supposed to feel this way? No one had ever told her what to expect on her wedding night.

"Do not be afraid," Sanza whispered. "I will not hurt you."

"I'm not afraid of anything, not anymore."

She moaned softly as his hands caressed her. Why hadn't anyone told her how wonderful it was to lie with a man? But not just any man. She couldn't imagine anyone but Sanza touching her so intimately, stroking her with such restrained passion. She loved his touch, loved the contrast between his bronzed flesh and her own pale skin.

Taking a deep breath, she began an exploration of her own, letting her fingertips slide over his broad chest and shoulders, then down his long, muscular arms. A low groan rose in his throat as her hands slid downward to caress his taut belly. It was a sound of mingled pleasure and pain, and it brought a smile to Dani's lips. It gave her a sense of purely female pleasure and power to know that her touch aroused him.

She pressed herself against him, wanting to be closer,

to feel the length of his body against her own. He undressed her slowly, his eyes hot with admiration as he bared her body to his gaze. She shivered with pleasure, felt her cheeks grow warm under his blatant regard. He caressed her, his hands gentle, arousing her still more until, suddenly bold, she removed his clout. Her eyes grew wide as she stared at him.

"Oh, my," she murmured. She had never seen a fully naked man before, let alone one who was aroused. It was an impressive sight!

With a grin that bordered on smug, he drew her into his arms once again. Ah, the wonder, the ecstasy of lying beside him with nothing but desire between them.

She was ready when he rose over her, his dark eyes aflame. A quick thrust, and she was no longer a maiden. She clutched his shoulders at the pain, but it was soon over and forgotten in the ripples of pleasure that spread through her.

Then he was moving deep within her, slow, soft strokes that grew faster, harder, deeper, until she writhed beneath him, reaching, searching, until she thought she might explode, until her body was slick with sweat. She moaned, frantic in her pursuit of something that remained elusive, and then, with one last stroke, pleasure such as she had never imagined broke over her. It was so wonderful, so beautiful, tears welled in her eyes.

Sobbing his name, she closed her eyes and rode the wave back down to earth.

"Da-ni?"

With a sigh, she opened her eyes and stared up into her husband's face. And then she smiled the smile of a woman who had been well and truly pleasured by the man she loved.

Sanza grinned at her, his chest puffing out. "You are all right?"

"Oh, I'm better than all right," she said, trailing her fingertips over his sweat-sheened chest.

His grin widened, a look of supreme satisfaction spreading over his face.

"Not bad for the first time," Dani remarked, then blushed at her own boldness. What a wanton she was becoming!

Sanza grinned down at her. "Perhaps the second time will be better."

"Second time?"

He nodded, and she felt his erection against her belly. "If I did not please you the first time, then I must do it again."

Well, she thought, what was she supposed to say to that? If she told him he had pleased her, he might not make love to her again. But if she said he didn't please her, it might hurt his feelings.

"You pleased me very much. But," she added quickly, "there's always room for improvement, don't you think? For instance, this time I could do this. . . ." Drawing his head down, she ran her tongue along the seam of his lips and then slid past to explore the dark depths inside.

Sanza let out a startled gasp but quickly followed her lead, his clever hands moving over her until she was on fire for him. There was no pain the second time he took her, only waves of pleasure that built and crested, carrying her higher, higher, until the world exploded once more.

Dani rolled onto her side and stared at the man sleeping beside her. She was in love with him, in love with an Apache warrior. How had such a thing happened? What would Marty say when she found out? Would she be shocked? Outraged?

Dani lightly traced the outline of Sanza's jaw, surprised to find that she no longer cared what her sister, or anyone else, thought. She knew it wouldn't be easy, learning to live with the Apache. She would have to win their friendship and trust, learn their customs and beliefs and their language. Sanza had already taught her a few words. *Ashoge* meant "thank you," *gowa'a* was the word for "wickiup," *yadalanh* meant "good-bye," *dah* was the word for "no." *Shil'-nzhoo* meant "I love you." That was her favorite word of all.

"What are you smiling about, wife?"

"I was just thinking how happy I am." Her gaze moved over him, lingering on his manhood, which was fully aroused. "What are *you* thinking about, husband?"

She laughed out loud as he rolled her onto her back, his body covering hers. "What do *you* think I am thinking?"

"Oh, I know what you're thinking," she replied with a giggle. "But I'm hungry."

He nodded solemnly, his dark eyes hot. "I, too, am hungry."

She looked up at him through the veil of her lashes. "Are you?" She ran her hands over his chest and buttocks, wondering when she had learned to flirt so shamelessly. "What are you hungry for?" she asked, stifling a grin. "Ash cakes, perhaps?"

He made a low growl in his throat as he cradled her head in his hands. All thought of food and flirting fled her mind at the touch of his lips on hers. He kissed her until she was mindless, breathless, her body aching with need. How could she want him again so soon when they had made love all night long? But want him she did.

Her last thought, before being swept away, was to hope that someday Marty would find the happiness she had found.

Chapter 23

Marty stared up at the tiny slice of blue sky visible through the smoke hole of the wickiup that she shared with Ridge. This morning marked their ninth day at the Apache stronghold. His wound was healing nicely and he was feeling better, so much so that they had spent the day before watching the final phase of a young girl's puberty rite, known as *Na-ih-es*, or the Sunrise Ceremony, something all Apache girls went through when they began their menses.

Marty had found it fascinating and had listened attentively while Ridge explained what was going on.

According to Ridge, the Apache believed that the *N'dee*, the People, had emerged from the center of the Earth and that their lives had begun when *Is dzán naadleeshe'*, or Changing Woman, was washed ashore and emerged from a seashell.

The Apache believed that *Is dzán naadleeshe'* sat cross-legged in front of her *gowa'a* one morning. Sitting there, with her arms raised toward the sun, she prayed to the Great Spirit. As she prayed, she bent low to touch Mother Earth, first on the north side and then on the south side. As she prayed, a crimson ray of light from the sun penetrated her woman's place and so her menses began.

Shortly after that, *Is dzán naadleeshe'* became pregnant. Her first child was named *Naye' nazgháné,* or Slayer of Monsters. A short time later, she gave birth to *Túbasdeschine,* or Born of Water Old Man.

During the ceremony, the girl sat on a blanket facing the east. The shaman, known as the *diiyin,* and the singers stood behind her. Marty thought it odd that they kept their hands over their mouths, and Ridge explained it was so that no evil spirits could create mischief while the singers were singing.

Marty thought the most fascinating part of the ceremony was when some masked dancers had burst upon the scene to the accompaniment of a bullroarer and the jingle of bells to banish whatever evil might be present. Ridge told her they were called the *Ga-an* and that they represented the Mountain Spirits. The *Ga-an* danced during the beginning of the ceremony to chase away evil spirits. With their garishly painted bodies and elaborate wooden headdresses, they were an awesome and frightening sight. Ridge told her that the *Ga'an* had the power to know if a person had done wrong. He remarked that when he had been a young boy, a friend of his had told his mother a lie. That night, when the *Ga'an* danced, one of the dancers had looked his friend in the eye. With a yelp of guilt, Ridge's friend had jumped to his feet and run into his lodge.

Marty found it odd that, during the Sunrise Ceremony, the girl could not wash herself. She wasn't allowed to scratch herself, either, unless she used a special stick anointed for that purpose, and that she couldn't drink except though a special tube.

At sunset on the first day, the girl began to dance, and she would dance for the next four days. She danced hour after hour with her head held high and her eyes fixed on the rising sun.

Marty had felt sorry for the girl. She danced for hours while the sun rose higher and hotter. Now and then another girl stepped forward to wipe the sweat from the face of the dancing girl.

Finally, after all the songs had been sung, the girl was allowed to sit down. She swayed back and forth, recreating the moment when *Is dzán naadleeshe'* was penetrated by the sun's light.

There was much more to the ceremony, most of which had made no sense to Marty. She had watched while the medicine man "painted" not only the girl but her clothing as well. Ridge told her that sometimes the *Ga'an* painted the girl and sometimes many people performed the task. When she asked Ridge how the girl would ever get all that paint out of her hair and clothes, he told her that, once the paint dried, it was easily brushed away.

When the girl had been painted, she was given the basket of paint and she moved through the crowd with another girl, who dipped the brush into the paint and flicked it over the people, thus showering them with blessings. Marty had looked at Ridge and laughed as drops of paint had rained down upon them.

When the basket was empty, there was more dancing and singing. Ridge had told her that when the ceremony was over, the masks the *Ga'an* had worn would be broken and carried away to a secret and sacred place where the Mountain Spirits lived.

And then the girl danced again while members of the tribe stood in line to bless her. First in line was the shaman, who sprinkled a handful of hoddentin over her head. More prayers were offered as hoddentin was sprinkled over the medicine man.

There were times when the line didn't seem to move at all. Ridge told Marty that during the Sunrise Ceremony, the girl was believed to have Changing Woman's power to heal, so men and women who were sick or had sick children sought to be healed at the girl's hands.

Ridge said that once, when he was a young boy, the parents of a little girl who had been badly burned brought her to one of the girls who was enduring the Sunrise Ceremony. A silence had fallen over the crowd as the girl took the child in her arms and lifted her high over her head, offering a prayer to *Usen* that the child would recover. The next day, the little girl was completely healed.

All in all, it had been the most amazing thing Marty had ever seen. Her last thought as she had followed Ridge back to their wickiup had been gratitude that she would never be called upon to endure such a rigorous ordeal.

She glanced over at him now, murmuring, "Good morning," when she saw him looking back at her.

"Mornin'."

"How are you feeling today?"

"Better." He threw back the covers and she averted her eyes as he stood. Since they had been here, he had taken to dressing like the other Apache men. She still found it somewhat shocking to see him clad in nothing but a breechclout and the bandage swathed around his middle.

Slipping on a pair of moccasins, he left the wickiup, giving her privacy so she could rise and dress.

Taking her brush from her saddlebag, she began to brush out the tangles in her hair. As always, her thoughts turned immediately to Dani. It had been weeks now since her sister had been captured. Was she still alive? Was she being treated all right? What if the warrior who had taken her didn't return to the stronghold in the next few days? She couldn't wait here forever. She had to get back to the ranch. She had responsibilities there. She had to find out what Nettie intended to do with the ranch. She had to find out who had killed her father and why. But how could she leave here without Dani?

Putting her hairbrush aside, Marty stepped into her trousers, slipped on her shirt, pulled on her socks and boots. Then, taking a deep breath, she left the wickiup.

Ridge was sitting outside, his back to the sun, his eyes closed. At the sound of her footsteps, he opened his eyes and looked up at her, then gestured at the bowl beside him.

"Breakfast is here."

Marty nodded. The old medicine man's wife prepared their meals for them.

Sitting down across from Ridge, Marty picked up the bowl and began to eat. She had asked Ridge endless questions in the last few days. She had learned that the Apache had a great fear of the dead. The body was buried on the day of death, if possible. Oddly, the task of preparing the body for burial fell to the nearest male relative. The Apache preferred to bury their dead in a remote cave or in a crevice in the rocks; if that wasn't possible, a grave was dug and the body was buried with all its personal effects. The grave was then covered with rocks to discourage predators from ravaging the body. Once the dead had been buried, those in attendance brushed themselves all over with grass, then placed the grass on the grave. The wickiup of the deceased was burned, along with everything in it, and those who had interred the body also burned the clothing they wore at the time, and then purified themselves in sagebrush smoke. The name of the deceased was never mentioned again so that his spirit would not be called back from its journey to the afterlife.

She learned that Apache medicine men believed that, when they were in their full regalia, they were no longer mere men but that they became the power they represented. Curiously, the hair of the shaman was believed to hold some special sort of power, and they took great pains to make sure no one touched it. Among the sacred objects used by the shaman were the medicine hat, the medicine cord, and the medicine shirt, as well as other charms and amulets thought to hold power. She learned that the medicine shirt was made of buckskin and painted with symbols representing the sun, moon, and stars, as well as clouds, lightning, and a rainbow. Other symbols represented the snake, the centipede, and the tarantula. It was believed that the medicine shirt protected the wearer from the arrows and bullets of his enemy.

The Apache ate abundantly of meat, and liked mule meat most of all. They ate their horses, as well as deer, buffalo, beef, gophers, and lizards. The Apache did not eat anything that lived in water. They did not eat bear meat because the bear walked on two legs, like a man. They did not eat pork because hogs ate animals that lived in water. They did not eat the meat of the turkey, though they hunted turkeys for their feathers, as well as mink and muskrat and beaver for their skins. The Indians ate roots and berries and the seeds of grasses, as well as acorns, mescal, and mesquite beans. The pulpy head of the mescal plant was available nearly everywhere in the desert. The women gathered it and roasted it in pits. The mesquite bean, the acorn, and grass seeds were pounded into meal and made into cakes. They also ate the fruit from a variety of cactus and yucca.

The Apache were good swimmers, and groups of women and children could often be seen splashing around in the stream.

As far as she could tell, Apache children received little discipline. They were rarely scolded or punished and seemed to have the run of the camp.

The women made lovely baskets for carrying goods and water.

She was surprised to learn that, when a man married, he forever left his own family behind and went to live with his wife's people. From that time on, he was expected to provide meat and protection for his in-laws. Their welfare became his responsibility.

For all their strange ways, the Apache were a deeply spiritual and friendly people. They made her feel welcome among them, even though she could not speak their language.

Setting the bowl aside, Marty glanced around the village, then looked at Ridge. "Do you think he's ever coming back?"

He didn't have to ask who she was talking about. "Sooner or later, he'll come home and he'll bring Dani with him."

"I'm not sure I can wait much longer."

"That's up to you. Say the word and we'll leave."

"How can I go?" she exclaimed. "I can't just ride off and leave Dani here."

Ridge held up his hands in a gesture of surrender. "Hey, you just said—"

"Oh, I know what I said! I'm just so worried about her, I don't know what to do. I can't help worrying about her. And about my mother, and the ranch, and . . ." She shook her head, fighting tears of frustration. "Damn!"

Scooting toward her, he placed an arm around her shoulders. Though she hadn't mentioned her old man, he knew that was who the tears were for. So much had happened so quickly, she really hadn't had time to mourn her father's death.

Burying her face in the hollow of his shoulder, she let the tears flow, unmindful of the curious stares of the Apache.

Ridge patted her back, overcome by a sudden need to protect and comfort her. One way or another, he would find the man who had killed her father. It had been a job before. It was personal now, though he didn't want to think about what had wrought the change in his thinking. He was growing far too fond of Martha Jean Flynn, starting to care about her far too much. Since he'd left his mother's people all those years ago, he'd never given a damn about anyone else or what they thought of him. But somewhere along the way, Martha Jean's opinion had started to matter, and that bothered him.

Gradually her tears subsided, and still she remained in his arms. After a time, she drew a deep breath, let it out in a long, shuddering sigh, and then eased away from him.

"You're all wet," she murmured, sniffling.

He glanced down at his chest, now damp with her tears. "It doesn't matter. I needed a bath anyway," he remarked, pleased when his small jest brought a faint smile to her lips. "And speaking of baths, I think we could both use one."

Marty nodded. They hadn't bathed since they had left the ranch, though she had washed her hands and face each day.

He rose, grimacing as the movement pulled on his wound, then offered Marty his hand.

Returning to the wickiup, she pulled a change of clothes from her saddlebags, along with a bar of soap. Ridge handed her a piece of trade cloth to dry with, then took another for himself.

Marty looked around. "Where do you bathe?"

"In the creek."

She should have known better than to expect a hot bath in a place like this. Tucking her clothes under one arm, she followed Ridge out of the wickiup and down a narrow dirt path that led to a tree-lined stream. He continued on until he came to a place where the stream widened.

Sunlight glinted off the face of the water. Marty looked at Ridge, wondering if he intended for them to bathe together. True, they had shared a few soul-deep kisses, but she wasn't ready to undress in front of him, or have him undress in front of her.

One corner of his mouth went up in a wry grin as he read her thoughts. "I'll go downstream a ways."

She nodded.

"Stay here until I come for you."

"All right."

She watched him walk away, noting the play of muscles in his back, the width of his shoulders, the way the sun's light cast blue highlights in his long black hair. He really was a gorgeous man.

When he was out of sight, she glanced around to make sure she was alone. Undressing hurriedly, she slipped into the water. She had expected it to be cold, but it was surprisingly warm.

She washed quickly; then, reluctant to get out, she sat in the shallows, her thoughts wandering toward home. She had never been away from the ranch this long before, and while she was certain Scanlan and Smitty and the others would look after the place, she couldn't help wondering—and worrying—about what Nettie was doing. Had she already put the ranch up for sale? And what about Victor Claunch? No doubt he'd been sniffing around again. Now that Marty was away, how hard would it be for him to persuade Nettie to sell the home place?

And what about Dani? What if Ridge was wrong and the warrior who had taken her sister didn't return to the stronghold? What if something had happened to the warrior? Dani could be wandering out in the middle of the desert, lost and alone. . . .

Marty stared up at the vast blue sky, thinking that, at the moment, she was feeling pretty lost and alone herself.

A movement caught her eye, and she saw Ridge striding toward her. Instinctively, she crossed her arms over her breasts, felt the heat rush into her cheeks when he came to a halt beside the stream, one brow raised as his gaze moved over her in a long, lingering glance. Heat rushed into her cheeks.

"Don't look!" she exclaimed.

He made a sound low in his throat. "How can I help it? You're the prettiest thing I've ever seen in that creek."

"Turn around! I'm naked."

"Yes, ma'am," he said appreciatively. "You surely are."

Her cheeks were burning now, the fire spreading through her whole body. "Ridge Longtree, stop staring at me like that this instant!"

Ridge let his gaze move over her one last time; and then he turned his back to her, knowing that the image of Martha Jean Flynn sitting waist-deep in the slow-moving water would be a sight he would never forget. Her skin was a pale golden brown, her forearms and neck tanned from hours spent outdoors. The sunlight had danced and sparkled in the drops of water in the wealth of her hair. The flush in her cheeks had been most becoming.

He heard splashing as she climbed out of the creek, the sound of cloth being dragged over wet skin as she dressed. He was sorely tempted to turn around for one more look but something—respect for Martha Jean, perhaps—kept him from doing so.

Marty stared at Ridge's back while she dressed. What was it about him that drew her gaze again and again? It was more than the fact that he was tall and ruggedly handsome, though she couldn't put her finger on exactly what it was. All she knew was that he filled her thoughts by day and her dreams by night, and that she felt empty inside when they were apart, even for a short time.

Was she falling in love with him?

She dismissed the thought immediately. And as quickly as she banished it, it returned.

Was she falling in love with him?

The question, once asked, refused to go away. And if the answer, heaven forbid, was yes, what then? He was a hired gun, wanted by the law, hardly the kind of man to settle down and raise cattle.

Marty was fully dressed when he turned around. His gaze met hers head-on and she had the answer to her question.

Somewhere along the trail, she had fallen in love with Ridge Longtree.

Chapter 24

Ridge sat outside the wickiup he shared with Martha Jean, his forearms resting on his thighs, his hands dangling between his knees. Marty was asleep inside, and the camp was dark. He seemed to be the only one still awake save for the sentries who guarded the entrance to the stronghold.

A flash of lightning seared the sky in the distance. The Apache believed that lightning was a visible sign of supernatural power from the Thunder People. Long ago, the Thunder People had provided the Apache with meat. After a while, the Apache had started to take the Thunder People for granted. To punish the People for their ingratitude, the Thunder People had stopped providing them with meat. Lightning flashes were their arrows, which could be a good sign or a bad sign, depending on the omens.

Ridge stared into the distance. Across the stream, the horse herd was a drifting mass of shadows. A few dogs wandered through the camp, searching for scraps. A baby cried in the distance, the sound quickly muffled. Apache children weren't allowed to cry. Away from the security of the stronghold, a baby's cry could alert the enemy to the camp's whereabouts.

He had avoided this place for so many years, he'd almost been afraid to come back. Surprisingly, it still felt like home. Reaching down, he picked up a handful of earth and rubbed it between his hands, then ran his hands over his arms and legs, returning, symbolically, to the land of his birth.

Yet he was still filled with a sense of disquiet, and he knew it was due to the woman sleeping inside. Since the first day he had seen her, he hadn't been able to put her out of his mind. He wanted her with a single-mindedness he'd never known before, and it scared the hell out of him. He wasn't interested in settling down in one place. He had no intimate experience with decent women. He'd been on his own since he was seventeen, drifting, hiring out his gun, living for the moment with never a thought for the future. Until he met Martha Jean Flynn, he had forgotten what it was like to worry about anyone but himself.

Muttering an oath, he gained his feet. When they returned to the ranch, he would do his damnedest to find out who killed Seamus Flynn, and then he'd get the hell out of her life while he still could.

The next few days passed uneventfully. Marty watched the Indian men and women as they went about their daily tasks. She had heard that the Apache were a stoic people, cruel to those they considered their enemy, and anyone not Apache was considered the enemy. To her surprise, she found them to be a happy, fun-loving people. The children were adorable. The men appeared to be caring husbands and fathers. The women were like women everywhere, concerned with taking care of their homes, husbands, and children.

She watched the women cook and clean, gather

wood and water, nurse their young, do the sewing and the mending, and though their methods were primitive, they were not inferior.

Earlier in the day, she had watched a group of six boys, perhaps ten years old, under the tutelage of two warriors. To her amazement, the boys had formed two lines some distance apart and then, fitting stones into rawhide slings, began to hurl them at one another, all the while dodging stones hurled at them. She remembered seeing several boys doing the same thing when she had first arrived. She realized now it was some form of training. One boy was struck in the cheek, another on the arm. Neither boy stopped, even though blood was running down the first boy's cheek.

When the boys finished with their slingshots, they took up small bows and arrows and began to shoot at each other. After that, the boys ran a footrace.

Little wonder Apache warriors were so fierce, she thought, when they played such games as children!

Her awareness of Ridge Longtree grew ever stronger. Every look, every touch, sent shivers of delight skittering through her. He was in her thoughts by day and her dreams by night. She tried not to stare at him, but it was impossible. He drew her gaze like a flame drew a moth. She loved looking at him, loved his smile, the deep blue of his eyes, the way he walked, the bold air of self-confidence that was as much a part of him as the color of his skin.

She stayed close to his side, learning what she could of Apache ways, picking up a few words here and there. But always, in the back of her mind, was a nagging worry for her sister.

She needed to know that Dani was all right. She needed to return to the ranch. That, she thought, would be a mixed blessing. When she got home, she would have to face her mother again, which was bad enough. Even worse, she would have to visit Cory's parents and tell them that their son was never coming home. She thought of asking Reverend Waters to do it for her, and then dismissed the idea. Tempting as it might be, she would not take the cowardly way out. Still, it might be wise to ask the reverend to accompany her. Doreen Mulvaney and her husband would most likely have need of their minister at such a trying time.

She looked over at Ridge. He was sitting in a circle with a half dozen other warriors playing some kind of gambling game. She envied him his ability to speak Apache. Her being unable to speak the language served only to make the gulf between herself and the Indians wider. Only so much could be communicated with hand gestures and facial expressions.

She was mentally rehearsing the Apache words she had learned when there was a bit of a commotion near the center of the camp. Rising, she turned in that direction to see two people ride up.

"Dani!" With a glad cry, she ran toward her sister. "Dani, thank God!"

"Marty!" Dani slid off her horse's back, laughing out loud as her sister hugged her so hard she feared her ribs might break. "I'm so glad to see you!"

Marty drew back so she could see her sister's face, and then frowned. "Are you all right?"

"Never better," Dani said, a blush rising in her cheeks.

Marty glanced over at the warrior who had ridden in with her sister. He had dismounted and was staring at her, his expression impassive.

Marty looked at Dani again. "Are you sure? He didn't . . . didn't . . . you know . . . ?"

Dani laughed as if Marty had said something funny.

"Marty, this is Sanza. Sanza, this is my sister, Martha Jean."

Sanza nodded solemnly.

"Does he speak English?" Marty asked.

"Yes."

"Oh. Well, then, I'm . . . I'm pleased to meet you, Sanza," Marty said, wondering if she should offer him her hand.

He nodded again, but remained silent.

"How did you get here?" Dani asked, her gaze darting around the camp. "Is Cory here?"

"Ridge brought me," Marty said. "Now that you're here, we can go home."

Dani glanced at Sanza, then back at her sister. "Where's Cory? Have you seen him? Is he all right? I've been so worried about him. I . . ." Dani's voice trailed off when she saw the bleak expression on her sister's face. "No. No. I don't believe it."

"I'm sorry, Dani."

Dani shook her head. "No, not Cory," she murmured, and then she turned to look at Sanza, as if he could make everything better.

To Marty's surprise, the warrior drew Dani into his arms. Bending down, he murmured something in her ear.

Dani looked at Marty again. "How did he die?"

"He tried to escape and . . ." Marty lifted one hand and let it fall. There was no need to say the rest.

Tears welled in Dani's eyes and slid silently down her cheeks.

It was all too telling that she continued to stand in the circle of the warrior's arms.

"I'm sorry," Marty said again. She looked at the warrior, noting the protective way he held Dani, and felt a sudden coldness in the pit of her stomach.

"What's going on?"

Marty glanced over her shoulder to see Ridge coming up behind her.

He took in the scene at a glance. There was no need for an explanation. Everything that had been said was easily read in Dani's tears, in the solemn expression on Sanza's face, in the look of disbelief in Martha Jean's eyes.

Ridge looked at Dani again, at the way she clung to Sanza, her body pressed intimately against his. Unless he missed his guess, Danielle Flynn wouldn't be going back to the ranch anytime soon, if at all.

Marty stared at her sister. They were alone in Ridge's wickiup. Sensing that the sisters needed some time alone, Sanza had gone to look after his horses and Ridge had gone back to his game.

"What do you mean, you aren't going back to the ranch with us?" Marty exclaimed.

"Just what I said. I'm staying here with Sanza."

"But why?" Marty asked, though she was afraid she already knew the answer.

"I love him."

Marty blew out a sigh. It was just as she had feared.

"And we're married."

Marty stared at her sister. "Married! That's impossible."

"No," Dani said, a dreamy look in her eyes, "it's not. Oh, Marty, he's so wonderful."

"Who married you? When? Where?"

"We sort of married each other. He offered me his horses, and I accepted." Dani shrugged, her smile widening. "And now we're married."

"No," Marty said curtly. "You're not."

"Yes, we are, whether you like it or not. I'm his wife in the Apache way. In *every* way."

Marty groaned softly. It was even worse than she had imagined. Reaching out, she captured her sister's hands with her own. "Dani, how could you?"

"He's wonderful, that's how. He's sweet and tender and he loves me."

"Where are you going to live?"

"Here, of course. With my husband."

Marty sighed, wondering how she would ever convince Dani to leave this place. And then she grinned. Of course. She had the one thing Dani couldn't resist waiting for them at home, something Sanza could never give her.

"Nettie's waiting for you at the ranch."

Dani stared at her, her eyes wide with disbelief— and hope. "Mama's here?"

Marty nodded. "She arrived the day after you disappeared."

"Mama." Tears welled in Dani's eyes and trickled down her cheeks. "Oh, Marty, I never thought we'd see her again. How does she look? Is she all right?"

"She looks the same, a little older, that's all. She's worried about you."

Wiping the tears from her eyes, Dani jumped to her feet. "How soon can we leave?"

Sanza frowned at his wife. "What do you mean, you are leaving?"

After Dani's tearful reunion with her sister, he had brought Dani to his wickiup so they could clean up from their journey. He had been eager to get her alone, waiting for the time when he could hold her in his arms again, when he could lose himself in her soft, womanly warmth. "Does this have anything to do with the boy's death?"

Dani shook her head. "No, of course not. It isn't your fault that . . . that Cory's dead."

"But you blame my people?"

"Well, yes, in a way, but that's not why I have to go," Dani said. "My mother's come home. I haven't seen her since I was a little girl." She smiled up at him, her eyes shining with excitement. "I can't believe she's come back after all these years."

He nodded, his face devoid of emotion. She was his woman, his wife. Now that she was his, he would not keep her here against her will.

"When will you go?" he asked, his voice hard and flat.

"Tomorrow morning . . . What do you mean, when will *I* go? Aren't you coming with me?"

"No." He turned his back to her. "My place is here."

"But I thought . . . You have to come with me! You're my husband."

He grunted softly. "Your sister does not approve of me, or of our marriage. Your mother will not approve either."

"I don't care what they think! I approve!" She moved to stand in front of him, tilting her head back so she could see his face. "Say you'll come with me."

"No, Da-ni." He gazed deep into her eyes. "I do not belong in your world."

You do not belong in mine. The words, unspoken, hovered in the air between them.

"She's my mother," Dani said, her voice thick with unshed tears. "I have to see her. Don't you understand?"

"I understand."

"But you won't come with me?"

"No."

She stared at him while the tears she had been holding back spilled down her cheeks. "Then I won't go."

"Da-ni." Whispering her name, he drew her into his arms, one hand stroking her hair, her back. It grieved him to think he had caused her tears. How could he refuse her?

Gently, he wiped the tears from her cheeks. "Do not weep, Da-ni. I will take you home."

She looked up at him, smiling through her tears. And then she threw her arms around him and kissed him. And it was a long time before either of them thought of anything else but the fire that burned between them.

Sitting cross-legged on a buffalo robe in his wickiup, Ridge watched Martha Jean pace the floor.

"Can you believe it?" she exclaimed. "She married him! Ha! Married. They married each other." She shook her head. "He gave her some horses and now they're married, just like that."

"It's the way of my people," Ridge said calmly.

"Well, it's not *our* way!"

He shrugged, thinking how pretty she looked with her dander up and her eyes blazing.

"She'll forget all about him once we get her back home."

He lifted one brow, but said nothing.

"She will!"

"And if she doesn't? What are you going to do, lock her in her room?"

"If I have to," she declared, and then her shoulders sagged. "What am I going to do?"

"I don't see as how there's much of anything you can do."

"But she's just a child."

"Not anymore," Ridge said. There was no mistaking the way Dani had looked at Sanza, no doubt in his mind that they were man and wife in every way. "She's a woman now, whether you like it or not."

"Nettie will be mortified."

"She'll get over it."

"Oh, you!" Marty glared at him, her eyes flashing. "You have an answer for everything, don't you? What will people think when they find out Dani's married to an Apache? What will Cory's parents think? Oh, Lord, how am I ever going to tell Doreen that he's dead?"

Rising, he drew her into his arms. "You can't worry about what other people think, Martha Jean. Your sister has to live her own life, and so do you. She made her decision and now she'll have to live with it, same as everybody else. If she really loves him, they'll work out the differences between them. . . ."

He paused, wondering if he really believed that. What about the differences between himself and Martha Jean? Could they be worked out? Or were some things beyond fixing?

With a sigh, she rested her head against his shoulder. "Maybe you're right."

Ridge grunted softly. Only time would tell.

Chapter 25

L ater that night, after the camp was dark, Marty lay in her blankets, unable to sleep. Staring up at the handful of stars that were visible through the smoke hole of the wickiup, she tried not to think of her little sister sharing a bed with an Apache warrior. But the harder she tried not to think about it, the more impossible it was. Were they making love, even now?

Marty thought of the times Ridge Longtree had taken her in his arms, the way her body had instantly responded to his kisses, warmed to his touch. She wasn't sure why it seemed right for her to have those feelings and wrong for Dani. She supposed it was because Dani was younger, because she had looked after Dani for so long. Her sister had always been younger than her years, innocent of life's harsher lessons.

Marty blew out a breath. Well, Dani wasn't innocent any longer. Looking at her sister, there was no doubt that Dani was head over heels in love with the man who had kidnapped her and taken her virginity. No doubt at all. She and Dani had talked earlier that evening, and Marty had to admit that she had never seen her sister looking happier, or more beautiful. Dani's eyes fairly sparkled with love and a newfound enthusiasm for life. In fact, her whole face seemed to glow as though lit from a fire within.

Dani's initial eagerness to go home had cooled somewhat. Even though she was anxious to see her mother, Dani had decided she was going to stay with the Apache for a few weeks, saying that she wanted to spend some time with Sanza's people before she left.

"We'll be along soon," Dani had said. "Don't worry."

Marty sighed again, disturbed by the niggling thought that she was jealous of her sister's happiness, jealous that she had the right to be intimate with the man she loved. Marty knew what it was like to want a man. She longed to surrender to Ridge, to let him teach her the ways of intimacy, to unlock the mysteries between a man and a woman. But no matter how badly she wanted him, she wasn't willing to give in, wasn't willing to give a passing stranger that which should, by right, belong to her husband.

She longed to talk to Dani, to ask her what it had been like on her wedding night. Was it as bad as they had feared? Or as wonderful as they had hoped?

She flopped over on her stomach and punched the robe she had rolled up to use for a pillow. There was no way she would go to her little sister for answers! Dani had always come to her.

"You gonna settle down anytime soon?" Ridge's voice pierced the stillness.

"Sorry. I didn't know I was keeping you awake."

He grunted softly. "What's keeping you awake? As if I didn't know."

She rolled onto her side and peered across the wickiup. In the faint light of the coals, she could see that Ridge was staring back at her. "What's that supposed to mean?"

"Nothing. Go to sleep."

"Humph!"

"Got you all hot and bothered, doesn't it?"

"I don't know what you mean!"

"Is that right? So it doesn't bother you at all that your little sister's sharing Sanza's lodge, or that he's probably making love to her right now."

"Of course not!"

His silence mocked her.

"Why should it bother me? They're . . . All right, it bothers me. They're not even legally married!"

"They're married according to the laws of my people."

"Well, according to the laws of *my* people, they're not. And Sanza's not even—"

"Not even white," Ridge finished for her, his voice blade-sharp.

"I didn't mean it like that," she said sullenly.

"If it'll make you feel better, they can always get married again when she gets home."

"There isn't a preacher or a priest in the whole town who would marry the two of them, and you know it." Thinking about a preacher brought Cory to mind. His parents wouldn't even have the comfort of a funeral. "Ridge?"

"Yeah?"

"What did the Indians do with Cory's body?"

"Buried it, I reckon. Why?"

"I was thinking about his folks. They'll never know where their son was laid to rest, never be able to visit his grave."

"Happens to a lot of families in the West. Men get killed in battle or lost out in the desert. Sometimes their bodies are never found."

"It just isn't fair. Cory never hurt anybody." Marty shook her head. "Poor Cory. Dani got over him mighty quick."

"Puppy love," Ridge said. "That's all it was." Sitting up, he stirred the coals, then added a few sticks to the firepit. The kindling caught quickly. Flames licked at the dry wood and he added a few larger pieces.

Marty sat up, too, the blankets tucked under her arms. "She wanted to marry Cory; at least that's what she said. I'll bet that's what they were doing out there the night they were captured, getting ready to run off and elope."

"She's young. At that age, it's easy to confuse puppy love with the real thing."

"So how do you know that what she feels for Sanza is the real thing?"

He shrugged. "I don't. But if she'd really been in love with Cory, she wouldn't have fallen for Sanza so fast. And even though she's saddened by the kid's death, she doesn't seem to be brokenhearted."

Marty nodded. Everything he said was true.

Ridge studied her, one brow raised quizzically. "So what's really bothering you? Afraid you'll be an old maid?"

"Of course not!" Even though it was a wild guess on his part, it was a little too close to the truth.

"No?"

"No." She grabbed at the one thing guaranteed to shut him up. "I'm engaged to Victor Claunch, remember?"

Ridge muttered a vile oath under his breath.

Bull's-eye, Marty thought.

"So I guess you'll be getting married when you get back to the ranch."

She glared at him across the fire. "You know darn good and well I have no intention of marrying that despicable man."

"So," he said, keeping his voice carefully indifferent, "who do you intend to marry?"

He gazed at her across the fire, his eyes dark and enigmatic.

Who would she marry? It was a good question, and one she had asked herself on more than one occasion. There were a good number of single men in Chimney Creek. She danced with them at barbecues and church socials, discussed the weather and the price of feed when she met them on the street. Unfortunately, she wasn't attracted to any of them and had pretty much resigned herself to being an old maid until Ridge Longtree kissed her.

He was still watching her, his gaze intent upon her face.

"I'll find someone," she said defiantly, and knew it for the lie it was. Now that she had met Ridge Longtree, she knew she would never be happy with anyone else. He was the man she had been waiting for her whole life, the reason no other man had ever been good enough.

"Good night." She slid under the blankets and turned her back to Ridge. She could still feel his gaze on her back when she fell asleep.

Marty removed her hat and ran her fingers through her hair. They had been riding for a little over two hours and the sun was high in the sky. It amazed her that Ridge could find his way across the seemingly trackless desert. There was little to see and few landmarks to show the way. A hawk circled high in the sky. A lizard sunned itself on a rock. Other than that, nothing moved as far as the eye could see.

Replacing her hat, Marty slid a glance at Ridge. They had said little since they left the stronghold that morning. He had bid farewell to Nochalo and to some of the other warriors, then packed their gear. She wondered if Ridge was sorry to be leaving the Apache so soon after such a long absence. Did he resent her? Resent the fact that he had to leave his people to take her home? If he felt that way, he could have said so. She could have waited and gone home with Dani and Sanza. Lordy, what was Nettie going to say when Dani showed up with an Apache husband?

Marty blew out a sigh. When had life gotten so complicated? Victor Claunch expected her to marry him. Dani was married to an Apache warrior. Nettie was waiting for them back at the ranch. Cory's parents were doubtlessly worried sick over their son's whereabouts. She had asked Smitty to ride over and tell Cory's folks that Dani and Cory had been kidnapped. Now, when she got home, she would have to go over and tell Doreen and her husband their son was never coming home. She was no closer to finding out who had killed her father. And Ridge would probably ride out of her life as soon as they returned to the ranch. The thought left her feeling empty inside. She was going to miss him desperately when he was gone.

She glanced at him again, wondering exactly what their relationship was. He was more than a hired hand. They had shared several sizzling kisses. She knew he wanted her the way a man wanted a woman. And she wanted him. Yet no words of affection had been spoken between them. She couldn't help thinking that, even if they had made love, he would still ride out of her life.

"Hey," he called softly. "You all right?"

She lifted her chin and squared her shoulders. "Why? Don't I look all right?"

"You look like you're about to cry."

"Don't be ridiculous."

He shrugged. "You asked."

She stared straight ahead, her throat thick.

"You wanna talk about it?" he asked.

"No!"

He lifted one hand. "Hey, no need to bite my head off."

"I'm sorry."

Ridge pulled his horse to a halt alongside a shallow water hole. "We'll rest awhile."

With a nod, she swung out of the saddle. Loosening the cinch, she let her horse drink. She stared into the water. Were her thoughts so transparent that Ridge could see what she was thinking? Lordy, that was a horrible thought!

She was aware that he had come up beside her to let his own horse drink. Even though her back was toward him, even though they weren't touching, her skin tingled at his nearness. Why did this man, of all the men she had known, have such power over her? She had only to look at him, hear his voice, and it was as if her whole body came awake from a deep sleep. She yearned for him the way a flower yearned for the sun after a cold and bitter winter.

He moved closer. His nearness sent a shiver of excitement down her spine. She wished she had the nerve to turn around, to rise up on her tiptoes and press her lips to his, to run her hands over his chest, to slide her hands up and down his back, to thread her fingers through his hair. A sharp stab of jealousy pierced her heart. She had always envied Dani. Dani was the pretty one. Dani was the talented one. She played the piano as though she had been born to it. Every year, her apple pie won the blue ribbon at the church bazaar. She had a fine hand for needlework. In spite of all that, Marty had never envied her sister more than she did now, because, no matter whether Marty approved of Dani's choice of a husband or not, Dani had the right to hold Sanza anytime she wanted.

She gasped as Ridge's hand closed over her shoulder. "Martha Jean?"

She swallowed the lump in her throat. "Wh-what?"

"Look at me."

She shook her head. "No." She would rather face a herd of stampeding cattle than look at him now.

His hand tightened on her shoulder as he slowly turned her around to face him. "What's wrong?"

She lowered her head, refusing to meet his gaze. "Nothing."

Ridge muttered an oath. He didn't know much about women, but one thing he did know was that "nothing" always meant "something."

"You might as well tell me what's bothering you. We're not leaving here until you do."

She looked up at him. "What's wrong? What *isn't* wrong? Dani's married to an Indian. My mother not only owns the ranch, but she's there, waiting for us. I still don't know who killed my father. Victor Claunch thinks I'm going to marry him. And you . . . you . . ."

Her words stammered to a halt, like a clock winding down.

"What about me?"

"Nothing."

He swore again, his gaze intent upon her face, and then his expression softened. "Nothing? Is this what you want, Martha Jean?" he asked softly, and, lowering his head, he kissed her.

It was exactly what she wanted. There was no point in lying to herself, or to him. Her arms went up around his neck and she kissed him back, pouring out all her love and longing in that one glorious, heart-slamming, soul-stirring kiss.

When the kiss ended, she stared up at him boldly. "Yes," she said breathlessly, "that was just what I wanted."

"Well, honey," he drawled, drawing her close once more, "why didn't you say so?"

And so saying, he kissed her again, a slow, deep kiss that drove everything else from her mind. His tongue feathered across her bottom lip, teasing, tantalizing, irresistible. The world spun out of focus as his hand slid under her shirt, caressing her bare skin, his thumb stroking the curve of her breast. Moaning softly, she clung to him, wanting his touch more than her next breath, yet knowing she would hate herself if she let her body succumb to the urgings of her heart. No matter how badly she wanted him, no matter how she burned for his touch, it was wrong—wrong to let him make love to her like this. She was Seamus Flynn's daughter, not some floozy whose time could be bought with a dollar and a couple of drinks.

With a muffled cry, she pushed Ridge away. "I can't do this."

"Sure you can," he said, his eyes hot and heavy-lidded with desire.

She glared at him, anger replacing passion. She made a broad gesture that encompassed the desert around them. "I'm not hiking up my skirts in the dirt for you or any other man." Especially for a man who had never said, or even hinted, that he cared for her, let alone that he loved her.

He nodded slowly. "We might as well get moving then." Turning away from her, he tightened the saddle cinch, swung into the saddle, then sat there, looking down at her. "You coming?"

Blowing out a sigh of exasperation, she tightened the cinch and mounted her horse. She had been right to stop him, she told herself. If he had felt anything at all, he wouldn't have been so willing to stop, would he? She was probably just a pleasant diversion, something to pass the time on the long ride back to the ranch.

Ridge shifted uncomfortably in his saddle, his body still hard with wanting her. Women! If he lived to be a hundred and ten, he would never understand them. Especially this one. One minute she was as hot as a Fourth of July firecracker; the next she was as cold as a high mountain lake in midwinter, and he had no idea what had caused the change from one to the other. Damn! His palm still tingled from the warmth of her skin. Her scent lingered in his nostrils. He could still taste her sweetness on his lips.

He slid a glance at her, riding stiffly beside him. What the hell had he done wrong? Had it been any woman other than Martha Jean, he might have thought she was just playing hard to get, but one look in her eyes and he'd known she was dead serious. The last time he had seen that look in someone eyes, he'd been looking down the business end of a Colt .45.

Damn. It was going to be a hell of a long ride back to the ranch.

Chapter 26

Nettie stood on the porch, one hand gripping the rail as she stared into the gathering dusk, searching for some sign that her daughters were on their way home. Her girls were the first thing she thought of when she woke in the morning, the last thing she thought of at night. She prayed as she had never prayed before, petitioning the Almighty to bring them safely home. She had missed out on so much. She couldn't lose them now. She never should have stayed away for so long. She knew that now. She should have called her husband's bluff. He might have told the girls the truth, but maybe he wouldn't have. In hindsight, she realized it had been a mistake to let Seamus send her away. She should have stood her ground, should have threatened to tell the girls the truth about their father. But she had been so young then, afraid of her husband's temper, afraid that telling her daughters the whole ugly truth would destroy them.

With a sigh, she went back into the house and closed the door. After lighting the lamps in the parlor, she went into the kitchen to fix a lonely dinner.

Later, sitting in front of the fire, she thought about the future. It was obvious that Martha Jean didn't want her here. If Danielle felt the same, what then?

Even though the ranch now belonged to her, Nettie knew she couldn't stay if they didn't want her here. She could always sell the ranch to Victor Claunch, but that would only make her daughters hate her more. This was the only home Danielle and Martha Jean had ever known.

Victor. He was another problem she was going to have to deal with. He had come courting every day, bringing her flowers and candy, and a book of poetry, which, to her surprise, he had insisted on reading to her. Sitting beside her on the porch, he had assured her that everything would be all right, that he would be there for her, no matter what.

Last night, he had started talking about how lonely he was, and the next thing she knew, she was confiding in him, admitting that she, too, had been lonely since she went east. He had put his arm around her and she had let him, finding comfort in being held in a man's arms after such a long time. She had a niggling feeling that he was going to ask her to marry him one day soon. She wasn't at all sure how she felt about that.

For the first time, she wondered if Victor had had anything to do with Seamus's death. She dismissed the idea as soon as it occurred to her. Victor might be tough and powerful, but a murderer? No.

Still, she couldn't put the thought out of her mind. Victor was a ruthless man, but then, Seamus had been ruthless, too. Men who couldn't be decisive and weren't willing to fight for what they wanted rarely got anywhere in the West. It was a hard land, and it took a hard man to conquer it. But murder?

Frowning, she stared into the fire. Soon after she had married Seamus and arrived in Chimney Creek, Jim Blackmer, the man who had owned the ranch that bordered the other side of Victor's spread, had been found dead in the river. It had been during the spring, when the river was running high and fast, and everyone had assumed that Blackmer's horse had gone down and that he had drowned. Four days after the man's funeral, Victor had bought Blackmer's ranch from the bank.

She shook her head. There was nothing incriminating about that. If Seamus had had the money to spare back then, he, too would have put in a bid for Blackmer's land. That didn't make him a murderer.

Was it merely coincidence that both of Victor's neighbors had died violently? It was possible, she supposed. After all, it was a wild land. Still, it seemed mighty fortuitous that both men owned land that Victor had coveted. Maybe tomorrow she would ride into town and have a talk with the sheriff. She didn't really expect to learn much, but it couldn't hurt. And while she was there, she could buy presents for her girls.

She tapped her fingers on the arm of her chair. She knew she couldn't buy Martha Jean's affection with a new gown or a pretty bauble. Then she smiled.

She knew exactly what to give Martha Jean.

Chapter 27

"How much longer until we get to the ranch?"
Ridge looked over at Martha Jean. It was
the first time she had spoken to him other than to
answer a direct question since he had kissed her a few
days back. "We should be there tomorrow afternoon."

With a nod, she stared straight ahead once more.

It was the last straw. He didn't know what had set
her off, didn't know what in the great green hell she
was so upset about, but he'd had just about enough.
Urging his mount up alongside hers, he took hold of
her horse's reins and brought both animals to a stop.

Dismounting, he grabbed Martha Jean around the
waist and set her on her feet. "All right," he said,
"what's eating you?"

"I'm sure I don't know what you mean."

"I'm sure you do. Now spit it out."

She glared at him, her arms crossed over her breasts,
her chin thrust out.

He suppressed the urge to put her over his knee
and give her a good thrashing. "We're not leaving this
spot until you tell me what a burr under your tail."

"I don't have a burr under my tail, Mr. Longtree.
And stop looking at me like that."

"I'll look at you any damn way I want, Miss Flynn.

Now, stop being so damn stubborn and tell me what's wrong."

"Nothing's wrong. What's the matter—are your feelings hurt because I didn't fall into your arms?"

He lifted one brow. "Honey, that's just what you did. And as long as you brought it up, what changed your mind?"

"I told you."

"Ah, yes. You said you weren't hiking up your skirt"—he glanced pointedly at her trousers—"for me or any other man."

She made a face that seemed to say, *That's right; so what?*

Ridge frowned at her. "I don't recall asking you to hike up your skirts *or* drop your drawers. Seems to me that all we were doing was kissing."

Her eyes shot sparks at him even as her cheeks turned bright pink.

"So are you mad at me, Martha Jean, or are you mad at yourself for wanting something I hadn't asked for?"

Bull's-eye. Her eyes widened. Her mouth opened, but no words came out.

"There's nothing wrong with what you felt," he said quietly. "It's perfectly natural. You're a young, healthy woman. . . ." He held up one hand, silencing her. "You can deny it all you want, but that doesn't change a thing." His eyes grew hot, his voice thick. "You want me. And I want you."

She didn't argue, merely stood there staring at him as if he had lost his mind. But he knew the truth. It was evident in the sudden intake of her breath, the quiver in her lower lip. She wanted him. She might not want to admit it, but it was still true.

And he wanted her.

Moving slowly, so there could be no mistaking his intentions, he reached for her. He had expected her to slap him or tell him to stop. Instead, she just stood there, her eyes wide as he drew her into his arms. She had beautiful, deep, dark brown eyes fringed by thick lashes. He ran one finger over the curve of her cheek. Her skin was warm and smooth, soft as a newborn baby's bottom.

"What are you doing?" she asked tremulously.

"What do you think?"

"Don't." There was no heat in her voice, no conviction.

"Want this to be all my idea, do you, so you can blame me for it later?" His forefinger traced the seam of her lips, back and forth, back and forth. "When we make love, it'll be because you asked for it, not because I forced you."

She noticed he said "when," not "if."

He jerked his chin toward a patch of grass. "We could spread a blanket over there and spend the rest of the afternoon making love."

She shook her head. Not here. Not out in the open. Even though they would be able to see anyone approaching long before they arrived, she wanted privacy and the cover of darkness, especially the first time.

With a nod, he kissed the tip of her nose, then released her and took a step backward. "You let me know when and where," he said, "and I'll be there."

Marty stared at him as he swung effortlessly into the saddle. Did he honestly think she was going to *ask* him to make love to her? Even as she vowed it would never happen, she was reliving every kiss, every caress. Though it shamed her, she had to admit she had hoped he would take her by force, thereby absolving her of guilt.

Head high, she took up the reins and stepped into the saddle. Suddenly, going home and facing Nettie didn't seem near as disconcerting as spending another restless night under the stars with Ridge Longtree.

Marty felt a sudden tension in her shoulders as the landscape grew familiar. They were almost home. Another mile or two, and the ranch house would be in sight. She felt a sharp pang as they approached the family cemetery.

Drawing her horse to a halt, Marty dismounted. Opening the gate, she made her way to her father's grave. If only he were still alive. Since his death, she had felt as though a great weight had been placed on her shoulders.

Kneeling, she ran her hands over the ground. If Pa were still alive, he wouldn't have been any happier with Dani's choice of a husband than Nettie would be when she found out. If Pa were still alive, Nettie wouldn't be here, Marty thought, and her home and her future would still be secure. If Pa were still alive, Ridge Longtree would have been long gone.

Ridge. She could feel him watching her from beyond the fence. She was tempted to stay by her father's grave a little longer, but she knew putting it off wouldn't solve anything. Sooner or later, she was going to have to face her mother. As Pa always said, it was better to get unpleasant tasks over and done with, and with that in mind, she stood up and brushed the dirt off her trousers.

Ignoring Ridge, she mounted her horse and headed for home.

At the sound of hoofbeats in the yard, Nettie hurried to the front window. Drawing back the curtains, she peered outside, felt her heart sink when she saw Marty and Longtree ride up to the porch. There was no sign of Danielle. Or Cory. Did that mean Longtree had been unable to find them, or . . .

She stood there, feeling numb inside, unable to accept the fact that she would never see her younger daughter again. She pressed her hand to her chest, wondering if it was possible to die of a broken heart.

She heard Martha Jean's footsteps on the porch stairs, the faint creak of the screen door opening, footsteps behind her, but she didn't turn around. If she didn't look at Martha Jean, if she didn't hear the words, it wouldn't be real.

"Nettie?"

Not "Mother" or "Mama," but Nettie. "Did you . . . did you find her?"

"Yes."

"Is she . . . ?" She couldn't say the word aloud, couldn't stay the quaver in her voice.

"She's fine."

"Thank God." Nettie turned to face her daughter. She felt light-headed, almost giddy with relief. "Where is she?"

"Why don't you sit down?"

Nettie's heart caught in her throat. No one asked you to sit down to hear good news. "What is it? What's wrong? You said she was all right. . . ."

"Just sit down."

Nettie moved to the sofa and perched on the edge of the cushion. "What is it? What's wrong with Danielle? Why didn't she come home with you?"

Marty sat down in the chair across from the sofa. "Nothing's wrong with her, except I think she's lost her mind."

"What?"

"She got married."

Nettie blinked several times as she digested that.
"She wasn't captured by Indians then?" She pressed
a hand to her heart. "Thank God." That explained
Danielle's absence. She was on her honeymoon with
Cory. Nettie wasn't pleased with the idea that her
daughter had eloped, but at least it was better than
the horrible alternatives she had been imagining.

"That's what I'm trying to tell you," Martha Jean
said flatly. "She married an Apache."

Nettie stared at her daughter in stunned disbelief.
"What?"

"You heard me. She'll be home in a few weeks."

"But . . . an Indian? That's impossible. No one would
marry a white girl to an Indian. And what about Cory?
Where's he? His father came by right after you left. He
said he was going out to search for Cory. Then, I think
it was last Thursday, he came by again. He said they
had lost the trail and wondered if I'd heard anything. I
promised to let him know as soon as I had any news."

Marty took a deep breath. There was no easy way
to say it. "Cory's dead. He was killed while trying
to escape."

Nettie sank back on the sofa, her mind reeling. Her
baby was married to an Indian. Cory Mulvaney was
dead. It wasn't possible. Poor Doreen!

"I'm going upstairs," Martha Jean said, rising. "I
need a bath, and then I need to go and talk to Cory's
folks."

Nettie watched her daughter leave the room. It had
to be a nightmare. Of course, that was it. She would
wake up in the morning and find that it had been
nothing but a bad dream.

Marty sat in the tub, submerged up to her chin.

When had anything ever felt so good? She had borrowed some of Dani's scented soap, and the smell of lavender filled the steamy air. Marty loved working on the ranch. She loved roundups and branding. She loved riding, and all the other chores that came with running a cattle ranch. But at the end of the day, her one luxury had always been a long soak in a tub of hot water.

Eyes closed, she let her thoughts drift. Not surprisingly, they immediately drifted toward Ridge Longtree. Scoundrel. Fast gun. Heartbreaker. Well, he wouldn't break *her* heart, but she had to admit it was badly dented. Thank goodness she had come to her senses before she completely lost her head—and her virginity! Bad enough she had lost her heart to the man. But he would never know that.

Later this evening, after she went to see Cory's folks, she intended to talk to her mother and find out exactly what Nettie's plans were for the ranch. Until then, there was no way for Marty to plan for her own future. She wondered if Dani really meant to live summer and winter with the Apache. She simply couldn't imagine her little sister spending the rest of her life in a brush-covered hut, cooking over an open fire, sleeping on the ground. And yet she couldn't forget the glow in her sister's eyes when Dani looked at her husband, couldn't forget the happy lilt in Dani's voice whenever she spoke Sanza's name. Maybe love did conquer all.

She stayed in the tub until the water grew cool. Stepping out, she toweled herself dry, then went into her bedroom and, in deference to the task ahead, donned one of the few dresses she owned. She brushed her hair and tied it back with a ribbon, then sat on the edge of the bed to pull on her stockings and shoes. And all the while, she tried to think of the best way, the gentlest way, to break the sad news to Cory's parents.

With a sigh, she put on a straw bonnet, took a last look in the mirror, and left the house. Wishing she were going anywhere but to the Mulvaneys', she walked down to the barn, intending to ask Smitty to hitch the team to the wagon, when Ridge appeared in the barn's doorway.

He lifted one brow as his gaze moved over her. "You going to church?"

"No," she replied curtly. "I'm going to see Cory's folks."

He grunted softly. "I'll hitch up the team for you."

"Thank you."

She tried not to watch him as he hitched the team to the buggy, but it was impossible. He had cleaned up, too. Now, clad in a pair of clean black trousers and a dark gray shirt, his hat pushed back on his head, his holster strapped to his thigh, he drew her gaze like a magnet. The other men on the ranch carried weapons; some wore gun belts; but Ridge wore his Colt as if it were a part of him. She doubted she would ever tire of watching him. He moved with an economy of motion, and a kind of confidence she could only envy him. She admired the play of muscles across his back and shoulders as he worked. She had felt the easy strength in those arms. . . . She thrust the thought from her mind. She would not think of that, not now, not ever again!

Offering her his hand, he helped her onto the seat, then swung up beside her.

"What do you think you're doing?" she asked.

"I think I'm going with you."

"I think you're not." She smoothed her skirts, then

reached for the reins. "I'm quite capable of driving myself, thank you."

"I'm sure you are. But I'm still going with you."

"Will you at least tell me why?"

He shrugged. "Think of me as your knight in shining armor."

She stared at him. "You must be kidding."

"Then let's just say I don't think it's a good idea for you to be wandering around on your own."

"Why ever not?"

"Your old man was killed. Dani and Cory were kidnapped. Let's just say I believe in being cautious where you're concerned."

"Don't tell me you think my life's in danger."

"No." Lifting the reins, he clucked to the team. "And I intend to keep it that way."

Careful to keep her eyes straight ahead, Marty sat back in the seat, her arms folded over her chest. He really was the most insufferable man she had ever known! She tried to ignore him, but every time the buggy hit a rut in the road, her shoulder and thigh brushed against his, sending little frissons of awareness skittering through her. Why hadn't he just stayed at the ranch? And yet, in a little corner of her mind that she refused to acknowledge, she was glad he was there beside her. She had never had to deliver news like this before, and she spent a few minutes trying to compose her thoughts. It reminded her that she had intended to ask Reverend Waters to accompany her. He would have known what to say, what to do, under the circumstances, but it was too late to think about that now.

Her thigh bumped against Ridge's again, and she silently cursed her attraction to the man. Maybe she should have taken Nettie with her after all, she thought sourly. Of course, then she would have had to contend with another kind of tension. She wasn't sure which would have been worse.

"How'd your mother take the news about Dani?" Ridge asked after a while.

"How do you think?"

"I guess she wasn't too happy about it."

"No."

"Did you talk to her at all?"

"What do you mean? Of course we talked."

"Uh-huh."

Marty glared at him. "I'm going to talk to her later tonight about the ranch." She blew out a sigh of exasperation, certain this was one of the worst days of her life. First she had to give Cory's folks the bad news, and then she had to talk to Nettie and find out what her mother intended to do with the ranch. She wasn't looking forward to either one.

"Did you ask your mother why she went back east?"

"No, and I don't intend to."

"You might want to reconsider."

"I don't think so."

"She's still your mother. I think you need to hear what she has to say."

"I really don't care what you think!"

"One of these days, you might feel differently. People die sudden-like, you know. Like your old man. Sometimes, if we wait too long, we don't get the chance to say the things we want to before it's too late."

"Well, aren't you the philosopher," she retorted. But his words gave her pause. She would have liked to have talked to her father one last time, tell him that she loved him. But that was different. She didn't love Nettie anymore. . . . She bit down on the corner of her lower lip. What if Longtree was right? What if something happened to Nettie? Would she spend the rest of her life wishing she had done things differently, wishing she had taken a few minutes to hear her mother's side of the story?

"You know I'm right, don't you?" Ridge said quietly.

She nodded, even though she didn't want to admit it. Before she could say anything else, the Mulvaneys' ranch came into view.

She just wished she knew what she was going to say.

Chapter 28

Doreen Mulvaney opened the door at Marty's knock. She was a plain woman, with light brown hair pulled back in a tight bun at her nape and pale blue eyes that seemed to hold all the sadness of the world. It was evident from her loosely fitting brown dress that she had lost considerable weight since Marty saw her last.

"Martha Jean," Mrs. Mulvaney exclaimed softly. She glanced past Marty, the sudden flare of hope in her eyes quickly turning to disappointment when she realized the man standing behind Marty wasn't her son. "Come in, won't you?"

Wordlessly, Marty and Ridge followed Doreen into the house. "Here," Marty said, handing a casserole dish to Doreen. "My mother sent this over."

"Oh? Well, that was mighty kind of her. Please," Doreen said, indicating a worn sofa, "won't you sit down? I'll just put this in the kitchen."

Marty sat down. Removing his hat, Ridge sat beside her.

Marty glanced around the room. The Mulvaneys weren't nearly as successful at ranching as her father had been, and it was reflected in their surroundings. The furniture was well worn, the curtains a little faded, but Doreen took good care of what they had. Her house was neat, the windows were clean, the floors gleamed with a fresh coat of wax.

Returning to the parlor, Doreen took a seat in the rocking chair beside the sofa. Folding her hands in her lap, she stared at Marty, waiting for her to disclose the reason for her unexpected visit.

Marty cleared her throat. "I . . . Where's Mr. Mulvaney?"

"He's out in the barn. Did you want to see him?"

"Yes," Marty replied, grateful for the reprieve, however brief it might be.

"I'll get him," Doreen said, rising. "Just make yourselves to home. I'll be right back."

When they were alone, Marty looked at Ridge. "I can't do this."

"Do you want me to tell them?"

She did, more than anything, but it didn't seem right. Ridge was a stranger to the Mulvaneys. News like this should be delivered by a friend. "No, thanks. I think I should tell them."

"It's your call."

Marty stiffened as she heard the sound of footsteps coming through the kitchen, and then Mr. and Mrs. Mulvaney were there. Doreen sat down. Jacob Mulvaney stood behind her. He was a tall man with dark blond hair, close-set brown eyes, a nose that was too big for his face, and a generous mouth. Looking at the two of them, Marty thought they looked like they had aged ten years in the last few weeks.

"Do you have news?" Mr. Mulvaney asked. "News about Cory?"

Marty nodded. "I'm afraid it isn't good news."

Jacob placed his hand on his wife's shoulder. "Go on."

"Cory's . . . I'm so sorry, but he was killed trying to escape from the Apache."

Doreen Mulvaney stared at her, and then a high-pitched wail rose in her throat. "My boy! Oh, my boy!" With tears streaming down her cheeks, she looked up at her husband. "He's gone. Our boy's gone!"

Kneeling in front of his wife, Jacob took her hands in his, then looked over at Marty. "You're sure?"

"Yes."

"Damned Injuns!" Jacob said. "Ought to wipe out the whole bunch of 'em."

Marty glanced at Ridge. A muscle worked in his jaw.

"I'm sorry," she said again. "Truly sorry."

Jacob nodded. "I'm obliged to you for letting us know. Now, if you don't mind, we'd like to be alone."

"Of course." Rising, Marty gave Doreen's shoulder a squeeze, then headed for the front door.

Ridge followed her outside.

"Well, I certainly handled that badly," Marty said, descending the stairs.

"You did just fine," Ridge said. "There's no good way to deliver that kind of news."

"I knew I should have brought Reverend Waters with me. He would have known what to say."

"It's not too late. We can drive into town if you like."

"Maybe we should."

Nodding, Ridge handed Marty into the buggy. He climbed up beside her, took up the reins, and then released the brake. Clucking to the team, he pulled out of the yard onto the road that led into town.

"They don't even have a body to bury," Marty lamented. "It doesn't seem right, somehow."

Ridge grunted softly. Maybe it was better that way.

He would never forget seeing his sister lying on the ground with two bullet holes in her back, her dark eyes vacant, her body limp, lifeless. In all his life, he had never loved anyone the way he had loved that little girl.

They rode in silence the rest of the way. When they reached town, Ridge parked the buggy in front of the reverend's white picket fence, then handed Marty out of the rig.

"Are you coming in?" she asked.

He shook his head. "I'll wait out here."

With a nod, she opened the gate, walked up the narrow path to the minister's house, and knocked on the door.

The reverend answered it a moment later. He was a portly man, with black hair going gray, honest hazel eyes, an aquiline nose, and a perpetual smile.

"Miss Flynn, this is a pleasant surprise." He stepped back. "Come in, come in; I was just having a cup of tea."

"Thank you." She followed him into the parlor and took the seat he indicated.

"Can I have Mrs. Monson fix you a cup of tea?"

"No, thank you."

"Well, then," he said, sitting down across from her, "what brings you here on such a lovely day?"

"I think you should visit the Mulvaneys. Cory . . ."

The reverend leaned forward. "Has something happened to the boy?"

"He's dead."

"Dead! When? How?"

"It's a long story. He was killed by Apache."

The reverend stood. Picking up his coat, which was folded over the back of a chair, he slipped it on. "Dear Lord, I'll go to them immediately."

Marty rose. "Thank you."

Waters grabbed his hat and followed her out the door.

"That didn't take long," Ridge remarked. Swinging down, he helped her into the buggy, then took up the reins and turned the horses toward home.

They had gone only a few blocks when Victor Claunch flagged them down.

"Good afternoon, Martha. I need to talk to you, if you've got a minute." Victor looked pointedly at Ridge. "Alone."

"Can't it wait?" Marty asked.

"It concerns your mother."

Marty's eyes widened. "Has something happened to her?"

"No." Reaching up, Victor took hold of her hand and tugged gently. "This won't take long."

Marty glanced at Ridge; then, slipping her hand from Claunch's grasp, she alighted from the buggy.

"I'll wait for you over at the blacksmith's," Ridge told her. Giving Claunch a warning glance, he took up the reins and drove down the street.

Victor took Marty's arm and escorted her across the street and into the hotel dining room. He held out her chair, then sat down across the table from her. When the waitress came, he ordered a cup of coffee and a slice of cake.

Marty ordered a piece of apple pie, then sat back and regarded Victor. Today he wore black trousers, a blue shirt, and a long black coat. She didn't know why it annoyed her that he was always so well dressed. Perhaps because she always had the feeling that he was really a snake disguised as a gentleman.

"So what's this all about?" she asked impatiently.

Victor cleared his throat. "I know you and I talked

about getting married. . . ." He held up his hand when she started to speak. "Hear me out. This isn't easy for me to say. I've been courting your mother. . . ."

"What?" Marty stared at him, unable to believe her ears.

Victor nodded. "I know I asked you to marry me, and you've every right to be upset."

"I'm not upset about that," Marty snapped.

He looked startled. "You're not?"

"Victor, I never said yes."

He stared at her a moment. She could almost see him searching his memory, trying to remember what her response had been the day he proposed. "Well," he said, "that makes what I have to tell you a mite easier. The truth is, I've always had a hankerin' for your mother, and now that Seamus is . . . gone . . . well, I'm going to ask your mother to marry me, and I wanted your permission first."

Marty stared at him in disbelief. "You want my permission?" She laughed mirthlessly. "That's something you'll never have! Tell me the truth, Victor. This is just another of your ploys to get your hands on the ranch, isn't it?"

Anger flared in Claunch's eyes. "Really, Martha," Victor said, looking offended. "How can you even think such a terrible thing?"

Marty leaned forward. "Because I know you," she said, keeping her voice low. "I know you've been after the ranch ever since my father died. I may not be able to prove it, but I know you're the one behind all the troubles we'd been having before I hired Ridge Longtree."

"That's absurd."

"Is it? Tell me, would you still want to marry my mother if she didn't own the ranch?"

The tips of his ears turned red. "Of course I would."

"I don't believe you."

"It doesn't really matter what you believe, does it?" He nodded at the waitress as she placed their order on the table. Picking up his cup, he took a drink. "I'm going to propose to your mother," he said when the waitress moved away, "with or without your permission." He smiled smugly. "And I'm sure she'll accept. So," he said, leaning back in his chair, "where have you been the last few weeks?"

"Didn't Nettie tell you?"

"No." He laughed. "I've been so entranced by your mother I never thought to ask."

"You must have been, if you didn't even notice that Dani's also been gone."

Victor stared at her a moment, then shrugged. "Now that you mention it, I haven't seen her. I just assumed she was busy elsewhere, perhaps with young Mulvaney."

Marty looked at the pie in front of her and pushed it away, her appetite gone. "Cory's dead."

"What?"

Marty nodded. "Apache stole some of our stock and captured Dani and Cory. Cory was killed trying to escape."

"And your sister?"

"She'll be home soon."

"I don't understand. Is she still with the Indians?"

Marty took a deep breath. "Dani married an Apache."

Victor stared at her in openmouthed astonishment. "She what?"

"You heard me. I hope you won't mind having an Apache for a stepson-in-law. And now, if you'll excuse me, Mr. Longtree is waiting."

Pushing away from the table, she rose and left the dining room.

Outside, she took a deep breath, relieved that she wouldn't have to worry about Victor Claunch's unwelcome attention anymore, horrified that he might become her stepfather. But surely Nettie wouldn't marry the man! And what if she did? Marty shuddered at the thought of Victor living in the house with them, and then frowned. If Nettie married Claunch, she would probably move into his house, which meant Marty might be able to stay on and run the ranch. It wouldn't be the same, though. Even if Victor let her stay, it would no longer be *her* ranch, but his. Would she want to stay under those circumstances? Where else could she go?

Lost in thought, she made her way down the boardwalk toward the blacksmith's shop.

Ridge was standing out front. Just the sight of him lifted her spirits. Although there were other men gathered around, Ridge Longtree was a man apart. It wasn't just the color of his skin, or the fact that he was taller than the men around him. He possessed an air of self-confidence and inner strength that was evident even when he was doing nothing more than passing the time of day with men he hardly knew.

As though sensing her approach, he glanced over his shoulder, then turned around, watching her walk toward him.

"So," he said when she drew closer, "what did Claunch have to say?"

"You're not going to believe this. He's going to propose to my mother, and he wanted my blessing."

Ridge grunted softly. "Didn't he propose to you not long ago?"

"Yes. At least I didn't have to tell him no."

"Do you think your mother will accept?"

"I hope not! Certainly even Nettie would have better sense than to marry a low-down snake like Victor Claunch."

Ridge laughed softly. "Are you ready to go?"

Marty nodded, and Ridge handed her into the buggy, then hopped up beside her. Taking up the reins, he clucked to the team.

With a sigh, Marty sat back and closed her eyes. She couldn't remember a more stressful day in her life. Talking to Cory's parents had been one of the hardest things she'd ever had to do. Then she'd had to sit and listen to Victor Claunch's shocking announcement.

She must have dozed off, because she came awake with a start when she realized the buggy had stopped. She looked over at Ridge. "Is something wrong?"

"No. I just thought we'd stop awhile."

"Why?" She glanced around, noting that he had pulled off the road and parked the buggy in the shade alongside a stream.

"You in a hurry to get home?"

She thought about that for a moment, then shook her head. She wasn't the least bit anxious to go back to the house and face her mother, but the ranch wouldn't run itself, and she had already been away far too long.

"We need to go," she said, even though spending the day here, with Ridge, was almighty tempting.

"Whatever needs to be done will still be there in an hour or two." Swinging down from the seat, he walked around to her side and lifted her out of the buggy.

"Ridge . . ." His hands were still around her waist, and he made no move to let her go.

"Shh." He drew her closer. "Just relax."

Relax? Ha! How was she supposed to relax when he was standing so close, when she could feel the heat radiating from his body, feel his breath fanning her cheek?

She looked up at him, waiting. He didn't disappoint her. She made no move to resist when he lowered his head and kissed her. Heat engulfed her, burning away every care, every other thought. How could she worry about Nettie or Victor Claunch or anything else when she was in Ridge's arms, when his hands were sliding up and down her back, when her whole body tingled from his touch?

Sweeping her into his arms, he carried her away from the buggy and lowered her onto a patch of grass. He sat down behind her, her back to his front, his legs on either side of her, and then, to her amazement, he began to rub her back and shoulders.

"What are you doing?"

"Taking care of my girl," he replied.

Startled, she glanced over her shoulder. "*Your* girl?" Excitement bubbled up inside her. Did he truly think of her as "his" girl?

"You got a problem with that?"

"Several," she retorted, tamping down the urge to turn and throw herself in his arms.

"Several?" He lifted one brow. "Want to tell me what they are?"

It was hard to think coherently with his hands moving over her back and shoulders. She held up one hand, ticking off the reasons. "One, you're a drifter. Two, you're a hired gun. Three, you're wanted by the law. Four, you've never said you . . . you cared for me at all. Five—"

He didn't give her a chance to finish. Tossing his hat aside, he cupped the back of her head in one big, capable hand and claimed her lips with his once again. It wasn't fair, she thought, dazed. It just wasn't fair that he could render her speechless with a kiss, make her forget all the reasons why he was wrong for her, make her want him with every fiber of her being.

It just wasn't fair, but it was the most wonderful feeling in the world. In his arms she felt beautiful, desirable. Heat flowed through her, making her feel as if she had swallowed a ray of sunshine.

Turning toward him, she wrapped her arms around his neck and kissed him back. Soon, all too soon, he would ride out of her life and she would never see him again. But she wouldn't think about that now, not when his tongue was teasing hers, not when his hands were caressing her.

Slowly he fell back on the grass, drawing her with him, until her body covered his. "Ridge . . ."

He nibbled her lower lip. "What?"

"I've never . . . you know."

"I know. But if you kiss me again, I'll let you have your wicked way with me."

It seemed wrong to laugh at such a time, but she couldn't help it.

"Think that's funny, do you?" he asked gruffly.

"No. It's just that you make me so happy, even now, when my whole life is falling apart."

He stroked her cheek with his knuckles. "It'll all work out, you'll see."

"Will it?" She traced the line of his jaw with her forefinger, ran her fingers over his cheek. "How can it? We still don't know who killed my father. The ranch doesn't belong to me anymore. Claunch wants to marry my mother. Dani's married to an Apache."

"I'm half Apache," he reminded her. "Would you mind marrying me?"

She blinked at him. "What did you say?"

"You heard me. Would you mind marrying a half-breed?"

"Are you . . . Is that . . . ?" She shook her head. "Did you just ask me to marry you?"

"Sure sounded like it to me."

She stared at him. "Are you serious?"

He nodded. "More serious than I've ever been about anything in my life."

"But . . . why?"

"Why do people usually get married?"

"Because they love each other, but—"

"I'm in love with you, Martha Jean Flynn. Do you think you might love me a little?"

"No."

A muscle worked in his jaw. "No?"

"No, you silly man," she said fervently. "I love you ever so much more than a little."

He laughed then, a deep, rich sound that seemed to come from the very depths of his soul. And then he kissed her again, a kiss that captured her heart and soul and branded her his woman forever.

When the kiss ended, she looked up at him, breathless. "So now what?"

His gaze moved over her, hotter than any flame. "I have a few ideas."

Marty felt her cheeks grow warm. She was pretty sure she knew what he was thinking, because she was thinking—and wanting—the same thing. Wanting to feel his bare skin beneath her hand, to feel his body joined to hers, to know, at last, what it was like to be loved by a man.

"So," he said, "tell me what you want."

"Don't you know?"

"I know what I want," he muttered, and kissed her

again, one hand spread across her back, the other cupping her buttocks, pressing her hips to his so there could be no mistaking what it was he wanted.

It was tempting, so tempting. She kissed him back, surrendering to the tide of emotions that flowed through her, pulling her first one way and then another. She wanted him desperately, needed him more than the air she breathed, and yet, in the back of her mind, she remembered how, as a young girl, she had dreamed of a big wedding, of saving herself for the man who would be her husband. How often had her mother told her that good girls did not lightly give away that which could only be given once? *It's a gift to be saved for your husband,* Nettie had often said. *No man wants another man's leavings.*

Marty frowned at the memory.

"What is it?" Ridge asked.

"Nothing. I was just thinking of something my mother said."

Ridge lifted one brow. "Now?" he asked wryly. "And what is it that she said?"

"She told me I should save myself for the man I married."

He grunted softly. Kissing her on the tip of her nose, he lifted her until she was sitting up, and then he sat up too. "She was right." Rising, he offered her his hand.

Disappointed in spite of herself, Marty took his hand and let him help her to her feet. She straightened her clothes; he dusted off his jeans and retrieved his hat.

"Come on," he said, giving her hand a squeeze. "You're far too tempting for your own good, and I'm far too weak to resist you."

She smiled, pleased that he found her so desirable.

"Just one thing," he said as he lifted her into the buggy.

"What's that?"

"You never said yes."

She grinned at him as he climbed in beside her. "Did you think for a minute that I'd say no?"

She was, he thought, the most beautiful woman he had ever seen, and he wondered, in that instant, how he could have ever thought otherwise. Her cheeks were flushed and pink, her brown eyes sparkled with an inner glow, her hair framed her face like an auburn cloud streaked with sunlight.

"You still haven't said yes," he reminded her with a wry grin.

"Yes, Ridge Longtree, I'll marry you."

Chapter 29

Dani brushed a lock of hair from her brow, then, taking a deep breath, she returned to scraping the hide pegged to the ground. It took skill and a steady hand to skin a deer without ruining the hide.

She had never worked so hard in her life as she had since they arrived at the stronghold. And to think she had once thought life on the ranch was hard!

She'd had to learn which plants were good for food or for healing, and which were poisonous. Sanza was unfailingly patient with her as she sought to learn the ways of his people and endeavored to learn his language.

Cooking on the stove in the kitchen back home was child's play compared to cooking over an open fire. Her first few attempts had turned out rather badly. Either she burned the meat from having the fire too hot, or she served it only partially cooked because the fire was not hot enough. Since Apache didn't eat three regular meals a day, but whenever they were hungry, food had to be available at all times. She had been proud of herself when she caught several fish in the river and served them for dinner, only to learn that the Apache did not eat fish because they believed they were related to snakes, and snakes were cursed.

Remembering her Bible study, Dani thought it interesting that the Indians believed snakes were cursed, since it had been a snake that deceived Eve in the Garden of Eden.

Thinking of Adam and Eve reminded Dani of a story Sanza had told her one night, a fable of how Old Man created people. As so many Apache stories seemed to, this one started with, "Long ago, when the world was new . . ." At that time, there were no people in the world except for Old Man, Coyote, and a few buffalo. One day, because Old Man was lonely, and maybe a little lazy, he was sitting by his fire trying to think of a way to pass the time. He had food and he had shelter, but he thought it would be nice if he had someone to talk to. Suddenly it occurred to him that he was the Old Man, and he could create people if he was of a mind to. And so he decided to make people. First he studied his reflection in a pool of water, and then he counted his bones and studied how they fit together. Then he made some clay and fashioned some bones and baked them in the fire.

When they were done, he took the best ones and made the figure of a man from the bones, then tied them together with sinew and covered the baked bones with buffalo fat. He added layers of clay mixed with buffalo blood to fatten them up, and then covered it all with a piece of buffalo hide. He was so pleased with what he had done that he made some more, and when he was finished, he blew smoke into the eyes, nose, and mouth of the clay figures and they came to life. And Old Man was happy because he had someone to smoke with and was no longer alone. Then, one day, Coyote came to visit. He looked at the men Old Man had created and said he thought he could do better, and asked Old Man what he was going to do with all the leftover bones.

Old Man said he didn't think they could make men out of the discarded bones, but the two of them got together and made creatures out of the best of them. When they were finished, Old Man blew smoke in the eyes, nose, and mouth of each one. But, instead of creating more men, Old Man and Coyote discovered that they had created women. As soon as the women were created, they began to talk to one another. And so it is even to this day, Sanza had said, that men sit around the fire and smoke and women gather together and talk.

It was quite a surprising story, really, coming from a group of people she had once believed were savages.

She wondered what her mother would think if she could see her now. No doubt Nettie would be shocked to see her daughter kneeling in the dirt scraping bits of meat from the hide of a deer. Dani grinned. Sometimes she was shocked to find herself in the midst of an Apache encampment, surrounded by people she had once considered to be savages. But they were not savages. True, they lived in a primitive fashion, but they were an honorable people, kind and loving to their own, willing to share whatever they had with those in need. They laughed when they were happy and cried when they were sad. Husbands and wives had disagreements. Little boys played pranks. Little girls teased each other. Day by day, she felt more at home among the Apache.

Still, there were times when she woke in the night wondering where she was. But then Sanza would reach for her, his strong arms curling around her, his voice, husky with sleep, murmuring in her ear, and she knew she was where she belonged. It was Sanza who made every hardship worthwhile. As long as he was there beside her, she wasn't afraid of anything.

Sitting back on her heels, she glanced around the camp. Sights that had once seemed strange now seemed natural to her. Now, in the heat of the day, men and children wore only enough for modesty's sake. Once, the sight of so many near-naked men had shocked her, but no longer.

Across the way, a mother nursed her infant. Several old men sat in the shade, dozing. A handful of young boys were shooting arrows at a target while the fathers wagered on which boy would hit the target the most times. She saw a young girl learning how to make moccasins, watched a baby take its first steps.

Watching the people interacting with their loved ones, Dani felt a sudden overwhelming urge to go home, to be with her mother and her sister, to introduce them to Sanza. They would have to make the trip soon, she thought, for there would be little traveling once winter arrived.

As soon as Sanza returned from hunting, she would ask him to take her home.

Chapter 30

Nettie stared from Ridge to her daughter and back again. "You want to get married? The two of you? To each other?"

"Yes, ma'am," Ridge replied. He smiled at Marty. "And we'd like your blessing."

Nettie placed her hand over her heart. "Oh, my."

"Just so you know, we're getting married whether you approve or not," Marty said. "It was Ridge's idea to ask for your blessing, not mine."

Nettie flinched at the bitterness in her daughter's voice. "Martha, are you ever going to forgive me?"

"Why should I?"

"There are things you don't know."

Marty shrugged. "It doesn't matter anymore. You weren't here when I needed you. I don't need you now."

"I think you need to sit down and have a long talk," Ridge said. "Just the two of you."

"I don't think so," Marty said.

"Well, I do. I'll see you later."

"Ridge, wait."

"You need to get this settled." He looked from one woman to the other. "I'll see you at dinner."

Marty watched him walk out the front door. Sitting

back on the sofa, she folded her arms over her chest and slowly turned to face her mother. "So what do I need to know?"

Nettie took a deep breath. Now that the time had come, she didn't know how to begin. She didn't want to destroy Martha Jean's memory of her father. Yet Seamus was gone and it was time Martha Jean knew the truth.

"I was very young when I married your father," she said quietly. "I met him at a party, and he was so handsome and so charming. All the girls were crazy for him, but he never paid attention to any of them. Just me. I was flattered. You know how he was: bigger than life. I think I fell in love with him that first night. It didn't matter that he was older, or that, as the weeks went by, he got terribly jealous if I so much as looked at another man. Once he'd decided I was his, he wouldn't allow me to dance with any of the other boys, not even the ones I'd grown up with.

"I didn't see anything wrong with that. In fact, it was rather endearing. He loved his whiskey, too. Again, I didn't see anything wrong with that. My own father drank, and so did all the other men.

"My parents warned me not to marry him. But I was young and in love, and the more they tried to talk me out of marrying Seamus, the more determined I was to be his wife. I told them that if they wouldn't give me their permission, I'd run away. Against their better judgment, they relented, and we set the date.

"My parents gave us the biggest wedding the town had ever seen. Everyone came. I was so happy. He had told me so much about the ranch, I couldn't wait to see it, even though it meant leaving everyone I knew, everything I was familiar with.

"It was on our way to the ranch that I got the first

taste of his temper. We had stopped in a little town to spend the night. While I stayed in our room to bathe and do my hair, Seamus went to a saloon. We went out to dinner when he returned. As we were leaving the hotel, a man smiled at me. Seamus accused him of flirting with me, and when the other man denied it, Seamus hit him.

"I was horrified. A crowd gathered around, and then the sheriff came and hauled Seamus and the other man off to jail.

"Your father apologized over and over again the next day, swearing it would never happen again. But it did. Often. His accusations grew worse as time went on. He accused me of leading men on, of wanting to have an . . . an *affaire d'amour*."

Nettie laughed softly. "I know now all those accusations were born out of his own guilt. He was the one having midnight trysts. I was devastated when I found out. Of course, he promised me it would never happen again. But it did, so many times I lost count. One night we had a huge fight and he stormed out of the house. I thought he'd gone to be with his latest paramour.

"I went outside so you and Danielle wouldn't hear me crying. We had a young man working for us at the time—Danny Arnold. He was a few years younger than I, a sweet boy. He heard me crying and he tried to comfort me. I let him hold me. It was all perfectly innocent, at first.

"I started looking for Danny whenever I knew Seamus was in town visiting his mistress. At first, all we did was talk. Danny told me about how he was saving money to go back home and marry his childhood sweetheart. A few months later, he received a letter saying that his intended had tired of waiting and married someone else. Soon after that, Seamus and I had a terrible argument. That night, while Danny and I were comforting each other, he kissed me."

Nettie looked away, her cheeks flushed with the memory. "What happened between us never should have happened. I'm not making excuses for what I did. It was wrong, and I knew it. But I was lonely and unhappy and so was he, and . . ." She shrugged. "One thing led to another. Seamus found us in each other's arms. He wouldn't listen to my explanation, wouldn't listen to anything. He beat that poor boy and then he fired him and turned on me. He slapped me and called me every horrible name he could think of. He accused me of sleeping with every man on the ranch, and then he told me to get out, that he never wanted to see me again.

"I looked at him and I knew I didn't love him anymore, that I couldn't stay in the house another minute. I was tired of his lying and his drinking and his irrational jealousy. I told him I was leaving and that I was taking my girls with me.

"He laughed at that. He said I was the one who was leaving, and that if I didn't go, he would tell you and Danielle that I was a whore, that I had had affairs with every man on the ranch, and that Victor Claunch was my lover."

"Victor!" Marty exclaimed. "I saw the two of you in the kitchen one night, kissing. I told Pa."

"I know. If you had been older, I would have tried to explain it all to you, but you were too young to understand such things. And I was so ashamed of what I'd done. I knew you idolized your father, and I was afraid that after what you had seen, you would believe Seamus and hate me, so I ran away. I know now it was a horrible, cowardly thing to do. But after seeing what Seamus did to Danny, I was suddenly afraid of what he might do to me if I stayed. I intended to send for you when I got back East, thinking that by then he would have cooled off and realized that my girls belonged with me. I couldn't go home to my parents. They had been against my marriage, and I simply couldn't face them, or ask them for help. It took me a while to find a place to stay and a way to earn a living. When I was finally settled, I wrote to Seamus, but he wouldn't answer my letters. It didn't take long to figure out that he was intercepting my mail to you and Danielle.

"I thought many times of coming back here to see you, but I could never summon the nerve. And the longer I put it off, the more difficult it became." Nettie shook her head. "So many wasted years. I missed out on so much." She wiped her eyes. "Can you ever forgive me? Can you ever understand?"

Marty blew out a deep breath. She couldn't condone what her mother had done, but she could understand her reasons for doing it. Ridge had been right, she thought. Seamus had left Nettie the ranch in hopes that it would bring Nettie home and somehow heal the breach between them.

And it had worked.

Rising, Marty went to her mother. "I understand."

Nettie rose. "And can you forgive me?"

With a nod, Marty drew her mother into her arms, her eyes filling with tears, tears that washed all the anger and resentment from her heart and soul. "Welcome home, Mama."

Ridge glanced over his shoulder at the sound of the front door opening. Martha stepped onto the porch. She stood there a moment, looking right and left.

Then seeing him standing near the corral, she hurried down the stairs.

"So," he said, stubbing out his cigarette with his boot heel, "how'd it go?"

With a sigh, she moved into his arms. "I'm not mad at her anymore."

"Want to tell me about it?" he asked, and listened intently as she related what Nettie had told her.

"I guess I can't blame her for running away," Marty said. "But I wish she'd had the nerve to stay. I can't believe Pa would have ever hurt her."

"What would you have done in her place?"

"I don't know."

"You wouldn't have run away."

"How do you know?"

"Because I know you." He smiled down at her. "Your courage is one of the things I love about you."

"What courage?"

He laughed softly. "The same courage that wouldn't let you stay home when I went after Dani. The same courage that made you hide your own feelings and shed your tears out in the barn where no one could see you when your old man was killed."

"Humph! *You* saw me."

"And I loved you for it."

She pressed her cheek against his chest. "And I love you."

"So when are we getting married? It had better be soon if you expect to be a maiden on our wedding night."

Cheeks flushed, Marty looked up at him. "We're still in mourning for my father. We really should wait at least a year."

"A year!" He swore under his breath. "Is that what you want?"

"Not really."

"Well, if it were up to me, we'd get married tomorrow morning."

"That might be a little too soon. Anyway, it will take at least a couple of weeks to find a dress and send invitations. And I'd really like for Dani to be here, you know, to be my maid of honor."

"Well, if they expect to get here and back before winter sets in, they'll have to leave right quick."

"Back? You don't think Dani means to live with the Apache, do you?"

"I don't know, but I'm pretty sure Sanza isn't planning to stay here."

Marty bit down on her lower lip. Until this moment, it hadn't occurred to her that Dani might actually live with the Indians. She had assumed that when Dani came back to the ranch, it would be to stay.

Suddenly, observing proper etiquette and proper periods of mourning no longer seemed important. She had waited her whole life for the man holding her in his arms, and she wasn't going to wait any longer.

"I'll talk to Nettie tonight," she said, "and we'll start making plans for the wedding."

"You're not going to turn this into a three-ring circus, are you?"

"No. But a girl gets married only once. I want it to be wonderful."

He couldn't argue with that. "All right," he said, brushing his lips over the top of her head. "Just name the day, and I'll be there. But I'm warning you, it had better be soon."

His fingertips lightly grazed her cheek. His arm tightened around her waist, drawing her up against him, fitting her body close to his.

A ragged sigh escaped her lips as her breasts were flattened against his chest. Tiny flames of desire seemed to spring to life everywhere his body touched hers and she lifted her face, eager for his kiss, reveling in the touch of his hands as they roamed up and down her back. Her breasts felt full, heavy, aching for his touch. She moaned softly when he broke the kiss.

Ridge gazed deep into her eyes. "How long did you say we have to wait?" he asked, his voice husky.

"I don't want to wait, but what about Dani?"

"Forget Dani," he growled, and claimed her lips once more.

She was breathless when he released her. "I'll talk to Mama tonight."

Marty was sitting on the front porch a few days later, making a list of people to invite to the wedding, when Dani and Sanza rode into the yard.

With a happy cry, Marty leaped to her feet and ran down the porch steps. "Dani!"

Dismounting, Dani hurled herself into her sister's arms. They hugged for several moments, then held each other at arm's length.

"You're glowing," Dani exclaimed as she studied her sister's face. "What's happened to you to put that sparkle in your eyes?"

Marty glanced at Sanza, then back at Dani. "The same thing that happened to you."

"You got married?"

"Not yet."

Dani blinked at her sister. "Who's the lucky man?" she asked, and then her eyes widened. "Not Longtree?"

Marty nodded, then burst out laughing at the look of utter astonishment on her sister's face.

"And you were upset because *I* married an Apache," Dani said, grinning.

Marty glanced over Dani's shoulder to Sanza. Still

mounted, he watched the sisters intently. "Do you still feel the same about him?"

"More than ever," Dani said, her eyes shining. "I have to admit, living in a wickiup isn't easy, but somehow it doesn't matter, not when he's with me." She looked up at the house. "Where's Mama?"

"She was baking bread last time I looked."

"Look after Sanza, will you?" Dani asked. She gave Marty a squeeze, then hurried into the house.

Marty looked up at her brother-in-law. "Welcome to our home," she said.

He nodded, reminding Marty that the Apache rarely said thank-you.

"Come on," she said, and taking up the reins to Dani's horse, she started toward the barn.

Sanza's gaze darted right and left as he followed the woman. He had never been among the White Eyes before. He had seen their lodges, but only from a distance. His people had forged an uneasy peace with the White Eyes. Of course, that didn't mean the Apache didn't occasionally steal horses or cattle from the whites; after all, the White Eyes had chased away most of the deer and buffalo. It seemed only fair that they should replace the game that had once roamed the land in abundance.

He dismounted when they reached the barn.

"Here." She handed him a brush.

He turned it over in his hand; then, following her lead, he began to brush the dirt from his horse's coat. He checked the mare's feet for stones, then led the horse into the stall she indicated. He rubbed the horse's neck, speaking to the animal in soft Apache for a few moments before stepping out of the stall and closing the door behind him.

"Can we talk for a minute?" the woman asked.

Sanza nodded.

"Do you intend to take my sister back to your people?"

He nodded again.

"Would you consider staying here? At the ranch?"

He frowned. "Why would I do that?" He glanced around, noting the big house, the well-stocked corrals.

"This is Dani's home."

He had not considered that. Among the Apache, when a man married, he said good-bye forever to his own family. From that time forward, he was obligated to protect and provide for his wife and her family. Why had he not thought of that sooner? Why had he not considered the consequences of marrying a white woman? By Apache law, he was bound to live with his wife's family. And Dani's family lived here.

"Yes," he said heavily. "We will stay here."

A smile spread over his sister-in-law's face. "That's wonderful!" she exclaimed. "Come on; let's go tell Dani and Nettie."

"Who is Net-tie?"

"Our mother."

Sanza shook his head. "No."

"Why not?"

He should have known she would not understand. She was not Apache. She did not know Apache ways. "Among my people, a man does not look at, or speak to, his mother-in-law."

Marty stared at him. "That's . . . Why not?"

He shrugged. "It is our way."

"So you never speak to your mother-in-law? Ever?" She frowned, thinking that was going to make for some interesting family holidays.

"We will build our wickiup over there, facing west."

"There's no need for that," Marty said. "There's

plenty of room for you and Dani in the house." Of course, living in the same house would make it practically impossible for Sanza to avoid Nettie. Heavens, what would they do if Ridge practiced that peculiar custom?

And even as she thought of him, he was riding toward her. Her heart did a familiar flip-flop in her chest at the mere sight of him.

Dismounting, he tossed the reins over the hitching post, then drew her into his arms and swung her around. Setting her on her feet, he kissed her before turning to greet Sanza.

The two men grasped forearms. "Welcome, brother," Ridge said.

Sanza nodded.

"So," Ridge said, looking at Marty, "what did Nettie say?"

"Dani's with her now."

Ridge grunted. "I need to put my horse away."

"I will do it," Sanza said.

"Obliged," Ridge said.

"Can I talk to you?" Marty asked, tugging on his arm.

"Sure."

Moving away from the barn, they stopped in the shade of a tree near the side of the house.

"What's wrong?" Ridge asked.

"Nothing, really. I asked Sanza if he'd think about staying here and—"

Ridge nodded. "And he said yes."

"Yes, and then I wanted to take him up to the house to meet Nettie—"

"And he said no."

Tilting her head to one side, Marty stared at him, one brow raised.

"Sorry. Go on."

"Anyway, he said he didn't want to live in the house, that he'd build his wickiup over there, facing west."

"In the opposite direction of the ranch house," Ridge said. "It's customary for the bride to build her wickiup close to her mother's, but facing in the opposite direction."

"So, this avoidance thing, how long does it last?"

"As long as they're married."

"I was afraid of that. Oh! You don't believe in that, too, do you?"

"No." Ridge drew her into his arms. "Stop worrying. Everything will work out."

"I don't see how. What are we going to do at Christmas if Sanza and Nettie can't look at each other? Won't it be a little difficult for them to sit at the table together? And what about Thanksgiving?"

"Hey, that's not our problem. It's theirs, and they'll work it out. Anyway, I doubt if Sanza will have much interest in Christmas or Thanksgiving. Or any other holiday. They don't mean anything to him."

With a sigh, Marty rested her cheek against his chest. "You're right, of course. Did you talk to the sheriff?"

"Yeah. He doesn't know any more now than he did before."

"We'll never find my father's killer, will we?"

"I don't know. All I've got to go on is that the killer's horse leaves a distinctive track. If I can find the horse that leaves it . . ." He shrugged, thinking that the odds of finding that track by chance were pretty slim. The horse Claunch usually rode didn't drag its hind foot.

"About Sanza," Marty said. "Where can I put him up?"

"He can sleep in the barn."

"The barn! I can't ask him to stay in the barn."

"Trust me: He'll be happier there than in the house."

"No, I have a better idea. I don't know why I didn't think of it sooner. Our old foreman was married. Pa built him a house over near Salt Springs. It's been vacant for a long time, but Sanza can stay there."

"Alone?"

"What? Oh. I suppose Dani will want to stay there, too."

"Yes," Ridge said dryly, "I suppose she will." He drew her closer. "Enough about them. Have you set the date yet?"

"Yes. The first week in September."

Ridge did some quick mental arithmetic. "Three weeks?"

"You said you were in a hurry, and believe me, that's rushing it."

Nettie didn't know what to say. First Martha had come to her, telling her that, even though they were in mourning, she was going to marry a man she hardly knew as soon as possible, and now Danielle sat across from her, telling her that she was already married, and to an Apache Indian, of all people! There was no doubt in her mind that her daughters thought they were in love with these men, but how could that be possible? Longtree was a gunfighter, and while Nettie could understand why Martha had hired him, the idea of accepting the man as her son-in-law was almost ludicrous.

And now Danielle had married the very man who had kidnapped her!

"Where is he, this Indian?" Nettie asked.

"Outside, with Marty."

"Why didn't he come in with you? Does he speak English? Danielle, whatever were you thinking?"

"I love him, Mama."

"And does this . . . this Indian, does he love you?"

"Of course."

Nettie stared at her daughter. It had never occurred to her that anyone would love an Apache. Or that the Apache were capable of love. They were savages, fierce warriors who, not so long ago, had cut a wide swath of bloodshed and destruction throughout the Southwest. Everyone knew that.

Nettie took a deep breath. Whether she approved of Danielle's choice of a husband or not no longer mattered. What was done was done. And, judging by the look on her daughter's face, it had been done well!

"Are you determined to stay married to this man?"

"Yes!"

"Then I think you should be married again, in church."

"I'm already married, Mama."

"Perhaps in the eyes of the Apache," Nettie replied. "But not according to our laws." She held up her hand, stifling her daughter's protests. "What if there's a child, Danielle? You don't want your children branded bastards, do you?"

"No," Dani said quietly. "Of course not. I hadn't thought of that."

"Perhaps a double wedding?" Nettie suggested.

Dani shook her head. "No. This should be Marty's day."

"Then perhaps a private ceremony afterward, with just the family?"

"I think that's a good idea," Dani said. "As long as Sanza agrees."

"Yes, of course," Nettie replied. "I think it's about time I met the man who put that smile on your face, don't you?"

"About that," Danielle said. "He can't talk to you."

"He can't? Is there something wrong with him?"

"Apache men don't speak to their mothers-in-law."

"Why not?"

"I'm not sure, exactly. They just don't."

"I see," she said, though she didn't see at all.

Chapter 31

Later that night, sitting on the well-worn sofa in the foreman's cabin, Dani snuggled against Sanza, thinking she had never been more content in her whole life. It was so good to be home again, surrounded by the people she loved. She couldn't believe her mother was really here, couldn't keep from touching Nettie every chance she got, simply to assure herself that it wasn't a dream. It was going to be hard, leaving this place when the time came. But she had made her choice. Her place was with her husband now. Perhaps Sanza would bring her home again in the spring.

Nettie had invited her and Sanza to dine up at the main house, but Dani had declined, reminding her mother that Sanza couldn't look at her or speak to her. Nettie hadn't argued. Instead, she had filled a basket with food and sent it home with Dani.

The foreman's cabin wasn't much, just a parlor, a kitchen, and two small bedrooms, all sparsely furnished, but sitting there, with her husband's arm around her and a cheerful fire in the hearth, she couldn't think of any place she'd rather be. She glanced around. Besides the sofa on which they sat, there was an overstuffed chair covered with a hand-made quilt, a small table, and a footstool. A colorful rag rug brightened the plank floor in front of the hearth. Faded gingham curtains hung at the window.

It wouldn't take much to spruce it up, she thought. Some new furniture, a coat of paint, new curtains, a few pictures and knickknacks, maybe some flowers outside the front door, and the place would have been charming. It would have been fun to fix the place up, but they weren't staying, so there was no point even thinking about it.

With a sigh, she wondered how best to approach the subject of having the Reverend Waters marry them. Would Sanza be offended? Or would he understand?

She felt his hand on hers and looked up at him.

"You are very quiet," he remarked. "Something troubles you?"

"No. Yes. Not really." She laughed softly. "I need to ask you something."

"Ask me."

"I'm afraid you'll get mad."

"I will not get mad."

"My mother thinks we should get married again."

"We are already married."

"I know, but an Apache marriage isn't recognized by my people."

He snorted disdainfully. "I do not care what the White Eyes think."

"Maybe not, but if we have a baby, my people will look at it with scorn if they think we are not married according to the laws of my people."

"And will they look at you the same way?"

She nodded. "It doesn't matter," she replied. But it did. For the first time, it occurred to her that she would be ostracized by the town when people learned she had married an Apache. The thought hurt. She could live with it if she had to, but she couldn't bear the thought of any social stigma being attached to her children.

Sanza frowned as he considered her words. For himself, he did not care what the whites thought, but he would not bring shame on his wife or his children.

"Very well," he said. "I will do as you ask."

She threw her arms around his neck and kissed him soundly. "Thank you! We'll have the reverend marry us after Marty's wedding. You don't mind staying here that long, do you? We can leave for the stronghold the next day, if you want."

"We will not go back to the village," he said dispiritedly.

"We won't? Why not? Where are we going to live?"

"We will live here, with your mother."

Dani blinked up at him. "Do you want to stay here?"

"No, but it is the way it must be."

"I don't understand."

"When a man marries, he cuts all ties with his own family. From that time forward, his wife's people become his people."

"I didn't know that," Dani murmured. His words reminded her of a Bible verse in the Book of Genesis that she had been taught in Sunday school, something about a man leaving his father and his mother and cleaving unto his wife. Odd, that the Apaches believed in something similar.

"Your family is here," he said heavily. "And here is where we will live."

She looked up at him, her emotions torn. The thought of staying here on the ranch with Marty and her mother, filled her with happiness. It would be so

wonderful to be close to them, to see her children and
Marty's grow up together, to go to church together
and celebrate holidays as a family. But at what cost?
She looked into her husband's eyes, her heart aching
at what she saw there. Sanza would never be happy
living here. The people in town would probably never
accept him. They would always look at him warily,
never trusting him. She couldn't ask that of him.

"We don't have to stay here," she said. "We can
go back to the stronghold. I know you'll be happier
there."

"And what of you?" He stroked her cheek lightly.
"Where will you be happy?"

"Wherever you are."

"You would leave here?" he asked.

"If that's what you want." Rising up on her knees,
she kissed him. "I just want you to be happy."

"It is my wish for you, as well." He grew thoughtful
a moment. "What if we spend our summers with my
people and our winters here, with yours?"

She beamed at him. "That's a wonderful idea!"

Pleased because she was pleased, he drew her onto
his lap, then buried his hands in her hair, loving the
way the silky strands curled around his fingers. Closing
his eyes, he inhaled her scent, and then he kissed her.

As always, his body responded immediately to her
nearness.

She giggled softly as she felt his arousal push against
her fanny.

"You dare to laugh at me?" he growled.

She looked into his eyes and laughed all the harder.
"Is that a spear under your clout?" she asked in wide-
eyed innocence.

"Shall I show you?"

"No, I'm much too frightened."

He moved her off his lap so that she was lying on her side. "Do not be afraid," he whispered as he stretched out beside her.

"But it's so big," she said in mock horror. "And so long."

"I will be very gentle," he promised.

She looked at him, her eyes glowing, her body trembling with desire. "Not too gentle," she murmured, and, drawing him into her arms, she guided him home.

Marty stood at her bedroom window, one hand holding the curtain back while she gazed into the distance. She had kissed Ridge good-night earlier, longing for the day when they wouldn't have to kiss goodnight, when she could follow him into their bedroom and close the door and shut out the rest of the world.

She thought of Dani and Sanza, thinking how lucky they were. Were they making love, even now?

She drew her thoughts away from that path. So much had happened in such a short time. Her father had been killed. Her little sister was married. Her mother had come home and, like it or not, seemed to be planning on marrying that snake Victor Claunch. But, most surprising of all, was the fact that Marty herself was in love.

Warmth spread through her at the mere thought of Ridge. He was everything she had ever dreamed of, and more. Tall and strong, proud and self-confident, a man who could take care of himself, and her. She had never known anyone who could make her so mad, or so happy. She had never wanted another man the way she wanted him.

Happiness bubbled up inside her. Soon, she thought, soon she would be his wife.

She was about to turn away from the window when she saw the faint glow of a cigarette. Excitement thrummed through her. Belting her robe tightly around her, she hurried out of her room, down the stairs, and out the front door.

Though her footsteps made no sound, he turned as she approached.

"Hi," she said breathlessly.

"Hi, yourself. What are you doing up so late?"

She shrugged. "I couldn't sleep."

"Why not?"

"Oh, I don't know. Probably because I was thinking about a man."

"Is that right?" He took a deep drag on his cigarette, then snubbed it out beneath the toe of his boot. "Any man in particular?"

She looked up at him through the veil of her lashes, a faint smile hovering over her lips. "Maybe."

"Maybe?" He slipped his arm around her waist and pulled her up against him.

"You shouldn't be out here this late. Any number of things might happen to you."

Her eyes widened. "What kind of things?"

"You never know. Some man might grab you and drag you into the bushes, and . . ."

"And what?" she asked, her voice low and breathy.

"And this." His lips claimed hers, his tongue plundering her mouth while one hand untied her robe and then slid inside to explore the warmth of her body.

She moaned softly as his hand slid over her breasts and belly. She was going up in flames, she thought, like dry grass touched by lightning.

He deepened the kiss, devouring her, until she couldn't think, until every fiber of her being knew only him, wanted only him.

She clung to him, yielding to his touch, willing to give him anything. Willing to give him everything.

He groaned, a sound filled with pain and longing, and then, with hands that shook, he put her away from him.

She looked up at him, dazed. "What are you doing? Why did you stop?"

"I was about to take you right here, right now, and then I remembered something you said."

She stared at him. "What did I say?"

"You told me once you weren't brought up to roll around in the dirt with a man you hardly knew."

"Oh," she said. "That."

"Uh-huh."

She wrapped her arms around his waist. "But I know you so much better now." She kissed his cheek, the point of his jaw. "And I want you so much more."

"Dammit, Martha Jean, you're not making this easy for me."

"I don't want to." She ran her hands over his chest, down his belly. "I don't want to wait."

Taking a deep breath, Ridge summoned every ounce of willpower he possessed, and then he drew her bathrobe around her and tied the sash tight. "Go to bed, Martha Jean. As much as I'd like to, I'm not going to take you out here, or in the barn, like some . . ." He reconsidered his choice of words. "Like some saloon girl. When we make love, it'll be in a bed, and you'll be my wife. "

She nodded. "I guess it's a good thing one of us can think straight."

"You'd better get back to the house before I change my mind."

Nodding, she rose on her tiptoes and kissed him. "Good night."

He grinned at her. "Go on; get out of here while you can."

Feeling warm and cherished, she hurried back toward the house. She paused on the front porch, turned and waved, then disappeared into the house.

Ridge stared after her. And then he smiled. She was a hell of a woman, and she was all his.

Chapter 32

Victor Claunch paced the floor of his den, a cigar clamped between his teeth. So Martha Jean was engaged to Longtree, and that pretty little gal Danielle had come home claiming to be married to an Apache warrior. Old Seamus must be rolling in his grave.

Going to the window, he stared out into the darkness, wondering what effect these unexpected happenings would have on his plans. On the one hand, it might be good news. There was always a chance that Martha and that gunman might decide to move off and start a place of their own. Same with Danielle and that Apache buck. It wasn't likely that the Indian would want to stick around. With both girls gone, it would give him a clear path to Nettie and the ranch. If he couldn't convince her to marry him for love, he might be able to convince her that she needed a man to help her run the home place. After all, this was no place for a woman alone.

On the other hand, if the girls decided to stay on at the ranch, it could change things entirely. Damn!

Pulling his watch from his vest pocket, he turned it over in his hand, admiring the beauty of it before he released the catch. He stared at the small photo of the woman on the inside cover before he checked the time.

In a few days, after they'd had time to decide what they were going to do, he would pay a friendly little visit to the Flynn women and find out exactly what their plans were. Only then could he decide his next course of action.

Chapter 33

The next few days were interesting, to say the least. The fall roundup was under way, and the ranch hands were busy from morning till night. For the first time in years, Marty didn't ride out with the hands. She had a wedding to plan, and although, in deference to her father's death, it would be a small affair, there was still much to be done.

Marty and Nettie and Dani worked together to clean the house from top to bottom, dusting, waxing, polishing the silver, and painting the porch, and when they weren't at the main house, they were sewing new curtains for the cabin at Salt Springs. Marty had been delighted when Dani told her that she and Sanza would be living at the ranch for half the year. Nettie, too, had been overjoyed at the news.

Ridge and Sanza spent their days out on the range with the men. The cowhands were a little leery of having an Indian riding with them. The first two days, they spent most of their time looking over their shoulders, as if they expected him to attack them at any minute. Sanza bore their curious looks and distrust with stoic indifference.

On Saturday, the women went into town. Their first stop was at the dressmakers'. Marty had never both-

ered much about dresses and such, preferring pants to
skirts, but this was different. This was her wedding
dress. She looked through numerous patterns before
choosing a gown. While not the latest Paris fashion, it
was quite lovely. Made of cream-colored satin, it had
a round neck and short, puffy sleeves edged with tulle
and lace. The skirt was gathered at the back with a
modest bustle. The short train was edged with rows
of ruffles.

Dani chose a gown of dusty-rose silk with a square
neckline and short sleeves. The skirt was shirred at
the hips and tucked along the bottom. Nettie chose a
two-piece dress in a muted shade of gray.

After leaving the modiste, they made a quick stop
at the general store for supplies and then headed for
home.

It had been a pleasant day, Marty thought as she
pulled into the ranch yard, until she saw Victor
Claunch's horse tied at the hitching post.

"What's he doing here?" Dani asked.

Marty parked the wagon alongside the house, and
then she looked at her mother, remembering the conversation she'd had with Victor Claunch not so long
ago. "I've got a pretty good idea."

"You do?" Dani said.

"He's come courting."

Dani frowned. "Courting? Who could he be courting here?" she asked, and then clapped her hand over
her mouth.

"Yes," Nettie said, alighting from the wagon. "I'm
afraid it's me."

"You!" Dani exclaimed. She looked at Marty. "Did
you know about this?"

"Yes."

"And you didn't tell me?" Dani looked at her mother again. "Is it true?"

"I'm afraid so," Nettie said. "He came calling regularly while you two were away."

Marty and Dani exchanged looks, then turned to face their mother again.

"You're not thinking of marrying him, are you?" Marty asked. In spite of what Victor had said, it had never occurred to her that her mother might actually consider marrying Victor Claunch.

"I take it you're against it," Nettie said dryly.

"How can you even consider it?" Dani asked.

"You can't marry him," Marty said. "I'm sure he killed Pa, and if he didn't, then he was behind it."

Nettie looked startled. "Why would you think that?"

"He's been trying to buy us out for the last five years," Marty explained.

"That doesn't make him a murderer." Nettie shook her head. "No, I don't believe it. Victor was your father's friend."

"He did it," Marty said stubbornly. "I might never be able to prove it, but I know he did it. And he only wants to marry you to get the ranch! For goodness' sake, he asked me to marry him when he thought Pa left the ranch to me."

"Shh," Dani said, "here he comes."

Marty looked past her sister to see Claunch walking toward them. "Looks like he's been out snooping around," she muttered. "I wonder how long he's been here."

"Afternoon, ladies," Victor said.

Dani nodded. Grabbing a package from the back of the wagon, she muttered something and hurried into the house.

"Hello, Victor," Nettie said. She glanced at Marty, then back at Victor. "It's good to see you."

He looked prosperous, as always, Marty thought, from the crown of his gray Stetson to the soles of his boots. He wore gray trousers, a white shirt, and a black leather vest.

"You too. Here," he said, reaching into the back of the wagon, "let me help you with that."

Marty managed a thank-you between clenched teeth as he took a large box from her hand.

"So, Victor," Nettie said, "what brings you out here this afternoon?"

Victor glanced at Marty, then at Nettie. "Why, I came to see the three prettiest women this side of the Missouri," he said gallantly.

Marty scowled.

Nettie blushed. "Let's go inside, shall we?"

"You two go ahead," Marty said. "I'll be along later."

She watched the two of them disappear into the house, then turned and retraced Victor's footprints, wondering what he had been looking at before they arrived. The man had enough nerve for a dozen men, she thought sourly. He'd been inside the barn and walked around the well. His footprints led to the back of the house, then disappeared in the gravel. What mischief was he up to now? she wondered.

Knowing she couldn't put it off any longer, she took a deep breath then went into the house. Victor and Nettie were in the parlor. There was a pitcher of lemonade and a plate of cookies on the table between them.

Nettie looked up and smiled. "Come," she said, "join us."

"I need to get cleaned up."

"Victor has something he wants to say to you."

Marty sat down on the sofa, certain that, whatever he had to say, she didn't want to hear it.

Victor cleared his throat. "As I told you earlier, I've been courting your mother for some weeks now." He smiled at Nettie and took her hand in his. "I've always had tender feelings for your mother, and now that she's free . . . well, I just asked her to marry me."

Marty couldn't help herself. She gasped, not in surprise, but horror.

"I don't blame you for being surprised," Nettie said quickly.

"She hasn't answered me yet," Victor said. "I think she wants your approval."

Marty sprang to her feet. "Well, she doesn't have it. Not now. Not ever!"

"Martha Jean!" Nettie exclaimed. "Where are your manners?"

Marty was too upset to reply. With a shake of her head, she turned and ran out of the room.

Nettie stared after her, then looked apologetically at Victor. "I'm sorry. She's been under a lot of pressure lately, what with her father's death and Dani being kidnapped."

"Yes, of course," Victor said. "But none of that has anything to do with us. So name the day, my dear."

"I'm afraid I can't say yes now, not when Marty objects so strongly."

A muscle twitched in Victor's jaw, and his eyes narrowed ever so slightly. "You're going to let her feelings come between us?"

"I'm afraid so, at least for the time being. Try to understand, won't you? I'm sure she'll come around in time."

"Yes, of course," he said. "In time."

*   *   *

Sunday morning, Marty put on her church dress and went downstairs to fix breakfast, only to find Ridge looking out the window, a cup of coffee in his hand.

He turned as she entered the room. "You're up early."

"It's Sunday," she said.

He lifted one brow.

"Church," she said.

"Ah." She wore a pale yellow dress. The neck was square and edged with rows of tiny ruffles. The sleeves were short and the skirt was full, pulled up on one side to reveal rows of ruffled lace. "You'll be the prettiest girl there."

"Thank you. Would you like to come with us?"

He shook his head. He couldn't remember the last time he'd been inside a white man's church.

"Will you come with us?"

"Do you think I'd be welcome?"

"It's a church, Longtree. Everyone is welcome." Walking up to him, she rose on her tiptoes and kissed him. "Please come."

"How can I resist?"

After breakfast, Ridge, Marty, and Nettie stopped by to pick up Dani, and then they were on their way.

"I guess Sanza wasn't up to coming to church, eh?" Ridge asked.

"No," Dani said, settling her skirts around her. "But he didn't mind my going. Do you suppose our God and the Apache god is the same?"

"Of course it is," Nettie said. "There's only one God."

Marty looked at Ridge. "Is that what you think?"

"I don't know. Can't say as I ever gave it a lot of thought."

A short time later, he parked the buggy in front of the church. Alighting, he handed Marty out of the conveyance, then helped Nettie and Dani out of the backseat.

Marty frowned at him as he reached for her hand.

"What's wrong?" he asked.

"Do you think you could leave your gun in the buggy?"

"No."

She didn't argue. Taking his arm, they walked up the stairs and entered the vestibule. Marty looked over at him and smiled.

"Relax," she whispered.

He grunted softly as he let Marty lead him to a pew about midway down the aisle. He was studying the stained-glass window over the altar when he felt Marty tense beside him. A glance to his left showed Victor Claunch sliding into the pew beside Nettie. Moments later, the organist began to play.

Ridge was dozing when Marty pinched him. He frowned at her; then, following her gaze, he saw what had upset her. Victor was holding Nettie's hand.

When the service ended, the church members gathered together. Gradually, the men moved off to talk about crops and cattle, politics and the weather, leaving the older women to gossip while the younger ones talked about babies and birthing and female complaints. Dani and Marty stood with the younger group. Nettie and Victor stood apart from everyone else.

Ridge glanced at Marty. She was glaring at Victor, her hands clenched into fists at her sides.

When she broke away from the other women, obviously intending to confront her mother and Claunch, Ridge intercepted her before she could cause a scene.

"Not now," he said quietly.

"Let me go!"

"Behave yourself. You don't want to cause a scene, do you?"

"I don't care!"

"Is that right?"

She stared up at him. Too late, she noticed the mischievous expression on his face. Before she could protest, he drew her into his arms and kissed her, long and hard.

She blinked at him when he finally released her. From the corner of her eye, she could see people staring at them. She felt herself blush from the tips of her toes to the top of her head.

"Are you ready to go home now?" Ridge asked innocently.

"What? Oh, yes."

Back straight, she marched toward the buggy. She didn't look back.

Stifling the urge to grin, Ridge followed her.

"What was that all about?" Dani asked, coming up behind him.

"Just trying to keep your sister from making a scene."

"Really?" Dani exclaimed. "I'd hate to see what you'd do if you were trying to cause one!"

The next few weeks passed in a flurry of activity. Nettie began planning the menu for the gathering after the wedding. Marty redecorated her bedroom in shades of blue and beige, bought new pillows and new sheets. She emptied several drawers in the highboy and made room for Ridge's belongings in the armoire. She went into town again and bought a new nightgown that was so revealing she blushed every time she thought of wearing it for Ridge. She also bought new undergarments to wear with her wedding dress, as well as a new pair of shoes.

The day before the wedding, all the men except Sanza went into town for haircuts. Before they left, Marty took Ridge aside and asked him to leave his hair long.

"Anything for you, darlin'," he had replied with a lopsided grin.

They met that night under the stars, as had become their habit. Ridge opened his arms and she made herself at home, her cheek snuggled against his chest, her arms wrapping around his waist.

She slipped one hand under his shirt. "One more day," she murmured.

He laughed softly. "Think you can wait?"

"Yes, but no longer than that."

"It's been a long three weeks," he muttered. It was getting harder and harder to let her go at night, to settle for a few kisses and a quick caress, to lie in bed at night and picture her lying in her own bed just down the hall. More than once, he'd gotten up and paced the floor, fighting the urge to go to her room and slide under the covers beside her. In spite of his honorable words to the contrary, he wanted her more than he'd ever wanted anything in his life.

"We've never talked about what we were going to do after we get married," Marty remarked.

"I plan to carry you to the nearest bed just as fast as I can," Ridge replied, his voice husky with longing.

"I don't mean *that*," Marty said, grinning. "I mean, I just assumed we'd stay on at the ranch, even though we never talked about it."

"Honey, we can live wherever you want."

"We can?"

"Sure."

"Don't tell me you're independently wealthy."

"Not quite, but I've got a few dollars put away, so if you get the urge to move on, you just let me know."

"And you won't mind sharing a house with Nettie?"

"Not as long as she sleeps in her own room."

"Oh, you!" she exclaimed, punching him on the arm. "Do you ever think of anything else?"

"Not when you're around."

They spent the next few minutes kissing and cuddling, spinning daydreams of their future.

"There's one other thing we haven't discussed," Marty said when they came up for air.

"What's that?"

"Children."

"What's to discuss? They'll come or they won't."

She laughed at that.

"Do you want a big family?" Even as he asked the question, he was imagining a little girl with reddish-brown hair and freckles.

"Yes, do you?"

He cupped her buttocks and drew her up against him. "Making them is half the fun. And now," he said, kissing the tip of her nose, "I think you'd best go to bed."

She didn't argue. After all, a girl needed her beauty sleep, especially when she was getting married in the morning.

Chapter 34

It was her wedding day. Marty woke early after a restless night. She stared up at the ceiling for a moment, her stomach all aflutter at what the day—and the night—would bring.

Tonight she would be Ridge Longtree's wife. The thought sent a thrill racing down her spine. Sitting up, she wrapped her arms around her waist and giggled like a schoolgirl.

Mrs. Ridge Longtree. She laughed out loud, giddy with excitement.

Three hours later, Marty sat on a stool in the middle of her bedroom while her mother arranged her hair.

"Martha, for goodness' sake, stop fidgeting!"

"I can't help it. I've never been a bride before. Weren't you nervous the day you married my father?"

"Oh, Lord, yes," Nettie replied, smiling.

"You had a big wedding, didn't you?"

"Yes. My folks insisted on it. I think they invited the whole city. Most of the day was just a blur, there were so many people there. I didn't even know most of them." Nettie paused. "I never told you anything about what to expect on your wedding night."

"Mama!"

Nettie shrugged. "And I don't know what to tell you now. If you love him . . ."

"Oh, I do!"

Nettie gave her shoulder a squeeze. "Then just let nature take its course."

She put the last hairpin in place, then stood back, her hands on her hips. "Perfect!" she declared.

Rising, Marty looked at herself in the mirror. A stranger looked back. Her mother had gathered her hair up and back, so that it fell down her back in thick waves. A few tendrils framed her face.

There was a knock on the door, and then Dani entered the room. "Marty! You look gorgeous. Wait until Ridge sees you!"

"Do I really look all right?"

"You look better than all right." Dani laughed. "No one will recognize you."

Marty made a face at her sister, and then began to change her clothes. Her new undergarments felt cool against her heated skin. And then her mother helped her into her dress, and when Marty looked in the mirror again, she saw a bride with rosy cheeks and eyes that were sparkling with excitement.

"Why, I'm beautiful," she murmured.

"Yes, you are," Dani said, grinning. "It must be love."

"It is, indeed," Marty agreed, and they all laughed.

"All right," Nettie said, "let's go."

Sanza drove the women in the buggy. Marty was by turns talkative and silent, nervous and eager. But she had no doubts about marrying Ridge Longtree. None at all.

She took a deep breath as the church came into view. She wished suddenly that her father were there to walk her down the aisle. Nettie had suggested that

Victor escort her, but Marty had flatly refused. Instead, she had asked Sam Bruckner.

Alighting from the buggy, she hurried to the church. Opening the door a crack, she peeked inside. The first few rows were filled with their closest friends and neighbors. The Mulvaneys were noticeably absent. Victor sat in the first row, on the aisle.

She smiled at Sam. He looked handsome in a dark brown suit, white shirt, and black string tie.

He shifted from one foot to the other. "New boots," he explained.

Taking Nettie's arm, he escorted her to her seat, then came back for Marty.

The organist began to play.

Dani handed Marty her bouquet. "You look lovely, Marty."

"So do you," Marty replied, thinking it wasn't fair that the maid of honor was prettier than the bride.

Dani kissed Marty on the cheek, gave her a quick hug, then turned and started down the aisle.

Sam placed Marty's hand on his arm. "Ready?"

She nodded. Walking down the aisle, she was hardly aware of her surroundings. Her whole being was focused on the tall man standing at the altar beside Reverend Waters. Ridge wore black trousers, a white shirt, a black vest, and a long black coat. His hair, neatly trimmed, fell to his shoulders. She grinned inwardly. No gun in sight. It was the first time she had seen him unarmed.

When they reached the altar, the reverend stepped forward, and Sam Bruckner backed up and sat down across from Nettie.

The reverend turned his gaze on Marty and Ridge and then looked out over the wedding guests.

"We are gathered here today to join this man and

this woman in holy matrimony, which is an honorable estate, and not to be entered into lightly. If there is anyone here present who knows of any impediment to this union, let him speak now."

The reverend paused, his gaze sweeping the congregation. "Who giveth this woman to be married to this man?"

Nettie stood up. "I do."

Reverend Waters nodded at her, then looked at Ridge and Marty. "Please join hands. Ridge Longtree, do you take this woman to be your lawfully wedded wife, to love her and cleave only unto her so long as you both shall live?"

Ridge gazed into Marty's eyes. "I do," he replied, his voice deep and rich and firm.

"And do you, Martha Jean Flynn, take this man to be your lawfully wedded husband, to love him and cleave only unto him so long as you both shall live?"

"I do," she said softly, fervently.

"Then, by the power vested in me, I now pronounce you husband and wife." Waters smiled at Ridge. "This is it, son. You may kiss the bride."

Slowly, almost reverently, Ridge lifted her veil and took her in his arms. "I love you, Mrs. Longtree," he murmured, and then he kissed her.

Heat spread through Marty, not the tingling warmth of desire, but the soothing warmth of belonging, of being where she was meant to be.

When he broke the kiss, she smiled up at him, and he winked at her.

Waters spoke to the wedding guests again. "I give you our town's newest couple, Mr. and Mrs. Ridge Longtree."

Hand in hand, Ridge and Marty turned to face their guests.

"Nettie Flynn has asked me to tell you that you're all invited out to the ranch to celebrate the nuptials," the reverend said. "May God bless you all. Amen."

Ridge and Marty walked down the aisle and left the church, then circled around the building to where Sanza was waiting, and then the three of them hurried into a side entrance.

When all the guests had left the building, Sanza and Dani stood before the preacher and exchanged their wedding vows.

Reverend Waters looked a little uncomfortable at officiating at a ceremony where the groom wore leggings, a buckskin shirt, a clout, and moccasins, but, all things considered, Marty thought he carried it off rather well.

He cleared his throat when he came to the part about kissing the bride, making her wonder if he didn't know if Indians kissed or if he was just opposed to Indians kissing white girls.

Dani glanced at him, and then, taking matters into her own hands, she stood on tiptoe and kissed Sanza.

Marty looked at her mother and Ridge and they all burst out laughing.

Ridge paid the preacher for both weddings, then turned to his bride. "What do you say, Mrs. Longtree— are you ready to go home?"

"That I am, Mr. Longtree," she replied. "That I am."

Their guests were at the ranch waiting for them when they arrived. Ridge helped Marty out of the buggy and they walked around to the side of the house, where several long tables had been set up. Nettie had outdone herself. There was cold ham, potato salad, applesauce, fresh-baked bread, fried chicken, and a cake decorated with pink roses.

Marty and Ridge circulated through the crowd, thanking people for coming and accepting their gifts and good wishes and congratulations.

There was a stir when Dani appeared with Sanza by her side. Ridge knew the warrior had not wanted to attend the reception, but Dani had finally persuaded him. Nettie hurried to greet them, and then, approaching each of their guests, she introduced Sanza as Dani's husband. Most people smiled politely and shook his hand. A few didn't smile, but no one refused to shake his hand. It was, Ridge supposed, the best that could be hoped for under the circumstances.

A few of the men had brought their instruments, and after everyone had eaten their fill, they began to play a waltz.

Marty looked at Ridge. "Do you dance?"

"Not much."

"Me, either."

He grinned as he took her by the hand. "Shall we?"

"I'm game if you are," she replied.

They danced the first waltz, and then other couples joined them, including Victor and Nettie.

Marty scowled at them.

"Hey, quit that," Ridge chided. "People will take one look at your face and think we're fighting already."

"Why did *he* have to come?"

Ridge didn't answer. Instead, he kissed her, right there on the dance floor. Whistles and catcalls rose from those on the sidelines.

Marty looked up at him and laughed, all else forgotten.

The afternoon shadows grew long. The kids played games. The adults danced or sat in the shade, the men talking about the price of wheat and cattle, the women reminiscing about their own weddings or speculating on how long it would be before Martha Jean was in the family way.

At dusk, their guests began taking their leave. Marty glanced at her husband, who hadn't left her side since that morning. He looked handsomer than the law allowed. Every time his hooded gaze met hers, she felt a rush of heat, followed by a longing so intense it was almost frightening. Soon, she thought, soon they would be alone. What if, after all the waiting, she disappointed him? What if he disappointed her? Lordy, no wonder brides were nervous!

When the last farewell had been said, Nettie and Dani started cleaning up the tables. When Marty started to help, they both shooed her away.

"You don't want to get that dress soiled, do you, now?" Nettie asked. "Besides, this is your wedding day. Go spend it with your husband."

Husband. What a strange and wonderful word.

Ridge smiled as she walked up to him. "Did I tell you how beautiful you look?" he asked, wrapping his arms around her.

"No," she said, pouting prettily.

"Well, you're the most beautiful, beguiling woman I've ever seen."

"Beguiling? Me?"

"You." He kissed the tip of her nose. "I'll do my best to make you happy, Martha Jean."

"I'm already happy." She glanced past his shoulder. "I'd be a lot happier if *he* went home."

Ridge blew out a sigh. He didn't have to look to know whom she was talking about. Though all the other guests had gone home, Victor lingered. Just now he was sitting on the front porch, idly thumbing through the newspaper. He didn't seem inclined to leave anytime soon. Had it been up to him, Ridge would have asked the man to leave, but it wasn't his place to do so. Hell, maybe Nettie wanted him here.

Later, when the tables were cleared and the food put away, Nettie called the family together.

"I haven't given you your wedding present yet," Nettie said. "Wait right here."

She went into the house, returning a moment later with a large envelope tied with a white satin ribbon. Smiling broadly, she handed it to Marty.

Marty looked at her mother and then at the envelope.

"Go on," Nettie said, "open it."

Removing the ribbon, Marty opened the envelope and withdrew a sheet of paper. It was the deed to the ranch. "What's the meaning of this?"

"Isn't it obvious?" Nettie asked. "I'm giving you the ranch as a wedding present. It's only in your name now, but you can have Ridge's name added the next time you go into town."

Marty stared at Nettie, speechless. And then she put her arms around her mother and kissed her on the cheek. "I don't know what to say."

"Try 'Thank you,'" Ridge said, slipping his arm around his wife's shoulders.

"'Thank you' doesn't seem like enough," Marty murmured, still stunned by her mother's generosity.

"I know how you love this place," Nettie said. "And if I know Seamus, he knew that eventually I'd give it to you."

Tears pricked Marty's eyes at the mention of her father.

"No tears, Martha Jean," Nettie said, blinking back tears of her own. "This is a happy occasion." She looked over at Victor, who was standing on the porch, one hand clutching the rail. "Isn't that right?"

"Yes," Claunch said. "A happy occasion."

But he wasn't smiling.

Chapter 35

Ridge had had enough chitchat for one day. Taking Martha by the hand, he nodded to Nettie and the others then swung his bride into his arms and carried her into the house, up the stairs, and into her bedroom.

He continued to hold her while he looked around. It was the first time he had been in her room since she redecorated it. He grunted softly. "Looks real nice."

"I'm glad you like it. Hmm," she murmured as she ran one hand over the muscle in his arm. "I like this."

He lowered her to her feet, then drew her up against him, one hand sliding up and down her back as he rained kisses over her nose, her cheeks, the curve of her throat.

She moaned softly as he pressed his lips over her breast, the heat of his breath penetrating the silk of her gown.

Lifting his head, he grinned at her. "Like that, do you?"

She nodded.

He smiled, pleased. Placing his hands on her shoulders, he turned her around then began unfastening the long row of buttons down the back of her gown.

Marty shivered as his fingers brushed her skin. Stepping out of her dress, she turned to face him. His gaze moved over her, his eyes smoldering.

"You're even prettier than I thought you'd be."

Kneeling, he removed her shoes and stockings. Then his hands slid up the length of one leg, and slowly slid back down.

Rising, he removed the rest of her undergarments until she stood bared to his gaze, a faint blush tingeing her skin under his warm regard. Lastly, he removed the pins from her hair. Freed of the pins, her hair fell down her back and over her shoulders in lush waves.

"Beautiful," he murmured, his voice thick.

"Am I?" It had always been Dani who was the pretty one.

He nodded. "Honey, you're more than beautiful."

She flushed, pleased by his compliment, by the admiration in his eyes, the love in his voice. Then, feeling a little uncomfortable at being the only one who was undressed, Marty slipped his coat over his shoulders and tossed it on a chair. She removed his vest and his shirt and tossed them both on top of his coat, then started to unbuckle his belt.

"Wait," he said. Reaching behind his back, he withdrew a derringer and dropped it on the dresser.

Marty grimaced. "I should have known," she muttered, reaching for his belt buckle again.

His hands skimmed over her body while she unfastened his belt. He stepped out of his trousers, then sat on the edge of the bed and pulled off his boots and socks. Naked now, he stood, one brow arched as her gaze moved over him.

His skin was a smooth copper color, puckered here and there with scars. His arms and legs were well mus-

cled, his shoulders broad and strong. She blushed as
she slid a glance at that part of him that made him
a man.

Ridge grinned. "Haven't you ever seen a naked
man before?"

"Not from the front. It's quite . . . um . . ." Her
cheeks grew hotter as she sought a word to describe it.

Laughing softly, he drew her into his arms. She mar-
veled at the feel of his skin, so warm and firm against
her own. She'd had no idea it would feel so wonderful
to be naked in a man's arms. She stroked his cheek,
the faint indention in his jaw. She had heard other
women describe the act of love as something a woman
had to endure. Surely they could not be talking about
what she was experiencing, for she would gladly endure this bliss, these exciting feelings, every day for
the rest of her life. She ran her fingers through his
hair, loving the feel of it.

"You're beautiful, too," she said shyly.

He looked down at himself and laughed. "Scars
and all?"

"Scars and all. There's so many of them. Where on
earth did you get them all?"

"I'll tell you someday," he said. "But not now."

And then he was kissing her again, his lips trailing
fire, burning a path from her neck to her navel and
back again, his tongue a clever flame that had her
gasping with pleasure.

Murmuring her name, he carried her to their bed
and stretched out beside her, wooing her with his
hands and his lips, whispering that he loved her,
adored her, could not live without her. His words
warmed her heart and soul because she knew, deep
inside, that he had never said them to anyone else
before.

Passion made her bold, and she began an exploration of her own, letting her hands wander where they would, measuring the width of his shoulders, making him flex his arms so she could squeeze the muscles in his biceps. She loved the way his muscles tensed and rippled beneath her hands, the sense of latent strength beneath her fingertips. He was brown all over, and not just where the sun had touched him. She loved looking at him, touching him, breathing in the sheer masculine scent of him.

She discovered he liked it when she ran her fingernails over his chest and down his belly, and laughed with delight when she discovered his feet were ticklish. Her hands roamed over every inch of him, from head to foot and all the delicious places in between.

He groaned low in his throat when she stroked the inside of his thigh. "You're playing with fire, girl," he warned.

The heat in his eyes seared a path to the very heart of her being. "Am I?"

"Keep it up and you'll find out."

She caressed him ever so lightly, teasing him with her fingertips until, with a low growl, he rose over her, his dark eyes aflame with desire.

She knew a moment of trepidation, and then, with one quick thrust, his body was a part of hers. She let out a soft cry of pained surprise.

Rearing back a little, he gazed down at her. "You all right, sweetheart?"

"Yes." She clutched his shoulders. "Don't stop."

"Never," he whispered, and then he was moving deep inside her. He kissed her and caressed her. All the while he moved within her, every stroke bringing pleasure, until she writhed beneath him, chasing something that seemed forever elusive until she reached the pinnacle of desire and pitched over the edge. Wave after wave of ecstasy rippled through her. She felt him convulse, heard her name on his lips as he collapsed on top of her, breathing heavily.

They lay that way for several minutes, and then he rose on his elbows and looked down at her. "Still all right?"

"Hmm," she purred. "Better than all right. Can we do it again?"

"Yes, ma'am," he said with a smile. "As often as you wish."

It was, she thought, a decidedly masculine, satisfied smile. Pulling his head down, she kissed him. "Thank you for making my first time wonderful."

"It'll be even better this time," he promised.

She shook her head. "It couldn't be."

"Wait and see," he said.

And she did.

And it was.

Marty woke slowly, aware of a heavy weight across her stomach and a soreness between her thighs. She frowned, and then she smiled. The weight was her husband's arm, and the soreness was no doubt due to the fact that they had made love all night long.

She grinned. He had been right. Making love to Ridge just got better and better. Glancing at her husband, she saw that he was awake and watching her.

"Mornin', wife," he drawled.

"Good morning, husband," she replied. His skin looked very brown against the crisp white sheets. Her gaze moved over the width of his shoulders, down his chest, to his waist. The sheet covered the rest of him, but did nothing to hide what he was thinking.

"How are you feeling this morning?" he asked.

She grinned at him. "Wonderful!"

Rolling onto his side, he gathered her into his arms. "So what do you want to do today?"

"The same thing we did last night," she replied with a saucy grin.

Laughing softly, he tossed the sheet aside and lifted her on top of him. "Your wish is my command, Mrs. Longtree," he drawled, and spent the next two hours fulfilling her every desire.

Marty couldn't stop smiling as she made her way downstairs. She ached in places she'd never known she had, but it was a pleasant kind of pain.

When she entered the kitchen, she found Nettie there, rolling out a pie crust.

"Well," her mother said, glancing at the clock, "it's about time you got up."

Marty blushed under her mother's knowing look. "Good morning, Mama."

Nettie grinned. "Ridge came down a few minutes ago, wearing that same silly smile."

"I think I'm going to like being married," Marty remarked. Pouring herself a cup of coffee, she carried it to the table and sat down. "Isn't it a lovely day?"

"Lovely," Nettie agreed dryly. "Are you hungry?"

"Famished!"

"Well, you just sit there and relax a minute and I'll whip up some scrambled eggs and bacon."

"Thanks, Mama. Has Ridge had breakfast?"

"He grabbed a cup of coffee and a couple of biscuits."

"Oh. He said something about going out to check on the north pasture. I think I'll ride out and see if I can find him after I eat."

A short time later, Marty saddled her favorite horse

and headed for the north pasture. It was a pretty piece of land watered by a narrow, winding stream. Tall trees provided shade. There was a line shack up on a ridge. Marty grinned inwardly. It was vacant this time of year, a perfect place for them to be alone.

With a laugh, she urged her horse into a gallop. Marriage had certainly turned her into a shameless hussy, she thought. All she could think of was the past night in her husband's arms and how eager she was to be there again. What a tender lover he had been, so patient and gentle with her, letting her explore every inch of his muscular body until she knew it as well as she knew her own, arousing her until she was ready to receive him. They had made love all night long, and it wasn't enough. She wanted him again, wanted to experience the unbelievable pleasure of his body melding with hers.

She had almost reached her destination when she felt something slam into her shoulder. A moment later she heard the sharp crack of a rifle.

Her first thought was that someone was hunting on her property. Then she looked at her shoulder and saw the blood soaking her shirt. Pain lanced through her arm as she stared at the blood.

She'd been shot! It was her last thought before she tumbled from her horse into oblivion.

Ridge drew his horse to a halt, one hand automatically reaching for his gun, as the rolling sound of gunfire split the peaceful afternoon air.

Reining his horse around, he rode in the direction of the gunshot. It was probably nothing, he told himself. One of the hands shooting at a snake or a mountain lion, or maybe putting an injured cow out of its misery. But deep inside, he knew something bad had happened.

Emerging from a stand of timber, he saw Marty's horse grazing a few yards away, its nose buried in a patch of grass. Alarm skittered down Ridge's back as he glanced around, searching for Martha. And then he saw her. She was lying facedown, one arm flung out.

He was off his horse and running toward her before the animal came to a halt. Kneeling, he turned her over, swearing a vile oath when he saw the blood that stained her shirt. He ran his hands over her, relieved that there were no other wounds save for a rather large lump on the back of her head. But she was alive. Thank God the bullet hadn't hit anything vital, though it had plowed a deep furrow in her shoulder.

Gently, he stroked her cheek. She moaned softly but didn't open her eyes. Cursing softly, he removed his kerchief, folded it in half and then in half again, and slid it inside her shirt, pressing it over the wound.

Lifting her in his arms, he carried her to his horse and placed her in the saddle. She slumped forward and he swung up behind her. Wrapping his right arm around her waist, he picked up the reins and headed toward home. Her horse trailed after them.

Who had shot her, and why? The question pounded in his brain. Was it an accident? Or had the man who killed Seamus struck again?

When he reached the house, he hollered for Nettie.

He saw her peering out the kitchen window, and then she was running down the stairs, her eyes wide with fear.

"She's alive," Ridge said.

"Thank the Lord." Reaching up, Nettie held her daughter while Ridge slid over the stallion's rump.

After tossing the horse's reins over the hitching post, he lifted Marty from the saddle and swiftly carried her into the house and up the stairs to their bedroom.

Nettie hurried in after him and drew back the covers.

Gently, Ridge placed Marty on the mattress.

"We'll need some hot water," Nettie said. "You'll find some clean cloths in the kitchen cupboard. There's some carbolic acid there, too. Hurry!"

With a nod, Ridge left the room.

"Martha, oh, Martha," Nettie murmured. "Who did this terrible thing?" Fighting back tears, she pulled off Martha's boots and socks, then eased her Levi's over her hips and down her legs. Next, she removed Martha's shirt and camisole, then drew a blanket up to her waist, her gaze riveted on the bloody kerchief that covered the wound in her daughter's shoulder.

Ridge returned a short time later carrying a bowl of hot water and the other items Nettie had asked for.

Ridge prowled the room while Nettie washed and treated the wound, then bandaged it with a length of clean linen.

"She'll be all right," Nettie said.

Ridge nodded. "Sure she will."

Marty stirred, a whisper stealing past her lips. "Ridge? I want Ridge."

He was at her side in an instant. "I'm here," he said, taking her hand. "Everything's all right."

Her eyelids fluttered open. "What happened?" She glanced around the room. "Why am I in bed?" She stared at him and then her eyes widened. "Someone shot me!"

"Shh, just take it easy. You're gonna be fine."

"I'll go down and make her a cup of tea," Nettie said. "It will help her relax."

Nodding, Ridge sat down on the edge of the bed. "How do you feel?"

"My shoulder hurts. And my head."

Leaning forward, he pressed a kiss to her brow. "Damn, girl, you gave me quite a scare. What were you doing out there, anyway?"

"Looking for you, of course."

"Why? Is something wrong?"

"No. I just wanted to see you." She shrugged, then winced as the movement sent a sliver of pain lancing through her shoulder.

Ridge stroked her cheek. "Missing me, were you?"

She nodded. "There's a line shack up there. I thought we could—"

"Here we go," Nettie said, hurrying into the room. "Drink this. You'll feel better."

Ridge helped Marty sit up a little. Nettie held the cup for Marty, who took a drink, then gasped, her eyes wide.

"What is that?"

"Tea," Nettie replied, "with a wee bit of whiskey. Come, drink it. It will do you good."

When the cup was empty, Ridge tucked Marty under the covers.

"Stay with me," she murmured.

"I will."

She reached for his hand. Her eyelids fluttered down, and she was asleep.

Nettie smoothed a lock of hair from her daughter's brow, then looked at Ridge. "Who do you think did this?"

"My money's on the same man who killed your husband."

"Marty thinks it was Victor."

"I know. I'm inclined to agree with her."

Nettie took a deep breath. "Then we'd better find out."

Thirty minutes later, Ridge left the house. Swinging into the saddle, he turned the stallion toward the north pasture, riding hard until he came to the place where he'd found Marty.

Dismounting, he searched the ground in ever-widening circles until he found what he was looking for—a set of hoofprints cut into the earth. The same irregular track he'd seen near the body of Seamus Flynn. There were no footprints.

Stepping into the saddle, he followed the prints to the edge of Claunch's spread.

Reining his horse to a halt, Ridge leaned forward, his forearms crossed on the saddlehorn, his eyes narrowed as he got his first glimpse of Victor Claunch's domain.

The house was large, three stories high, sparkling in the afternoon sun with a new coat of white paint. The door was dark green, there were matching shutters at the windows. A big red barn stood to the right of the house; there were several corrals filled with horses, another filled with yearling calves.

There was no sign of Claunch.

Ridge sat there for an hour, watching. He considered confronting Claunch but knew it would be futile. The fact that the tracks ended here didn't prove that Claunch was the killer, but it made him look guilty as hell.

Ridge grunted softly. If Claunch wasn't the killer, then someone sure wanted it to look that way.

Dismounting, Ridge tied his horse to a tree out of sight of the house, and then, using all the skills his grandfather had taught him, he made his way to the barn. He stood at the back door a moment, listening. Deciding the barn was empty, he opened the door and slipped inside.

He paused just inside the door, letting his eyes adjust to the dim light. The smells of hay, horse, leather, and manure filled the air. Moving quietly, he followed the irregular track to the second-to-last stall. It wasn't the horse Claunch usually rode, but the fact that it was in the man's barn was damning enough.

With a grunt of satisfaction, Ridge retraced his steps to the back of the barn and went out the back door.

Skirting the edge of the yard, he made his way back to his horse. Swinging into the saddle, he turned the stallion toward home, all the while contemplating his next move. His first instinct was to confront Claunch and then kill the bastard. But he was wanted in too many places already. He couldn't afford to run afoul of the law now, not here. He had too much to lose. His best bet was to talk to the sheriff and let him handle it.

Ridge snorted softly. Bruckner seemed like a decent guy, but Ridge didn't have much faith in his ability as a lawman.

When he reached the ranch, Ridge left his horse at the barn, then hurried up to the house.

Nettie looked up from the sofa, where she was doing some mending, when he entered the room.

"How is she?" Ridge asked.

"Sleeping. Did you find anything?"

"I found some tracks near where she was shot. They led straight to Claunch's place."

Nettie stared at him, then shook her head. "I can't believe it," she murmured, and then her eyes widened.

"I think you're right. I remember the look on his face yesterday when I gave Marty the deed to the ranch. What do we do now?"

"Go to the sheriff, I reckon."

"Do you think we have enough proof?"

"No."

Looking thoughtful, Nettie set her mending aside. "Martha told me Seamus's watch was missing when she found him. Whoever killed Seamus most likely took the watch I gave him the day we got married. If Victor killed Seamus, he must have the watch."

"I don't know. He'd be a damn fool to keep it."

"Maybe, but if he wasn't going to keep it, why take it?"

Ridge nodded. "True enough."

"So all we have to do is find the watch."

"How do you propose to do that? Just waltz in and look around?"

"No, but I'll bet I could get him to invite me to dinner. Or I could go calling when I'm sure he's not home and then wait for him inside. Yes, I think that's a better idea."

"It's too dangerous."

"The man shot my daughter and killed my husband," Nettie exclaimed, her voice rising. "I'm not going to let him get away with that! Are you?"

"No, ma'am."

"Good. Victor told me yesterday that he had some business to take care of at the bank tomorrow afternoon. I'll go over for a visit, and when his housekeeper tells me he isn't home, I'll tell her I'm going to wait."

"It's too risky."

"I'm going, and that's that."

"You know, your daughter's a lot like you," Ridge muttered.

"Thank you."

"It wasn't a compliment," he retorted.

Nettie laughed. "Maybe not, but I'm taking it as such. We'd better not say anything about this to Martha. I don't want her worrying."

"Right." No sense in worrying Martha Jean, he agreed. He was already worrying enough for both of them.

Chapter 36

Marty fretted constantly at being forced to stay in bed. Her mother had sent Smitty after the doctor. After examining the wound and the lump on the back of her head, the doctor advised her to spend the next few days taking it easy. Nettie and Ridge interpreted this as 'staying in bed.'

"But I feel fine," she argued, but to no avail.

Dani came to keep her company the next day. As always, Dani looked as if she had just stepped out of a bandbox. She wore a pretty pink gingham dress. Her hair was pulled back and tied with a matching ribbon. She made the day brighter just by entering the room, Marty thought. No wonder everyone loved her.

In no time at all, Dani was sitting on the edge of the bed, and the two of them were comparing notes on husbands and married life. Both agreed that the intimate side of marriage was far more wonderful and exciting than they had ever dreamed or expected.

Just before noon, Nettie poked her head into the room. "You girls doing all right?"

"Fine," Dani said.

"You don't mind staying a little longer, do you, Danielle?" Nettie asked. "I have an errand to run."

"I don't mind. Take your time."

"Good." Nettie started to go and then, on impulse, she kissed each of her daughters on the cheek. Just in case. "I love you both," she said, her voice thick, and then left the room.

Marty and Dani exchanged looks.

"What was that all about?" Marty asked.

Dani shrugged. "Maybe she's just trying to make up for lost time."

Ridge was waiting for Nettie at the barn.

She looked at the two saddled horses and then looked at him, one eyebrow raised.

"You didn't think I was gonna let you ride over there alone, did you?" he asked.

"No, I suppose not."

"Good." He helped her mount her horse, adjusted the stirrups, and handed her the reins. "You do know how to ride, don't you?"

"Of course, but it's been a while."

"We'll take it slow then," he said, and stepping into the saddle, he rode out of the yard.

She tried to concentrate on the beauty of the countryside, the clear blue sky, the cattle they passed, the birds flitting from tree to tree, but to no avail. Her heart was pounding like a blacksmith's hammer by the time they reached the outskirts of Victor's ranch. She folded her hands on the pommel to still their trembling and hoped Ridge wouldn't notice. She should have known better. The man didn't miss a trick.

"You don't have to do this," he said quietly. "We can always just turn around and go back."

"No." She squared her shoulders. "It's got to stop now. He might not miss the next time."

"It'll be a lot easier and quicker if I just call him out."

"Ridge, no!" she cried in horror. "What if he's innocent?"

"One more dead man on my conscience isn't going to make a hell of a lot of difference."

"So, it's true, what Joe Alexander told me."

"I don't know. What did he tell you?"

"He said you're wanted for murder in Dodge and Abilene."

Ridge nodded.

"Does Martha know?"

"You don't think I'd marry a woman without telling her about my past, do you?"

"No, I guess not. Is it true, what Joe said?"

"Partly. It was self-defense both times."

"So they let you go?"

"No, ma'am. I lit out just as fast as I could."

"But why?"

He grinned. It was the same question Martha Jean had asked, and he gave Nettie the same answer. "Because I'm Apache and they weren't."

She started to say she couldn't believe that would make a difference, that surely he would have gotten a fair trial, but she knew he was right. No Apache ever got a fair trial, at least not in this part of the country.

"You still determined to do this?" he asked.

"Yes."

"All right. I'll wait for you here. If you're not out of the house in thirty minutes, I'm coming in after you."

With a nod, Nettie urged her horse into a trot.

Ridge leaned forward, his arms resting on the saddle horn. From his vantage point, he could see the front of the house and part of the left side. He watched Nettie dismount and tie her horse to the hitching post. She smoothed her skirts, ran a hand over her hair, then climbed the stairs and knocked on the front door.

It was opened a moment later by a rotund woman wearing a white apron over a gray dress.

"Hello," Nettie said. "Is Victor home?"

"No, ma'am."

"Well, I'm sure he'll be back soon," Nettie said with a smile. "I'll just come in and wait."

The housekeeper regarded her a moment; then, with a shrug, she stepped aside. "Come on in."

Nettie took a deep breath. "Thank you," she murmured, and stepped across the threshold. She shivered as the door closed behind her.

The housekeeper led the way into the parlor. "You can wait in here, if you like."

"Thank you."

"Can I bring you something?"

"Not right now."

"Well, then, I'll get back to my washing."

"Of course." Smiling at the woman, Nettie sat down on the sofa and picked up the newspaper lying on the table.

The housekeeper watched her a moment and then left the room.

Nettie put the newspaper down and glanced at her surroundings. The furniture was heavy and dark; the walls were papered in a dark green stripes. Several rifles hung above the fireplace. Aside from the sofa on which she sat, there were two comfortable-looking chairs, and a rocker. There was a low table in front of the sofa. Expensive rugs covered the floor. A painting hung on one wall, depicting a herd of wild horses running from a storm. There was a long table beneath the window. It held a sparkling crystal decanter and several glasses, a pipe rack, and a stack of magazines.

She waited a few minutes and then tiptoed to the door and looked out. Seeing no one, she ran up the stairs. If Seamus's watch was here, it would most likely be in Victor's room.

Walking softly, she opened one door after another until she came to the master bedroom. Heart pounding, palms damp, she stepped into the room and closed the door behind her. Moving quickly, she looked through the drawers in the dresser and the small drawer in the bedside table. Going to the armoire, she opened the doors and searched inside, checking the pockets of his coats, his pants. Nothing.

Frowning, she looked around the room. Where could it be?

She whirled around, her heart leaping into her throat, when the door opened.

"Nettie Mae," boomed a deep voice. "What a pleasant surprise."

"Victor! You startled me."

"Mrs. Knox told me you were here." He glanced around the room, noting the armoire's open doors. "Did you find what you were looking for?"

"I don't know what you mean." She forced a shaky smile. "I was just . . . just curious about your house, and . . . well, since it might be my house one day, I . . ." She made a vague gesture with her hand. "I didn't think you'd mind."

His gaze held hers for stretched seconds. And then he held out his hand. "Shall we go? I asked Mrs. Knox to fix us some lemonade."

Keeping her smile firmly in place, Nettie took his hand and let him lead her down the stairs into the parlor.

"Please sit down." He indicated the sofa, then sat down beside her.

A plate of sandwiches, a pitcher, and two glasses sat on an engraved silver tray on the low table in front of the sofa. Victor poured a glass of lemonade and handed it to her. "Sandwich?"

"No, thank you." She wondered if he'd noticed the slight trembling in her hand.

"So." He leaned back, one arm draped over the back of the sofa. His gaze was intent upon her face, like that of a cat getting ready to pounce on an unwary mouse. "Can I hope you're here to accept my proposal?"

Stalling for time, she sipped her lemonade. She had to get out of here soon, before Ridge came after her.

"Nettie?" He took the glass from her hand and set it aside, then pulled her into his arms and kissed her hard, his lips bruising hers. "I want you," he said, his voice a low growl. "I've wasted half my life wanting you." His arms tightened around her until she could hardly breathe. "Don't make me wait any longer."

He kissed her again. She slid her hands between them, trying to push him away, and in doing so, she felt something small and hard and round in his vest pocket. A watch?

Abruptly, he released her. Eyes narrowed, his lips a cold thin line, he reached into his pocket. "Is this what you were looking for?"

She stared at the watch dangling from his hand. "So it was you."

At her words, a change came over him. His eyes grew hard, merciless; his mouth twisted in a cruel smile.

"How could you? Seamus was your friend. And Martha . . ." Nettie shook her head, unable to comprehend such evil.

"It would have been so much easier if you had just kept the ranch and married me."

"Why?" Rising, she began to pace the floor. "Why do you want the ranch? Yours is twice the size of ours, three times the size of any other spread in these parts."

"Because it should have been mine," he said brusquely. "Just as you should have been mine."

She stopped pacing. "So you killed him? Why, after so many years?"

"Water," he said succinctly. "You have more than you need, and I've never had enough."

"Seamus would have shared with you, if you had asked."

"I don't go begging of any man. He was supposed to be my friend. He knew my circumstances. He should have offered it."

She shook her head. "So you killed him because you were too proud to ask for a favor?"

He nodded. "And now I'm afraid I may have to kill you as well."

His words struck her like shards of ice. Feeling suddenly dizzy, she took a step backward, one hand pressed to her heart. She told herself to keep calm. He couldn't kill her, not now, not here, in his own house. She glanced out the window, wondering how much time had passed. There was no sign of Ridge.

Victor followed her gaze then looked back at her, his expression thoughtful.

"Expecting someone?" he asked.

She shook her head. "No."

"Uh-huh." Putting the watch back in his pocket, he took her by the arm and pushed her down on the sofa. "Have a sandwich."

She stared at him. Surely he didn't expect her to eat at a time like this!

Picking up a sandwich, he thrust it into her hand. "Eat."

She took a small bite, afraid to swallow for fear it would come right back up. Forcing it down, she glanced out the window again.

Victor pulled his gun from the holster and checked the loads. "I suppose Longtree is out there somewhere," he remarked. "Killing him will be a pleasure."

Moving to the front window, he closed the curtains, then took a place beside the front door, his gun hand dangling at his side.

Nettie sat there, hardly daring to breathe. Thirty minutes had surely passed by now. Where was Ridge?

A faint movement caught her eye. She turned her head toward the door that led down the hall toward the kitchen in time to see Ridge duck out of sight. She looked back at Victor. He was still standing beside the front door, looking out.

She glanced back at the hallway. Ridge appeared in the doorway, his gun drawn. Nettie didn't know what tipped Victor off, but he suddenly whirled around, his gun coming up.

Two gunshots echoed off the walls, one coming hard on the heels of the other.

Screaming, Nettie dropped to the floor, her hands covering her ears, the stink of gunpowder stinging her nostrils.

There was a moment of utter stillness, followed by a heavy thud. She glanced to her left, horrified to see Victor lying there, his gaze on her face. He reached toward her, his hand falling short.

"I . . . loved you." He whispered the words with his last breath.

Tears stung her eyes as she pulled herself to her feet.

Ridge stood in the doorway. A dark stain spread over the front of his shirt just above his waist.

Grimacing, he slid his gun into the holster. "It's over."

Nettie took a deep breath; then, gathering her wits about her, she went into the kitchen to find a cloth to bind his wound. She was startled to find Mrs. Knox sitting in a kitchen chair, her hands and feet bound, a gag in her mouth. Moving quickly, Nettie untied the woman.

"We need some bandages right quick," she said. Grabbing a towel, she hurried back to Ridge. Lifting his shirt, she pressed the folded towel over the wound to stanch the flow of blood.

Moments later, three men ran into the house, their guns drawn. "What the hell's going on here?" one of them asked. "We heard a shot and . . ." His voice trailed off when he saw Claunch sprawled on the floor. "Is he dead?"

"Damn right," Ridge said.

The man's eyes narrowed. "What happened?"

"It's a long story," Nettie said. "I suggest you go into town and get the sheriff." She glanced at the blood soaking the towel and Ridge's shirt. "And a doctor."

"Tell them to meet us at the ranch," Ridge said.

"You ain't going nowhere," the man said, his gun leveled at Ridge's chest.

Ridge fixed the man with a hard look. "Are you gonna try to stop me?"

The man took a step back. "No," he said, holstering his Colt. "No, I'm not."

"Are you sure you don't want to wait here?" Nettie asked anxiously. "You're losing a lot of blood."

"I'm sure," Ridge said. "Let's go home."

Marty sat up, grimacing as the movement sent a twinge through her side.

"What are you doing?" Dani asked.

"I'm getting up."

"The doctor said—"

"I don't care what he said. I feel all right, just a little sore. Besides, something's going on." She slid her feet over the edge of the bed. "Something's wrong. I just know it."

Rising, Dani reached to steady Marty as she gained her feet. "Are you sure you should be doing this?"

"Stop fussing over me."

Feeling a little light-headed, Marty left her bedroom and, step by slow step, made her way down the stairs.

"Do you know where Ridge is?" Marty asked.

"No. I thought he was out with the hands. You know, learning the lay of the land or chasing cows, or whatever it is they do out there."

"Dani—"

"Seriously, I don't know where he is. Are you sure you're all right? Should I go look for him?"

"No." Marty sat down on the sofa.

Dani pulled a quilt from the back of a chair and covered Marty with it, then stood there, one finger tapping her lower lip. "I'm going to go look for him," she said. "Don't move."

Sitting back on the sofa, Marty stared out the window, wondering where her mother had gone. An errand, Nettie had said. What kind of errand? And why had her voice sounded so odd when she told them she loved them, almost as if she was saying good-bye?

Overcome with a sudden sense of foreboding, she

wrapped her arms around her waist. Something was wrong; she was sure of it. And even as the thought crossed her mind, the front door opened.

"Dani! Dani, where are you?" Nettie yelled.

"She went looking for Ridge," Marty called. "What's wr . . ." She didn't finish asking. She knew what was wrong. Unmindful of the sharp stab of pain in her shoulder, she leaped off the sofa and ran to the front door.

Nettie stood just inside the door, her arm wrapped around Ridge's waist. An ugly red smear stained the right side of his shirt.

"What happened?" Marty hurried toward Ridge, needing to touch him.

"I'll be all right," he assured her. "Just let me sit down."

Marty looked at her mother as they followed Ridge into the parlor. He sank down in a corner of the sofa and closed his eyes.

"Where were you?" Marty asked. "What happened?"

"We went to see Victor."

"You did what?"

"It was my idea." Nettie glanced at Ridge. "He didn't want me to go."

Opening his eyes, Ridge looked at Marty. "You and your mother have a lot in common," he said with a wry grin, then closed his eyes again. "Neither one of you has enough sense to stay home where you belong."

"Go on," Marty said.

"Victor had your father's watch. He's the one who shot you. He shot Ridge, too."

"Where's Victor now?"

"He's dead," Ridge answered.

"Did you . . . ?"

"Yeah."

Marty blew out a breath. "Mama, shouldn't we get a doctor?"

"He should be on his way. I told one of Victor's men to notify the sheriff and send the doctor out here." She glanced at Ridge, who seemed to be sleeping, and lowered her voice. "The bullet's still in his side. I put some water on to heat. I could use a cup of tea, and the doctor will probably want some hot water."

Marty nodded absently, her attention on her husband. He looked pale beneath his tan. How much blood had he lost? How much could a man lose and still live?

Wishing the doctor would hurry, she began to pace the floor. Hearing Dani's footsteps on the porch, Marty went to head Dani off before she went into the parlor. Ridge was asleep, and right now, that was the best thing for him.

Dani listened in amazement as Nettie related what had happened at the Claunch place, unable to believe that her mother, always so quiet and demure, had had the nerve to search Victor's house.

"Ridge is the one who saved the day," Nettie said. "I don't know what would have happened if he hadn't insisted on going with me. Let me tell you, I was never so glad to see anybody in my life."

"Thank God you're both alive," Dani said fervently.

"Amen," Marty murmured.

Leaving Nettie and Dani in the kitchen to fix dinner, Marty helped Ridge up the stairs to bed. She pulled back the covers, and he sat on the edge of the bed while she pulled off his boots and socks, unbuckled his gun belt, removed his trousers and his shirt.

With a low groan, he lowered himself to the mattress and closed his eyes.

"Here." She placed his hand on the bloody towel. "Keep some pressure on that. Can I get you anything?"

"Some whiskey if you've got it."

"All right." She drew the sheet over him and left the room. She came back with a bottle of rye that her father had kept in his desk. She poured a shot, then held the glass to Ridge's lips. He downed it in one swallow.

"More."

She frowned at him. "Are you sure? That's pretty strong."

"So's the ache in my side."

Wordlessly, she poured another shot.

He was feeling no pain when the doctor arrived thirty minutes later.

Marty hovered nearby as the doctor drew back the sheet and removed the towel covering the wound. She held the bowl while the doctor washed the ragged, angry-looking hole, stood by with several clean cloths while he probed for the slug.

Marty swallowed the bile that rose in her throat.

Seeing her face, Ridge caught her hand in his. "Hey, you're not gonna be sick, are you?"

"Of course not."

He grinned crookedly, then swore, his hand crushing hers as the doctor dug deeper into the wound. Blood oozed from the nasty hole in his side.

Marty looked away. He might have been killed trying to protect her mother. The thought made her angry even as it made her love him all the more.

"Ah! Here it is," the doctor said. He held it up for

Marty to see, then dropped the small chunk of lead into a pan. "Wet a couple of those cloths, will you?"

Marty did as she was asked, grateful to have something to do.

A short time later, the wound was cleaned and bandaged.

The doctor closed his black bag with a snap, then looked at Marty. "Aren't you supposed to be in bed, too, Miss Martha?"

She nodded, and then, feeling like a child who had disobeyed the rules, she crawled into bed beside Ridge.

"That's better," the doctor said. He looked from one to the other. "See if you two can stay out of trouble for a while."

Picking up his bag, he left the room.

Ridge looked at Marty, a twinkle in his eye. "Not much of a honeymoon, is it?" he asked, his words slightly slurred. "I always wanted to get you into bed, but damn, not like this."

Sheriff Bruckner showed up at the ranch the next day. He listened to what Ridge had to say, then took Nettie into another room and listened to her version of the shooting.

"It sounds like self-defense to me, Longtree," Bruckner said, "but I'm not the judge or the jury. I'm afraid I'll have to take you in."

Marty stared at Ridge, her eyes wide. Would he go peacefully? Or would he run again? She could tell nothing of what he was thinking from his expression, which remained impassive.

"Longtree?"

"Can't he stay here?" Marty asked. "He's hurt."

" 'Fraid not." Bruckner's hand moved to his gun
butt. "Get dressed, Longtree."

Ridge drew Marty close and kissed her cheek.
"Don't worry, honey."

She nodded, tears welling in her eyes. Bruckner and
Nettie left the room so Ridge could dress.

Marty hovered around him, touching him, her eyes
caressing him. He'd hang if they found him guilty. The
thought made her sick to her stomach.

"Maybe you should make a run for it," she said.
"Hide out for a while. I'll meet you somewhere."

Ridge shook his head. "I'm through running."

He drew her into his arms and held her gently,
mindful of her injured shoulder. "I love you, Martha
Jean. Don't ever forget that," he said, and then he
kissed her, long and deep.

She was crying when he opened the door.

Bruckner was waiting in the hallway. He pulled a
pair of handcuffs from his back pocket and thrust
them at Ridge. "Put these on."

"You don't need 'em," Ridge said. "I'm not going
anywhere."

Bruckner studied him a moment, then nodded.

Marty slipped her arm around Ridge's waist and
hugged him tight. "I love you!"

"I know." He brushed a kiss across the top of her
head. And then he was gone.

Ridge was having second thoughts as he stepped
inside the iron-barred cell. It would have been easy
to overpower Bruckner and make a run for it. Ridge
was surprised the man had lived this long. He was far
too trusting to be a lawman. Then again, Chimney
Creek was a pretty quiet town.

He flinched when Bruckner shut and locked the cell

door behind him. Sitting on the edge of the cot in the corner, he stared at the floor, wondering if he had just made the biggest mistake of his life. He had been locked up only once before, and he'd sworn it would never happen again. But that had been before Martha. She was more important to him than anything in his life, even his freedom.

Glancing at the walls and the bars, he was filled with a sudden restlessness. Gaining his feet, he began to pace the narrow confines of his prison like a caged tiger, the tension in him growing with each passing minute.

Joe Alexander came to visit him, nosing around for a story. "I've got a couple of flyers in my office," he remarked, studying Ridge's face. "They look a lot like you."

"Is that right?"

Alexander nodded. "No name on either one. Good descriptions, though. Long black hair. Blue eyes. Some Indian blood. About your height and weight."

Ridge grunted. "You going anywhere with this?"

"Just wondered if there was anything you wanted to tell me."

"Not a thing."

Alexander tapped his fingers on one of the bars. "Want to tell me about the shoot-out with Claunch?"

"It was self-defense."

The newspaperman chuckled. "Of course."

"I've got nothing else to say."

"Well, I'll see you at the trial, then. Good luck to you."

Ridge watched Alexander leave, hoping that Bruckner wouldn't make the same connection the newspaperman had.

The trial was held two days later. Handcuffed, Ridge sat beside the lawyer Nettie had hired to defend him.

The trial was surprisingly short. Nettie related her reason for being at Victor's and seeing her husband's watch in his possession. In a voice that shook with emotion, she told how Victor had confessed to killing Seamus and trying to kill Martha Jean.

The fact that Marty was in the courtroom, her injured arm in a blindingly white sling, gave credence to Nettie's testimony.

The jury deliberated for less than half an hour and returned a verdict of self-defense.

Ridge breathed a heartfelt sigh of relief.

Marty wept.

Dani and Nettie hugged each other. Finally, it was over.

A few evenings later, the Flynn family sat out on the porch talking softly land sipping lemonade. It was a lovely, star-spangled night. A gentle breeze kept the heat at bay.

Marty and Ridge sat on the swing holding hands. Dani and Sanza sat on the top step. Nettie sat in the rocker, idly petting one of the barn cats that had curled up in her lap.

"I still can't believe you had the nerve to go search Victor's house," Dani remarked after a while. "You could have been killed."

Nettie shrugged. "That doesn't matter now. What matters is that we're all here together, where we belong."

Marty glanced from her sister to her mother. "Do you think this is what Pa wanted to happen when he left you the ranch?"

"I'm sure of it," Nettie replied softly.

"I guess things happen the way they're meant to happen," Dani said, smiling at her husband.

"I guess so," Ridge agreed. He counted himself the luckiest one of all. He had happened onto this place and found a home and a woman to share it with.

Marty looked up at him, her eyes shining with love, and Ridge Longtree knew he'd found what he had been searching for all his life.

Epilogue

Martha Jean shook her head, wondering if things would ever be peaceful again, as she tried to settle a squabble between her four-year-old son, Luke, and Dani's four-year-old daughter, Alyssa.

Nettie sat on the rocking chair on the porch, laughing softly as she watched her daughter and her grandchildren. She held Marty's four-month-old daughter, Katie, cradled in her arms, while Marty's three-year-old daughter, Marissa, sat on the porch step trying to put a sweater on one of the puppies.

The ranch had prospered in the last five years. Dani had used her inheritance to buy Victor Claunch's ranch, and she and Sanza lived there through the winter and spring, leaving the foreman to manage the place in the summer, when they went to stay with the Apache. Sanza had adapted well to ranch life.

Each summer, Sanza and Ridge drove two hundred head of cattle into the stronghold. Of course, Dani and Marty went, too. The more Marty got to know the Apache people, the more she loved and respected them. They could be fierce enemies, that was true, but they were also loyal friends, and she looked forward to spending summers with the People, hearing the old stories, renewing acquaintances. She intended to make sure that her children were proud of their Apache heritage, that they learned the language and the customs. No man or woman could be whole unless they knew who they were and where they came from.

Nettie had surprised everyone by marrying Joe Alexander, the newspaperman. Though she had moved into town, Nettie came to visit often, usually bringing presents or candy for her grandchildren. Marty declared that Nettie was going to spoil them something terrible, but Nettie just laughed and told her that was what grandmothers were for.

The squabble settled, Luke and Alyssa went down to the barn to look at the new kittens that had been born the week before.

"I think I'd better go along," Nettie said. She descended the stairs and placed the baby in Martha's arms. "She's a little beauty, isn't she?"

Marty nodded. Her children were all beautiful. They had their father's dusky skin and black hair and Marty's brown eyes.

Thoroughly content, she watched Nettie hurry to catch up with Luke and Alyssa.

She was about to go into the house when she saw Ridge striding toward her. Time had not dulled her reaction to him. He was still the most gorgeous man she had ever seen. Just looking at him made her insides turn to mush and her toes curl.

He smiled as he swept Marissa into his arms and swung her up on his shoulders. "How are my girls?"

"Never better," Marty replied. "How's our favorite fella?"

"Never better," Marissa echoed. "Want to see the kitty."

Side by side, Ridge and Martha Jean walked down to the barn, smiling at each other as their son ran out of the stable, the sound of happy laughter filling the air, the sun shining down on their family like a benediction.

Dear Reader:

I hope you enjoyed *Under Apache Skies*. I really had a good time writing this book. It was fun having two heroines and two heroes. Originally, Sanza was going to be the "bad" guy but, as happened with Ravenhawk in *Spirit's Song* my bad guy simply refused to be bad. Men can be so contrary sometimes!

Under Apache Skies is my thirty-second historical romance and my forty-fourth full-length novel. I'm happy to say that even after all those books, writing is still fun and I still get a thrill out of seeing my books in stores.

Thank you for your letters and support. I love hearing from you.

May God bless you and yours.

Madeline Baker
www.madelinebaker.net

Signet

New York Times bestselling author

Madeline Baker

Wolf Shadow

Kidnapped by Sioux Indians as a child, Teressa Bryant
was raised as a beloved member of their tribe.
Ten years later, a man known to his mother's people
as Wolf Shadow has been hired to bring her home.
Can she return to her old life—and leave her new love?

0-451-20916-8

**Available wherever books are sold or at
www.penguin.com**

S903

Sweeping prehistoric fables from
New York Times bestselling author

LINDA LAY SHULER

LET THE DRUM SPEAK 190955

Possessed with the same mystical powers as her mother, a young
woman follows her wandering mate to a fabled city in the
prehistoric Southwest. But here her beauty attracts the attention of
the city's supreme ruler—a man who will become her greatest
enemy. Far from her homeland, she must now struggle for her own
survival...and that of her only child.

SHE WHO REMEMBERS 160533

"Linda Lay Shuler....has brought to life the story of the Mesa Verde
and Chaco Canyon, and the ancient people who built those
mysterious hidden canyon cities. I admire her accurate research, but
I loved her compelling story of love and adventure even more."
—Jean M. Auel, author of *The Clan of the Cave Bear*

VOICE OF THE EAGLE 176812

Spanning ten years, this magnificent novel, rich in detail, gives an
intimate portrait of a strong and independent woman, who is also
the spiritual leader of her people. Set in the Southwest, this
enthralling tale brings to life the vanished ways of the
first Americans.

Available wherever books are sold at
www.penguin.com